THE END OF TIME

A COLONIAL FLEET NOVEL

NEXUS HOUSE BOOK 3

RICK CAMPBELL

Copyright © 2025 by Rick Campbell.

All rights reserved.

No part of this book may be reproduced in any form or by any electronic or mechanical means, including information storage and retrieval systems, without written permission from the author, except for the use of brief quotations in a book review.

Severn River Publishing
www.SevernRiverBooks.com

This is a work of fiction. Names, characters, businesses, places, events and incidents are either the products of the author's imagination or used in a fictitious manner. Any resemblance to actual persons, living or dead, or actual events is purely coincidental.

ISBN: 978-1-64875-703-7 (Paperback)

ALSO BY RICK CAMPBELL

The Nexus House Series

The Final Stand: A Colonial Fleet Novel

Descent into Hellios: A Colonial Fleet Novel

The End of Time: A Colonial Fleet Novel

The Synthec War: A Colonial Fleet Novel

Annihilation: A Colonial Fleet Novel

The Seed of Destruction: A Colonial Fleet Novel

To find out more about Rick Campbell and his books, visit
severnriverbooks.com

MAIN CHARACTERS

A complete cast of characters is provided in the addendum

NEXUS HOUSE
Rhea Sidener Ten (Placida) / Nexus One (The One)
Jon McCarthy Ten
Elena Kapadia Ten
Noah Ronan Nine (Primus) / Legion Commander / Department Head - Defense
Angeline Del Rio Eight / 3rd Fleet guide
Lara Anderson Eight / Nine trainee

CORVAD HOUSE
Lijuan Xiang Ten (Placida) / Princeps

COLONIAL COUNCIL
David Portner Regent - Inner Realm / Council president
Morel Alperi Regent - Inner Realm / Director of Personnel
Lijuan Xiang Regent - Terran (Earth) / Director of Material

COLONIAL FLEET
Nanci Fitzgerald Fleet Admiral / Colonial Fleet Commander
Jon McCarthy Admiral / Colonial Fleet staff
Natalia Goergen Admiral / 3rd Fleet Commander
Nesrine Rajhi Vice Admiral / Excalibur Battle Group Commander (3rd Fleet)

COLONIAL MARINE CORPS
Drew Harkins Major / Nexus escort platoon leader
Ed Jankowski Sergeant Major / Nexus escort platoon
Narra Geisinger Sergeant Major / Nexus escort platoon
Liza Kalinin Sergeant / Nexus escort platoon

KORILIANS
Mrayev Pracep (war campaign commander)
Krajik Pracep Mrayev's executive assistant

1

A half mile beneath Earth's surface, seated in her console at the back of the Fleet command center, Fleet Admiral Fitzgerald monitored the status of the Liberation Campaign assaults. Arranged before her in the dimly lit facility were six rows of consoles manned by men and women wearing the crimson-and-burgundy uniforms of the Colonial Navy, their faces illuminated by the blue glow of their console displays. After thirty-three years of war, the command center personnel were experienced and not easily rattled, but the tension in the air today was palpable. Fleet Intelligence had determined that the Korilians were about to launch a major offensive.

Fitzgerald's eyes moved across the large displays mounted along the command center's front wall, evaluating the status of the latest phase of the Korilian War. 1st, 3rd, and 4th Fleets were supporting ten planetary assaults as the Colonial Defense Force pressed forward, regaining the planets lost during the first thirty years of the war. The Liberation Campaign, normally supported by four fleets—sixteen battle groups—was short-handed at the moment, with 2nd Fleet in an extended refit taking on replacement starships. It would take another two weeks to finish replacing over two hundred warships lost during the assault on Hellios. 5th and 6th Fleets remained in Earth's orbit per the Colonial Council's edict, guarding against a surprise Korilian assault on humankind's home planet.

An adjacent display, monitoring the status of nearby star systems, caught Fitzgerald's attention. Red alarms were flashing in several sectors. Fifteen Korilian battle groups had been detected, divided into five task forces. The Korilians had launched their offensive—its first in three years—against five of the ten Liberation Campaign planets, attempting to drive the Colonial Fleet warships away. As Fitzgerald evaluated the incoming data, she realized that despite the forewarning received about the pending assault, the Korilians would succeed. They had committed fifteen battle groups while the Colonial Navy currently had only twelve available for operations beyond Earth's orbit.

Admiral Jon McCarthy, who had led the Fleet during its Final Stand three years ago, stopped beside Fitzgerald. Dubbed by the public as the Hero of the Korilian War, he had earned the title. With humanity on the brink of extinction, over two thousand Korilian warships had jumped into Earth's solar system. Admiral McCarthy had been given command of over half of the Fleet, spearheading an assault into the heart of the Korilian juggernaut, destroying the Korilian command ship. Had anyone else been assigned the mission, it would have assuredly failed, but McCarthy was no ordinary man.

McCarthy was a rare talent, trained by a secretive group of prescients able to perceive the future to some extent, depending on the complexity and volatility of the timeline being examined. Twenty-one years ago, at the age of sixteen, McCarthy had been assigned to the Fleet to assist in the Korilian War, working his way up from a junior officer to command of 1st Fleet, and was now assigned to Fitzgerald's staff, providing guidance to all six fleets.

He had provided the forewarning about today's assault, and as he prepared to offer additional insight, Fitzgerald knew he was assessing the situation in a way she could never comprehend. Not only could McCarthy discern the future, he could postulate various responses and evaluate the impact, selecting the optimal option. Not that his insight would help much today. 1st, 3rd, and 4th Fleets were outnumbered: fifteen battle groups to twelve. No matter how they arranged the pieces on the board, until 2nd Fleet became operational again, the Korilians would have the advantage.

McCarthy delivered the expected advice. "I recommend we abandon all ten planetary assaults. Until Second Fleet becomes available, any attempt to hold a planetary system will result in higher losses for us than the Korilians. Once Second Fleet completes refit, we'll have a marginal probability of success."

Fitzgerald acknowledged his input. After deliberating the matter a moment longer, she gave the order, pulling all Liberation Campaign battle groups back from the front line, abandoning ground support for the planetary assaults.

Fifteen minutes later, as the Colonial battle groups jumped away and reformed into their three fleets, the command center supervisor approached Fitzgerald.

"Ma'am, the Excalibur battle group has not acknowledged your order."

Fitzgerald examined the monitor displaying the status of the battle in the Antares star system. A Korilian battle group had jumped into the system and engaged the Excalibur battle group, and two more Korilian battle groups were only a few jumps away. None of Excalibur's warships had initiated the jump sequence. They were staying at Antares.

What in the hell is going on?

Seated at the battle group commander's console aboard her Resolute-class battleship, Vice Admiral Nesrine Rajhi monitored the status of the one hundred warships in the Excalibur battle group, orbiting the fourth planet in the Antares system. Through the bridge windows, white flashes announced the arrival and departure of supply ships and troop transports replenishing 7th Army's resources on the planet's surface, while red and blue pulses, accompanied by the yellow flash of impacted starship shields, surrounded her. A Korilian battle group had jumped into the Antares system, attempting to drive the Excalibur battle group away.

The sensor display updated, relaying video from a recon probe three jumps out. A full-strength Korilian battle group with one hundred warships had just jumped into the Draugor star system. Two minutes later, the Korilian battle group jumped again, this time to the Sarioca star system, two jumps from Antares.

Rajhi was fairly certain the Korilians would halt at Sarioca for several hours to let the physiological effects of the double jump dissipate before commencing another double jump into combat. As she considered how much longer to let supply ships off-load their material, another sensor display updated.

"Korilian battle group detected at Veles, three jumps away," the sensor supervisor reported.

Two minutes later, the battle group jumped again. There were now two more Korilian battle groups only a double jump away.

Rajhi weighed her options, which weren't many. The Excalibur battle group would soon be outnumbered three to one. The choice was obvious, but as Rajhi canvassed the men and women on the starship bridge, she saw the uncertainty in their eyes. Would she order a retreat or choose to stay and fight an unwinnable battle?

She had heard the whispers.

Admiral Rajhi has a death wish.

Two months ago, she had volunteered to lead 2nd Fleet's cruiser task force on a suicide mission supporting the assault on the Hellios system, deep within Korilian-controlled territory. The predictions had been correct; over half of Rajhi's two hundred cruisers had been destroyed in the surprise attack, which required the cruisers to emerge from a jump—before shields were formed—within firing range of Korilian warships.

Following the Hellios mission, Rajhi had been promoted to vice admiral and placed in command of the Excalibur battle group. With the situation at Antares rapidly deteriorating, Rajhi needed to decide how to respond. Despite what the rumors said, she did not have a death wish. She was simply not afraid of death, and would choose whatever option allowed her battle group—and her—to kill as many Korilians as possible. Under the present circumstances, the decision was clear.

Rajhi turned to her communications supervisor. "Inform Seventh Army Command that the Excalibur battle group will depart Antares once all supply ships have jumped."

Her words were odious. Rajhi would leave behind 7th Army's ten million men and women, stranding them on the planet. Instead of the Excalibur battle group in orbit providing ground support, red pulses from

The End of Time 5

Korilian warships would rain down, pulverizing exposed troops. 7th Army would not last long, two months at best.

Inside the Fleet command center on Earth, bright white flashes lit up one of the main displays, announcing the Excalibur battle group's departure from Antares. As the Liberation Campaign warships fell back to regroup, Fitzgerald reviewed her options.

Even after 2nd Fleet returned to operation, the Colonial Navy could muster only sixteen battle groups against fifteen Korilian. At relatively even odds, the Korilians had the advantage; they were a telepathic species able to coordinate their attacks more efficiently than humans. Only with McCarthy in direct command of a fleet or battle group could that advantage be overcome. That was an option, returning him to battle instead of assigned to her staff where his talent had been harnessed to provide valuable guidance for the entire Fleet.

"There are several issues to consider," McCarthy said, seemingly reading her mind, although she knew that wasn't one of his talents. "I need to confer with The One," he said.

Rhea Sidener, The One who ruled the Nexus House, was another level-ten prescient and the most powerful Nexus. At level ten, other talents emerged, and the Nexus One was both respected and feared. Fitzgerald had heard the rumor—Rhea could kill someone with a single thought.

Fitzgerald nodded her understanding. "Give my regards to The One."

2

An executive Fleet transport plunged through white cumulus clouds above the Caspian Sea, then sped northeast toward the snow-capped Ural Mountains. The shuttle approached a gap between two jagged mountain peaks, slowing to a hover above spaceport doors that had begun opening. A moment later, the shuttle descended to a gentle landing.

Admiral Jon McCarthy emerged from the shuttle, followed by his guard of ten Nexus praetorians—level-nine Nexi trained in every form of combat. Greeting McCarthy was Dewan Channing, the Deinde Eight—second in command of the Eights—who was tasked with training Nexus fleet guides.

"Welcome home, Jon," Channing said, extending his hand. The two men gripped each other's forearm in the traditional Nexus greeting.

"It's good to see you, Dewan," McCarthy replied, addressing the man who had helped McCarthy achieve level eight. Even in the short time under Channing's tutelage, McCarthy had developed an affinity for the older man.

"The One is in Tanum," Channing said, referring to the combat training arena, "awaiting your arrival."

McCarthy flicked a hand signal to his guard, releasing the ten praetorians from duty now that he was safe within the walls of Domus Praesidium.

The End of Time

Channing accompanied McCarthy down one of the radial corridors that ran through the north, west, and south wings of the Nexus stronghold, entering the Tanum complex in the south wing where the House trained its personnel for battle. In one of Tanum's hand-to-hand combat arenas, twenty students were working with Noah Ronan, the Primus Nine, in charge of all level-nine personnel and responsible for House Defense. The students were assembled in a line, catching their breath as they listened to Ronan explain the finer points of Letalis-Tutela, the deadly House martial art.

Nearby, observing the training, stood Rhea Sidener, a diminutive fifty-year-old woman, her silver hair woven into a circular braid behind her head. She wore the standard blue Nexus jumpsuit, with ten white stripes around each arm, plus a white sash with gold embroidery around her slender waist, signifying that she was The One who ruled the Nexus House.

McCarthy and Channing stopped beside The One, waiting for her acknowledgment. After a moment, she turned to McCarthy.

"What do you think of the praetorian candidates?" The One asked.

McCarthy surveyed the trainees, realizing that one of the students was Lara Anderson, which he found unusual. Lara was an Eight, and as far as McCarthy knew, only Nines were trained as praetorians. Nines had a clear view of the future, able to predict every move their opponent planned. The only way to defeat a prescient combatant was with a prescient opponent. Once engaged in combat, both Nines would view the future. The two views in proximity would disrupt each other, eliminating either participant's prescient advantage, reducing the conflict to skill alone.

Lara noticed McCarthy's arrival and smiled briefly as she caught her breath. He knew what she was thinking—*Will we have time to be together before you leave?*

During the intense preparation for the Final Stand and the battle itself, followed by the arduous assault on Hellios 4, McCarthy and Lara's relationship had evolved into a romantic one.

As Lara returned her attention to the Primus Nine, McCarthy noticed the dark circles under her eyes. She was exhausted; The One was pushing her hard. The One believed Lara had tremendous potential—McCarthy had sensed her latent power himself—but they had not been able to tap into it. Lara was stuck at level eight and was frustrated. But instead of spending more time developing her ability to view the future, she was training as a praetorian? For what purpose?

McCarthy turned to The One. "Lara?" He needn't say more.

The One replied, "Lara will eventually reach level nine and perhaps level ten, and Tens must be able to protect themselves in case they are caught without their guard. You also trained as a praetorian, did you not?"

"Of course," McCarthy said. "But not until I reached level nine."

"Lara is getting a head start in case she ends up in harm's way again."

McCarthy detected concern in Rhea's voice and nodded his understanding.

Thirty-three years ago, after defeating the Corvad House and ending the three-thousand-year House War, a calm—and complacency—had settled over the Nexus House. That calm was shattered three months ago when McCarthy and Lara were attacked by praetorians from an undeclared house. There was the possibility that a Corvad cell had survived, or perhaps an alliance between the hostile minor houses had been formed. Following the attack, Rhea had assigned a praetorian guard to McCarthy whenever he was outside the protection of a Fleet warship or command center, and had ordered the Primus Nine to rebuild the praetorian legion.

Although the Nexi had defeated the Corvads at the Battle of Domus Valens, the victory had been costly. Of the one-thousand-strong Nexus Praetorian Legion, only forty had survived. Afterward, Rhea had decided to reconstitute only one of the ten cohorts—only one hundred praetorians. The Nexus House was the only major house remaining, and most of the twenty-two minor houses that had survived the House War had been aligned with the Nexus House. There would be no need for a full legion. Or so it seemed until McCarthy and Lara were attacked, saved only by the arrival of Ronan and a team of praetorians dispatched by Rhea, who had foreseen the assault.

Ronan was training additional praetorians as quickly as possible, but Nines were rare, and those suited for combat even rarer, and he could add only fifty praetorians per year on average. It would take twenty years to fully rebuild the legion, assuming there were no significant losses along the way.

"Join me," Rhea said to McCarthy as she turned to depart Tanum. "We have much to discuss. The Fleet faces difficult decisions, and Elena has regained consciousness."

"When?" McCarthy asked. "Why was I not told immediately?"

"You just were," Rhea replied tersely. "I was informed this morning."

As they traveled through the busy corridors of Domus Praesidium toward Rhea's office, McCarthy's thoughts dwelled on Elena Kapadia. Aside from Rhea and McCarthy, Elena was the only other Ten in the Nexus House. Shortly after achieving level ten, both at the age of sixteen, McCarthy had been assigned to the Navy and Elena to the Army to assist in the Korilian War.

While the Fleet protected McCarthy, letting him gain experience over the next twenty years, working his way up from a lowly ensign to starship captain to battle group commander and finally command of 1st Fleet, the Army had wasted Elena's talent, sending her to assist on Darian 3, the bloodiest battle in the history of the Korilian War, a planet the Colonial Defense Force had chosen to hold at all costs, hoping to stop the Korilian advance. After five years of carnage and over one billion lives lost in the attempt to hold Darian 3, the Army's manpower was expended and the Fleet was forced to abandon the planet, sentencing Elena and what remained of 3rd Army Group to death.

Three months ago—eighteen years after Darian 3 fell—they had discovered that Elena had survived and been taken prisoner and incarcerated on a planet in the Hellios system. The perilous mission to Hellios, deep in Korilian territory and far from reinforcements, had been successful, but had come at a significant cost, losing over half of 2nd Fleet.

Additionally, it was possible that they had lost those warships and half of the Marine Expeditionary Force executing the ground assault, and accomplished nothing. Elena had been tortured physically and mentally for years. The Korilians had finally broken her, forcing her to view the future and aid the Korilians. By the time she was rescued, she was mentally unstable and had even tried to kill McCarthy. She was now in a sanitorium in Belgium, being treated.

After entering her office, Rhea settled into her seat behind her desk as McCarthy took one of three chairs facing her. Rhea said nothing for a moment, and McCarthy felt the cool sensation flow past him as she viewed the future.

"Let's discuss the Fleet situation first," Rhea said. "I assume you've reached the conclusion that returning Second Fleet to operation won't solve the problem?"

"I have," McCarthy replied. "The Korilians will be able to engage our Fleet with even or better odds anywhere they choose unless we combine all four Liberation Campaign fleets. That would give us sixteen battle groups to their fifteen, but that would still be insufficient. The Korilian superiority in command and control is too significant to overcome with a single battle group advantage."

"Your solution?" Rhea asked.

"I intend to convince Fleet Admiral Fitzgerald to return me to command of one of the fleets. I can overcome the Korilian advantage, even if we engage at even odds."

"That is not a complete solution," Rhea replied. "While you win with one fleet, the Korilians can defeat three others."

"My plan includes a reduction in the number of Liberation Campaign assaults, down to two or even one if necessary, letting us combine the fleets. While in command of a two-fleet task force, or even all four fleets in a single engagement, I should be able to defeat the Korilians. However," McCarthy added, "we will need the Council's permission to let me engage in combat. The Council has been reluctant to place me at risk since the Final Stand."

"I will assist where I can," Rhea replied, "but unfortunately, I have the power of command, not of suggestion."

Rhea's ability—command over a human's physical body—was powerful and dangerous, but also obvious and threatening. The inferior power of suggestion, being able to plant ideas into a person's mind, would have been more helpful in this situation. Unfortunately, no Nexus currently alive had the power of suggestion.

"What of Elena?" he asked, moving the conversation to undoubtedly the second topic Rhea wished to discuss.

The One replied, "If she's rational, determine what talents she developed during her incarceration on Hellios. We know she's a timeline blocker and a healer. We also know she can use her healing talent in reverse, draining someone's life force, which is prohibited within the Nexus House, I must point out."

"You shouldn't fault her," McCarthy replied. "She was tortured for years on Hellios and would likely be dead by now if she hadn't developed the ability to protect herself."

"My position on the matter is firm," Rhea replied, irritation obvious in her tone. "In her current condition, leeway is appropriate, but once she is stable, I will address the matter."

Anger built inside McCarthy; it was unfair for Rhea to condemn Elena for developing the *wrong* talent. She had no control over the talents she had.

He tamped down on his anger, lest Rhea detect his failure to maintain firm control of his emotions. He had heard the mantra countless times— *Emotion is the source of all evil.*

Rhea continued, "It's possible that Elena has developed additional talents, but I cannot make a prediction. Her thoughts are so fragmented that I can't follow her timeline very far forward or backward, evaluating what talents she has developed. Perhaps you will gain more insight when you visit her today."

McCarthy had just learned Elena was conscious and had not yet made plans to see her; it was obvious that Rhea had viewed the future, learning of the decision he would soon make.

"I have to warn you," Rhea added. "You and Elena were close, but she isn't the woman she once was, and may never be. I suspect your visit today will be difficult for you."

McCarthy nodded his understanding. Sensing their conversation was over, he stood, as did Rhea. She gripped his forearm, offering the standard Nexus farewell.

"The future is not set."

McCarthy replied, using the response reserved for a farewell between two Nexus Tens.

"Together, we will change it."

3

Lara Anderson hurried through the corridors of Domus Praesidium, working her way through the mountain fortress toward the garden atrium. Moments earlier, her praetorian training session had just finished when her wristlet vibrated: a message from McCarthy, requesting she meet him in the atrium. She had only thirty minutes to shower and report for her next training assignment, but couldn't disregard his request. She had hoped they could spend the night together before he returned to Fleet command headquarters, but a meeting jammed between her classes portended otherwise.

She tried to let the disappointment wash over her, letting the emotion dissipate as she was being trained to do, but she was ill-suited to be a Nexus. She was an emotional creature at her core, and the Nexus One knew it. Lara felt like she was being judged every minute of every day she spent in Domus Praesidium.

Lara entered the atrium, a circular chamber filled with tropical vegetation, its walls rising over a thousand feet through the mountain to a glass-dome roof. She followed the winding path through the foliage until she arrived at the center—a thirty-foot-wide circle with stone benches along the perimeter. McCarthy was the only one there, sitting on a bench, and he stood when she arrived. Her uniform was still damp with perspiration from her exertion in Tanum, but McCarthy seemed not to care. He pulled her close and leaned in for a kiss, which she eagerly accepted.

Their kiss lingered, and McCarthy's hands moved slowly over her curves. She let him enjoy her body, hoping to convince him to spend the rest of the day, or at least an hour with her after her training was over. She glanced around, and after verifying there was still no one else within view in the atrium, she pulled the zipper of her jumpsuit partway down her chest and rested her forearms on McCarthy's shoulders.

McCarthy pulled back, a grin on his face.

"How long will we be alone?" she asked. Dating a man who could see the future had its advantages.

McCarthy slowly pulled her zipper back up. "I can't stay long, only a few minutes. I need to see Elena this afternoon."

Lara's smile faded.

It hadn't taken long to realize that McCarthy had a special relationship with Elena, and Lara couldn't help but feel threatened. McCarthy insisted they had never been involved romantically—Elena was like a sister—but Lara wasn't convinced. Elena was a beautiful woman who offered what Lara could not: a relationship with a powerful Nexus Ten. However, as long as Elena was confined to a sanitorium, detached from reality, Lara's relationship with McCarthy was safe.

"How is Elena?"

"She's conscious now. I'll learn more this afternoon."

Lara's jealousy flared. *Elena is recovering?*

"I know the timing is bad," McCarthy replied. "I was planning to spend the evening with you, but now that Elena is conscious, I owe it to her to stop by. I don't know how fragile her mental state is, but I'm certain a visit from me will bring some measure of comfort to her."

Lara released her embrace and stepped back. "She tried to kill you."

"She was unstable and deranged."

"And that's changed?"

"I don't know. That's why I want to stop by. To see if she's more like herself, or still..."

His words trailed off. Then he sat on the bench, staring into the distance.

The End of Time 15

Lara sat beside him, waiting for her jealousy to subside.

McCarthy's eyes drifted to the ground. Then he felt the underside of the stone bench they were sitting on. When he found what he was looking for, his fingers traced something carved into the stone.

"When Elena and I were kids, we'd sometimes crawl under this bench and pretend no one could see us—that there was an invisible force field that protected our lines from view. It was silly, since we were in plain view and our lines could be easily followed. But you don't know what it's like growing up in Domus Praesidium, filled with Nines and The One who can view where you are and what you're doing at any time, even view your most intimate moments with another.

"Elena and I would talk into the night about what we'd do when we grew up and the war was over. We'd wonder what the future held in store for us. Before we were shipped off to support the war, we carved our names into this bench. We wanted to leave something behind, evidence that we once existed. Finding Elena on Hellios...it cuts both ways. I'm thankful she's alive, but seeing what's become of her..."

Lara caressed McCarthy's back. "I know that dealing with Elena's condition has been hard on you," she said, "but your relationship with her is difficult for me as well. I'm envious of your bond with her. I don't want to lose you."

McCarthy wrapped an arm around Lara and pulled her close. "You have nothing to worry about. I care for Elena deeply, but she could never take your place."

Lara forced a weak smile. "You had better never forget those words."

"I won't," he replied. After a short pause, he asked, "How have you been?"

"I'm exhausted. The One has added praetorian training, and I've also resumed training as a fleet guide. I'm getting barely five hours of sleep a night."

Her resumed training as a fleet guide took McCarthy by surprise. "Fleet guide?"

"We're down to zero backup guides. We've lost three guides in the last year, and Carson didn't fare well during our sprint from Hellios back to Colonial territory."

After 2nd Fleet and the 3rd Marine Expeditionary Force had retreated from Hellios, three Korilian battle groups had chased what remained of the battered Colonial task group, forcing it to jump more quickly than was prudent. Insufficient rest time between jumps steadily increased the body's internal pressure until organ failure occurred. Typically, the eyes went first, bursting after one jump too many, followed by brain hemorrhages. Carson Lieu, the 2nd Fleet guide at the time, had endured both. Although his eyes had been replaced, it would be a while before he fully recovered from the brain bleeds.

In the meantime, a replacement guide had been assigned to 2nd Fleet, leaving Lara next in line, although she was not yet a certified guide.

McCarthy placed a finger under Lara's chin, lifting her face toward his. "No wonder you're exhausted. Although I don't understand why you've begun praetorian training early. Perhaps..." His voice trailed off, and he seemed lost in his thoughts.

"Perhaps what?"

"It's a training strategy," McCarthy replied. "You've been stuck at level eight for a while, and there are two unique strategies that are sometimes employed to help a student progress. One is total isolation for an extended period. The isolation removes the daily distractions, letting the mind focus solely on the training regimen.

"Another tactic is overload. Overload a student to exhaustion with physical and mental tasks, and sometimes the mind becomes more efficient, more streamlined in its processing. Once the overload is removed, students sometimes make quick, significant progress, breaking through whatever barrier existed. I suspect that's what The One is doing with you."

"That makes me feel better; I was wondering if she was just trying to break me. I can't tell with her. She's so...cold and unreadable."

McCarthy's wristlet vibrated with a message from his lead praetorian, informing him that his guard was assembled at the spaceport. He stood to leave, helping Lara to her feet. She hugged him and tried to invoke a vision, attempting to foresee what might happen during his visit with Elena. But unlike a Nine or Ten, she could not view a desired future or control the subject of the premonition, or even invoke one at will. This time, no vision appeared.

The End of Time 17

She relied on her intuition—the basic level-one skill present in all humans to some extent—prickling the hair on the back of her neck. While incarcerated on Hellios, Elena had developed the ability to drain a person's life force. Lara had witnessed Elena's lethality firsthand, aboard the 2nd Fleet command ship. Elena, in a deranged fit, had killed two nurses, leaving behind only their skeletons with thin, leathery skin stretched taut over their bones.

"I have a bad feeling about her, Jon."

McCarthy stared at Lara, and she felt the chill from his view. When the cold faded, he said, "It's difficult to predict the future when another Ten is involved, and even more so with Elena for some reason. I can't foresee what happens more than a few minutes into our meeting."

He kissed Lara gently on the lips, then released her from his embrace.

"Be careful," Lara said as he turned to leave.

McCarthy paused for a moment, then nodded and departed the atrium.

4

Aboard the shuttle bound for the sanitorium in Belgium, McCarthy closed his eyes, attempting to follow his and Elena's timelines during their meeting. Neither strategy proved successful, as both lines dissolved only minutes after meeting Elena. However, additional insight would be gained once the meeting began, as McCarthy was reasonably confident that a small sliver of the future, advancing in time during their conversation, would provide him with enough forewarning should the situation turn hazardous.

As the shuttle descended through dark, moisture-laden clouds toward its destination, McCarthy's thoughts turned to the past, to the fateful day that had led him and Elena here. Shortly after they both reached level ten, they were tasked to the Colonial Defense Force to assist in the Korilian War, and Elena had been sent to Darian 3. Two years into what would become a five-year effort to halt the Korilian advance, Darian 3 had already earned a reputation as a meat-grinder, chewing through combat troops as fast as reinforcements arrived. Assignment to Darian 3 was considered a death sentence.

McCarthy had been livid that The One sent Elena to Darian 3. Rhea explained that it was out of her hands; the Council's edict required her to turn over all Tens to the Colonial Defense Force. It was then that McCarthy learned the devastating truth—that he was the one originally assigned to the Army, destined for Darian 3. Rhea had told Elena first, preparing her to say goodbye to her close friend, and Elena had begged Rhea to let her take McCarthy's place. Rhea had acquiesced, letting Elena sacrifice herself for him.

For eighteen years, McCarthy had carried the burden of Elena's death, learning only three months ago that she had survived 3rd Army Group's annihilation on Darian 3. The Korilians had realized that Elena had special abilities and had captured her instead, then incarcerated and tortured her on Hellios 4 until she agreed to view the future for them. By the time she was rescued, Elena was demented and unstable, unable to reliably discern reality from hallucinations.

Amid a light rain, McCarthy's shuttle landed on a circular landing pad leading to the sanitorium: a sprawling five-story stone mansion with lush, manicured gardens. Waiting at the edge of the landing pad under black umbrellas were two men wearing white uniforms. They greeted McCarthy as he stepped from the shuttle, then escorted him and his guard into the sanitorium, the front doors closing behind them with a heavy clank. Once inside, they led McCarthy to a conference room filled with a half dozen men and women—the team assigned to care for Elena Kapadia—while his guard waited outside.

Dr. Elijah Guptah, seated at the head of the table, stood as they entered. "Welcome back to Sint-Pieters," he said, extending his hand.

Guptah introduced the members of his team again, then provided an overview of Elena's condition.

"Elena in relatively good health, physically, especially in light of what she endured on Hellios 4, although she remains significantly underweight. Mentally, we've made progress. After she was unsedated yesterday, she regained consciousness and did not become aggressive like last time."

"What happens next?" McCarthy asked.

"The challenge we face is convincing Elena that this," he spread his arms out to signify everything around him, "is real and not a Korilian fabrication; that her rescue from Hellios actually occurred and isn't a cruel Korilian mind trick. Apparently, not only are Korilians telepathic, but they can create illusions in a human's mind and have likely done so to Elena many times.

"As long as Elena does not become aggressive, we plan to keep her unsedated and continue her therapy, building her confidence that what she is experiencing is real, and help her develop the ability to differentiate reality from fabrication. Trust is the biggest element, and Elena doesn't trust anyone, not even herself.

"Your visit is fortuitous," Guptah said, "since you and Elena were close friends. You may be able to help us establish the trust with Elena that will aid in her recovery."

Guptah added, "I have to warn you, Admiral. Elena's grip on reality is tenuous. We believe your visit will be helpful, but you should avoid subject matter that would invoke traumatic memories. I recommend you simply follow Elena's lead. At some point, she'll need to talk about what happened on Hellios, which is an essential element of her therapy. We believe she may open up to you more easily than one of us. Perhaps not in today's meeting, but eventually.

"Do you have additional questions?" Guptah asked.

"Not at the moment," McCarthy replied.

"Let us proceed, then." Guptah gestured toward the door. "I will escort you to Elena."

McCarthy and his guard accompanied the doctor through the sanitorium, working their way toward the center of the facility. They soon reached a ring of rooms surrounding a circular garden atrium lined with trees and several layers of flowering shrubs. Guptah stopped beside a door with a glass viewport. On the other side of the door was a room with an adjacent patio on the atrium's perimeter, which was open to the sky. Glass panels rose twenty feet on three sides of the patio, with the sanitorium forming the fourth wall, ensuring the patient could not escape into the atrium.

On one side of the patio, Elena sat on a stone bench in the light rain, staring into the distance. Her blonde hair was soaked, and her knees were drawn up to her chest with her feet on the bench, her arms wrapped tightly around her legs as she rocked gently back and forth. A hospital garment clung to her body, leaving little to the imagination. The outline of her frail form was apparent through the fabric, and though she had filled out somewhat since the last time McCarthy had seen her, she was still quite thin. Elena was barely five feet tall, and combined with her emaciated body, she appeared almost childlike, belying her deadly talent.

"She has not left the patio since we transferred her to this room today," Guptah said. "Once she learned we had rooms adjacent to an atrium, she requested one, and apparently," Guptah gestured to the rain, "the elements do not matter. After being incarcerated in a cave-like chamber beneath the planet's surface for eighteen years, the open area is therapy in itself."

A guard holding a carbine approached, stopping beside Guptah.

"We're not sure how Elena will respond to you; whether she'll believe you are real or a Korilian fabrication. We have reason to suspect that you were a central element in the Korilian mind manipulations, which led to her attacking you on Hellios. As a safeguard, we have given Elena medication that should make her less aggressive, but she will become drowsy in about thirty minutes. Additionally," Guptah gestured to the armed guard, "you will be monitored by a sentry with his weapon set on stun, should Elena turn violent."

McCarthy glanced at his praetorians. He had no need of additional protection; they would intervene if necessary. But he nodded his understanding to Guptah.

"Keep the guard out of sight," McCarthy said. "I don't want Elena to feel threatened."

"Of course," Guptah replied. "One more thing," he said. "It appears that Elena doesn't remember your encounter on Hellios or what happened on the Second Fleet command ship. We've told her the basics—that you helped rescue her—but left out the details. When she sees you today, it's likely that she will think it's the first time she has seen you in twenty years, since she left Domus Praesidium."

Guptah unlocked Elena's door, then added, "Good luck. I will remain nearby should things get out of hand."

After Guptah pulled back, McCarthy focused on Elena, realizing she was viewing. He decided not to view before engaging her. Two Nines or

Tens viewing in proximity created a disturbance, similar to attempting to view two videos on a single display, resulting in the dissolution of both views. He decided Elena would feel safer if her view wasn't disturbed. It was risky, deciding to approach Elena without knowledge of what would occur in the next few minutes.

The moment McCarthy entered her room, she noticed his arrival and scurried to the far end of the bench, facing him as she crouched on her hands and feet. Her eyes were focused on him, her muscles taut, and McCarthy was unsure if she was about to attack.

He stepped from the room into the rain, stopping at the other end of the bench. "May I join you?"

There was no response from Elena aside from a guttural growl.

McCarthy took her response as a no.

"It's me," he said. "Jon."

Elena uttered a series of guttural sounds, this time louder and more threatening, and McCarthy concluded she was speaking Korilian. Although Korilians were telepathic, they had a crude method of verbal communication.

McCarthy offered a curious expression, to which Elena replied, "Don't pretend you don't understand, professing to be human."

"It's me," he repeated, "and I do not understand Korilian."

"Get out of my mind!" Elena screamed, then turned sideways, returning to her previous position, her knees drawn up and arms wrapped tightly around her legs. She began rocking back and forth again, although at a faster pace than before.

McCarthy sat on the other end of the bench, waiting for Elena to make the next move.

After a few minutes, Elena spoke again. "If you're Jon, tell me something you know about me that I don't know."

It seemed that the telepathic Korilians had been able to read Elena's thoughts, then devise scenarios to torment her. Elena had asked him to provide proof he wasn't a Korilian, something he knew about her that the Korilians wouldn't have learned from probing her mind.

"Something I know that you don't?" McCarthy asked. "How do I figure that out?"

Elena stared at him for a moment, then a confused expression clouded her face. She turned away and began talking to herself.

"Yes, how does he figure that out? If he's human, he can't see into my mind; he won't know what I know and what I don't. But what if he makes something up? He can just lie and I won't know."

Her face hardened as she turned back to McCarthy. "I didn't survive all this time by being stupid!" Her face turned red and spittle flew from her lips as she spoke.

"I have a better idea," McCarthy said. "Can a Korilian do this?"

He began viewing, and their commingled views were disrupted by the turbulence.

Elena turned away again, rocking back and forth as she spoke quietly to herself, casting furtive glances at McCarthy. Slowly, she shifted to a normal sitting position, then gradually slid toward him, one foot at a time. After stopping an arm's length away, she poked his shoulder with a finger.

McCarthy placed his arm slowly around her, then gently pulled her close.

Her body was tense at first, then she melted into his embrace, squeezing him tightly with both arms, her face pressed against his chest. He felt the warmth of her tears mixing with the cold drizzle soaking his uniform. She sobbed softly, then began crying.

After several minutes, her tears ended. She released him and sat upright, taking one of McCarthy's hands in hers, staring across the atrium.

"Tell me this is real. Tell me you're really here."

"I'm real, and I'm here."

"What took you so long?"

"I didn't receive the last message you sent from Darian 3. The Korilians were jamming all outgoing transmissions, and your message arrived partially garbled. The communication center personnel thought you were delirious, talking about being able to see the future. They filed your message away instead of delivering it, and we didn't discover your message until three months ago."

"Do you know..." Elena paused as emotion gathered in her chest and tears formed in her eyes. "Do you know what I've done?"

Her question was cryptic, but McCarthy concluded she was asking whether he knew she had viewed for the Korilians; that her assistance had cost millions of human lives.

"I do."

Elena burst into tears again, burying her face in her hands.

"I tried, Jon, I tried," she said between sobs. "I tried to resist them, but they broke me."

Her body shook in anguish, so McCarthy pulled her close again. Slowly, her sobs subsided but tears continued to flow.

"I tried to prevent it," she said, still with her face in her hands. "I knew they would eventually break me, so I tried to kill myself. I stopped eating and drinking, but they injected nutrients into my body. Then I decided to slit my wrists, but I didn't have anything sharp enough. So I chewed through my own flesh."

Elena sat up and looked at McCarthy, taking his hand in hers again. The rims of her eyes were red and puffy, her lips quivering. "I remember the taste of my blood, remember bleeding out on the chamber floor, and a mind-numbing fog enveloping me as I drifted into the darkness.

"When I woke up, my wrists were healed with no sign of what I'd done, not even a scar. I eventually learned that I had developed the ability to heal myself, but that was my undoing."

She stopped, and McCarthy sensed the emotion gathering inside her again. She finally continued, this time her voice cracking in anguish. "Once the Korilians realized I could heal myself, you can't imagine the things they did to me." She turned away, staring into the distance.

Her voice turned hard. "Those bastards. I wanted to rip every one of them apart."

Cold seeped into McCarthy's hand and up his forearm. He glanced down. His hand and arm had turned gray and were shriveling.

"Elena," McCarthy said.

She didn't respond.

"Elena!"

She turned toward him, then followed his eyes down to his arm. Her eyes widened, and a pained expression appeared on her face.

"I'm sorry!"

The End of Time

McCarthy felt her hand grow warm, then heat flowed into his arm, reversing what she had done until his arm and hand returned to normal.

"Please forgive me," she said as she released his hand. Then she dropped onto the ground and scurried under the stone bench. She crawled to the far end, curling into a fetal position. "I'm sorry," she repeated over and over as she began crying again.

McCarthy knelt down and peered beneath the bench. Elena was still apologizing. He tried to caress her face, but she flinched as he reached toward her.

"It's okay, Elena," McCarthy said. "You didn't mean to hurt me."

Elena gradually quieted, but her body still trembled.

"You're safe now," he said. "You're safe."

She slowly crawled out from under the bench, and as she returned to a sitting position, she began shivering. She was soaked and had almost no body fat to help protect her from the elements.

"Let's get you inside and warmed up."

He took her by the hand, and she followed him listlessly. Once inside, she stood there while McCarthy retrieved a towel from the bathroom and dried her off, then found dry clothes in a drawer.

"Don't leave," she said, before entering the bathroom to change, and she left the door open, peeking into the room frequently to ensure he hadn't left.

While he waited, McCarthy dried himself off with the towel as best possible.

When Elena emerged from the bathroom, she sat on the edge of her bed and McCarthy joined her. They talked for a while and Elena became drowsy, as Guptah had predicted. Her eyelids began to droop.

"I'm so tired," she said. "Will you stay with me? Lie beside me like we used to do under the bench in the atrium?"

McCarthy hesitated, assessing the danger—her ability to drain his life force by touching his skin. He searched Elena's eyes for clues, realizing that at this moment, she was staring at him with the eyes of the five-year-old girl he had met in Domus Praesidium. The eyes of the child who had made a pact with him not long afterward. They would become brother and sister, creating a family to replace the ones they had left behind. But not only had they become family, they had become best friends.

If there was any hope for Elena's full recovery, she needed a friend. She needed him.

McCarthy agreed, then lay behind her as they had done as kids, wrapping an arm around her and pulling her close. Her body slowly relaxed, and she placed her hand over McCarthy's, intertwining her fingers with his, squeezing his arm tight against her waist. It wasn't long before her breathing slowed and she drifted off into an uneasy sleep. Her body twitched as she made guttural noises, speaking to the Korilians in her dreams.

As he lay beside her, McCarthy realized he was exhausted. He'd had little sleep since discovering the Korilians were planning an offensive, staying up late viewing as many timelines as possible, postulating various responses and the alternate futures they created.

His thoughts returned to Elena, evaluating how to proceed. He finally decided it was best if he was there when she awoke, rather than leave and let her wake up alone, abandoned.

He closed his eyes and drifted off to sleep.

McCarthy was awakened by a light touch of fingers brushing across his forehead. He opened his eyes to see Elena lying beside him, facing him, her green eyes almost glowing in the twilight as day faded to night. She was brushing a lock of hair away from his forehead, smiling.

She spoke softly. "I had forgotten how handsome you are." Her fingers kept moving, tracing the outline of his face. "At first, you gave me the strength to resist the Korilians. I knew it wouldn't be long before you destroyed the facility or rescued me. I waited, and waited. The months turned into years, and you didn't come. I thought you had abandoned me. My resolve wavered, and I began to lose the will to survive. But then my love for you turned into hatred, and it gave me the strength I needed to survive."

Her words caught McCarthy by surprise; it was the first time Elena revealed that she was in love with him. They had been close during their time in Domus Praesidium, but their relationship had never been romantic. He had dated Amira through his teenage years until she failed the level-ten Test and became a Lost One, permanently insane.

But perhaps he had misinterpreted Elena's statement. Perhaps she was referring to the love shared by siblings. After all, he and Elena were like family.

Elena seemed to know where his thoughts were. "Just because we never dated doesn't mean I didn't want to. I used to watch you with Amira. I wanted to be her, to be the one holding your hand, sitting in your lap with your arms wrapped around me. I should have said something earlier, but I was waiting for your relationship with Amira to end. I knew she'd fail the Test and become a Lost One. But then things happened so quickly afterward, and I never got the chance. Until now."

She smiled as she traced the outline of his face again.

McCarthy considered the sudden turn of events. Elena's mental stability was tenuous, and rejecting her romantically would likely have significant repercussions. The issue would need to be addressed—he would have to reveal his relationship with Lara—but now wasn't the right time.

Instead, he asked the question that had been on his mind for twenty years, since the day they both left Domus Praesidium.

"Why didn't you say goodbye?"

"I thought it was best that way. I didn't want to give you an opportunity to change The One's mind, convincing her to send you to Darian like she originally planned. I didn't want you to learn what I had done—taking your place—until it was too late."

McCarthy smiled. "You were smart to do so. I would have done anything to convince The One to reverse the assignment."

"I know," Elena said. "And I didn't have to be a Ten to realize it."

"I never got the chance to thank you," he said.

"You came for me on Hellios. That's enough."

As dusk faded to darkness, McCarthy realized he needed to get going. He had to be at the Colonial Defense Force compound in Brussels at eight a.m., and he still had a short journey plus timelines to evaluate.

"I need to go," McCarthy said. "I have a meeting at Fleet headquarters first thing in the morning."

Elena pushed herself to a sitting position, then took his hand in hers.

"I've missed you," she said. "I've missed us."

"I've missed you as well. I'll be back as often as I can." McCarthy stood, pulling his hand slowly from hers.

Her voice suddenly turned cold. "You'll be back, in more ways than one."

"In more ways than one?"

"Your relationship with *it* won't last long."

"With *it*?"

"That thing you call Lara. I learned much while you were sleeping, following your line into the past. Not far—you woke too soon—but far enough. Your relationship with *it* will end, just like it did with Amira. And I'll be there when you finally realize that you love me and no other."

McCarthy wasn't sure how to respond. Her words weren't threatening, but there was an edge to her voice, a clear animosity toward Lara.

"Goodbye, Jon," she said. "I'll see you in a few days."

He considered for a moment, then decided not to address her predictions about his relationships. He stepped closer, kissing Elena on the cheek. "I *do* love you, Elena."

"I know," she said as she stepped onto the patio again, even though it was still raining. "And you will eventually love me more."

Elena looked skyward, letting the drizzle fall on her face. "I've missed the rain, too."

She sat on the stone bench again and pulled her legs up against her body, wrapping her arms around her shins, then began rocking back and forth again, talking to herself as McCarthy departed.

5

Admiral McCarthy's shuttle pierced the thick gray clouds, angling for the Colonial Defense Force compound in the center of Brussels: three triangular-shaped skyscrapers joined together to form another triangle. The Colonial Navy, Army, and Marine Corps headquarters were connected to a fourth tower in the center—the Colonial Defense Force command center. As the shuttle descended toward the landing pad atop the center building, McCarthy was lost in his thoughts, shifting between Elena—and her impact on his relationship with Lara—and the pending assault to regain control of the ten planets where their ground forces were stranded, evaluating various options and subsequent outcomes.

He was met on the rooftop by a Colonial aide, who escorted him to the main conference room where he took his seat at the table, awaiting the arrival of the Joint Chiefs of Staff. Due to his prescient ability, his presence and guidance had been consistently requested during JCS meetings.

The Joint Chiefs of Staff entered the conference room, taking their seats, with Fleet Admiral Fitzgerald sitting between the Marine Corps Commandant and Army Chief of Staff. Beside them sat two white-robed members of the Colonial Council: Inner Realm Regent Morel Alperi—a man in his fifties with a gray goatee—and Terran Regent Lijuan Xiang—an attractive woman in her late forties with long black hair, representing

Earth. Alperi and Lijuan were the directors of Personnel and Material, respectively, and the two most senior members of the Council aside from its president.

Fleet Admiral Fitzgerald made a few introductory remarks, then handed the meeting over to Captain Tom Wears, Fitzgerald's liaison with Fleet Intelligence, standing at the front of the conference room.

"As you're aware from the pre-brief," Wears began, "with Second Fleet in extended refit replenishing its losses, the Korilian Fleet has a temporary numerical advantage at the front line, fielding fifteen battle groups to our twelve. As a result, they've forced us to abandon the ten Liberation Campaign assaults in progress, stranding our troops without Fleet ground support or resupply.

"Once Second Fleet is operational again, the forces at the front line will be approximately equal: sixteen battle groups to their fifteen. However, the challenge we face is that due to superior Korilian command and control, the Korilians have the advantage at these odds. The only battles where we have defeated the Korilians without a one-third numerical advantage were when Admiral McCarthy was in command of the engagement.

"To enable victory in our Liberation Campaign efforts, Fleet Admiral Fitzgerald plans to place McCarthy in direct command of the four Liberation Campaign fleets, with authority to allocate those forces as desired: break them into battle groups, strike groups, or strike forces, or combine them into whatever size unit he desires, even a four-fleet task force.

"The first phase of the Liberation Campaign, once it recommences, is to combine the four fleets into a single task force, which will resupply our ground forces trapped on the ten planets. We'll engage the Korilians in each star system long enough to create a protective jump zone for resupply ships and medical transports, doing so one planet at a time.

"The second phase will depend on the Korilian response. We're hoping they respond in kind, combining their battle groups to engage our four-fleet task force. That means they'll abandon the other nine planets, which eliminates Korilian ground support from warships in orbit. If that happens, we'll assess the strength of Korilian combat troops on each planet and decide whether to proceed or withdraw from each planet as the situation dictates.

The End of Time 31

"If the Korilians ignore the bait—our four-fleet task force—and simply withdraw their warships from whatever planetary system we attempt to engage them at, we'll have to reevaluate. While our fleets control one planetary system, the Korilians will control the other nine, and those planetary assaults will eventually fail."

Fitzgerald addressed the regents. "As of today, the fundamental strategy of the Liberation Campaign has changed. Instead of regaining our lost colonies as quickly as possible, the goal is to destroy as many Korilian warships as possible. The Korilian warship construction rate has increased significantly since the Final Stand, building two warships for each of ours. In order to win this war, Korilian warship losses must double ours until the additional construction yards in Earth's orbit are operational."

Fleet Admiral Fitzgerald finished with, "We request your support at the Council, approving my proposal to place McCarthy in direct command of the Liberation Campaign battles."

Regent Alperi replied, "I'm not sure it's wise to send Admiral McCarthy to the front line. Why can't he lead the Liberation Campaign from Fleet headquarters here on Earth?"

Fitzgerald answered, "McCarthy's ability to view the future is affected by his proximity to the timelines. To outmaneuver Korilian forces in battle, he needs to participate *in* the battle."

"I don't think that's a good idea," Alperi replied. "It's open knowledge that McCarthy is a Nexus Ten—his abilities are no longer a secret after you revealed them before the Final Stand. If the Korilians have somehow determined his value to us, they may target him during battle. We should keep him on your staff, out of harm's way as he provides guidance."

Lijuan joined in. "When are you going to learn to trust Fleet Admiral Fitzgerald? You voted against her request to let McCarthy lead a task force to capture a Korilian cruiser prior to the Final Stand, which was critical in reverse engineering their starship shield settings, and you opposed sending him on the mission to Hellios 4."

"I may have been incorrect on the first issue," Alperi replied, "but my position on Hellios was appropriate. We risked McCarthy unnecessarily, sending him down to the planet's surface and into the Korilian facility. Ten thousand Marines went inside, stepping directly into a Korilian trap, and only four escaped with McCarthy. He was extremely lucky."

"It was not luck, Alperi. It was McCarthy's talent that enabled him to survive. Plus, we rescued Elena."

"Elena," Alperi said with disdain. "Do not remind me. We lost two hundred warships and half of a Marine Expeditionary Force, and what did we gain? An unstable woman who betrayed us."

There was an uneasy silence in the conference room. No one could argue with Alperi's assessment.

"Fleet Admiral Fitzgerald's request was still appropriate," Lijuan replied, "and the Council was wise to approve it. The mission was accomplished without harm to McCarthy, which is what matters."

"We're playing with fire," Alperi insisted. "There's a saying, 'The third time's the charm,' or in this case—disaster. We can't risk losing McCarthy."

"No war is won without risk, Morel. When are you going to learn to let the military fight the war, taking the risks they deem appropriate, instead of substituting your judgment for theirs? Sending McCarthy to the front line is far safer than Hellios. He'll be aboard a heavily defended fleet command ship and should be able to detect any harm coming his way. Plus, if you disapprove, what is your solution to our current dilemma—how to regain the advantage without a one-third numerical superiority?"

Alperi considered Lijuan's words for a moment, then turned to Fitzgerald. "I will support your request at the Council."

"As will I," Lijuan announced.

Fitzgerald replied, "Thank you, Regent Alperi and Regent Xiang."

Addressing the entire Joint Chiefs of Staff, Fitzgerald announced, "We will recommence the Liberation Campaign once Second Fleet has received sufficient replacement ships, which should be in two weeks. In preparation, Admiral McCarthy will lead the operations brief at Central."

6

Krajik lumbered through the dimly lit Korilian Fleet command compound, the black fibrous floor giving slightly with each step of his six-hundred-pound body, eventually entering the command center supervising the war against the humans. When he stopped beside Pracep Mrayev, who commanded all fleet and ground forces assigned to the campaign, he sensed the pracep's irritation.

Responsible for the campaign's overall strategy, Krajik had leveraged the assistance of the human who could see the future—the one who called itself Elena. After eight years, they had finally broken the human, harnessing its aid for the last ten. However, three months ago, after the Colonial fleet reached Hellios and was about to be destroyed by the trap Mrayev had prepared, the human had betrayed them.

The ambush at Hellios failed, Mrayev said to Krajik, conveying his thoughts telepathically instead of using crude sounds. *Elena betrayed us and alerted the humans, giving them time to prepare for our assault.*

Still, Krajik replied, *we were able to destroy half of a human fleet.*

This was not a victory. It was a clear defeat—the humans have reclaimed the one who can see the future.

That may not be as devastating as it seems, Krajik replied. *We have reviewed the surveillance videos from Elena's rescue, and it appears the humans already had this ability. There is at least one other human who can see the future. One that calls itself McCarthy. The intelligence directorate believes it is the one who led the human fleet in battle in Earth's solar system. Its ability to analyze the future and provide guidance is likely the reason for our unexpected defeat three years ago.*

Elena lied to us. It said it was the only human who could see the future.

When are you going to learn that deceit is integral to human nature? They can never be trusted.

Mrayev considered Krajik's comments for a moment, then said, *I must brief the Rhysh on the results at Hellios and outline the path forward. The Rhysh grows impatient with the war's duration, and I must propose a plan to annihilate the humans quickly. Do you have a recommendation?*

We must eliminate the human named McCarthy.

How is that possible? Mrayev asked. *It can foresee the future and will be aware of our plans.*

We learned much from Elena, Krajik replied. *Prescient humans are not omniscient. They perceive the future in narrow timelines they focus on, and will be unaware of other events. If we can keep McCarthy focused on unrelated events, we may be able to catch it by surprise and kill it. We will then be able to make swift progress, eradicating the remaining humans.*

Krajik added, *Now is the perfect time to eliminate McCarthy.*

Why is that?

We have just halted the human advance, repelling their battle groups supporting their planetary assaults. The humans have ten armies stranded, and their Fleet will have to reengage, driving our forces away long enough to resupply their troops or evacuate them. As they prepare for this critical and difficult endeavor, their focus will be outward rather than inward.

Inward?

With our fifteen battle groups committed at the front line, supporting our assault on the ten planets, the humans will not be concerned about an attack on Earth. We have no additional forces, at least nothing approaching what would be required for a surprise attack on their home planet. However, we already have four additional squadrons formed from replacement warships, and we can commit them to my plan.

What do you propose? Mrayev asked.

If the humans adhere to their previous pattern, they will hold an operations brief at their lunar base prior to launching a major offensive. We have two reconnaissance probes hidden in Earth's solar system, and they have detected the human fleet commanders heading to this base. McCarthy will undoubtedly be there, giving us an opportunity to kill it.

Krajik continued, *This will be a difficult and costly effort, however. Their lunar base is heavily defended, and all warships committed to the assault will likely be lost. However, they need to last only a short time, shielding combat troops descending to the moon's surface long enough for them to breach the lunar facility.*

There is another critical issue to consider, Krajik added. *We do not know how many human ground troops are stationed inside their lunar base, and we must insert overwhelming force to ensure the mission is a success. We should consider committing slayers to the attack.*

Mrayev reacted with surprise and concern, as expected. Slayers were larger and more vicious than standard combat troops, but more important, they could surround themselves with a defensive energy shield, making them extremely difficult to kill. They were very rare, however, with a single slayer normally leading an entire Korilian army into battle. Committing a slayer to a suicidal mission to kill one human was problematic. Even more questionable was Krajik's next suggestion.

I recommend we commit four slayers.

Pracep Mrayev pondered Krajik's proposal for a moment, then decided. *I approve of your plan. Send a strike force with four slayers to kill the human named McCarthy.*

7

Admiral McCarthy's shuttle rose from the Domus Praesidium spaceport, accelerating between the mountain peaks as the heavy metal doors shut slowly below. Inside the four-person Nexus shuttle, Lara sat beside McCarthy as the transport sped toward Central, the sprawling moon base. As the primary backup fleet guide, Lara had been directed to attend the pending operations brief.

Traveling directly from Domus Praesidium to Central, McCarthy had left his praetorian guard behind, as well as his Fleet transport. For the trip to Central, McCarthy had selected the Nexus shuttle built for him prior to the Final Stand, which was unique in two aspects: it had a jump drive, a capability no other transport this size featured, plus McCarthy had given the shuttle's artificial intelligence a special name—*Elena*. The Nexus engineers had even modified the artificial intelligence to speak in Elena's voice.

Three years ago, Elena was thought to be dead, slain on Darian 3. Even so, Lara had felt a pang of jealousy when McCarthy had named his shuttle's artificial intelligence after his close Nexus friend. Lara noticed that during times of intense viewing, McCarthy preferred to travel in his Nexus shuttle, as if hearing Elena's voice—even though it was only a manufactured resemblance—helped him concentrate.

Shortly after they began their ascent into the darkness above Earth,

McCarthy energized the operations brief he would present at Central, which detailed the revised Liberation Campaign fleet command structure, task force organization, and objectives. When prompted, *Elena* produced three-dimensional images of the ten planetary systems where the Colonial Defense Force had stranded its ground forces, along with the disposition of Korilian warships in orbit. While McCarthy viewed the potential futures, his gaze shifted between the planetary systems as he attempted to evaluate the outcome of various Fleet strategies and tactics.

As McCarthy had explained to Lara and others many times, he was prescient, not omniscient. The future was affected by billions of individual timelines, and he could follow only one at a time. His experience helped guide his selections, following one, then another, and another, attempting to identify the critical events that determined the outcome of the issue being examined, as well as how to manipulate that timeline to produce the desired result. However, he could not follow all timelines an equal distance into the future.

In chaotic scenarios like battle, where thousands of decisions were made every minute, timelines dissolved quickly, sometimes only a few minutes into the future. It was clear there would be heavy fighting once the Fleet recommenced its Liberation Campaign assaults, and McCarthy was certain that this time, the Korilians would not retreat to avoid losses as they had over the last three years. The outcomes of the pending battles, however, were undeterminable, as all relevant timelines dissolved in a gray haze shortly after the battles commenced.

In the distance, Earth's moon grew slowly in the shuttle window. *Elena* adjusted the vehicle's trajectory as they approached the lunar surface, leveling off and skimming just above the flat gray landscape. A sprawling white facility in the distance grew larger, and Lara recalled the details about their destination.

Central wasn't the actual name of the lunar complex. Its official name was the Deep Space Exploration Control Facility. But that was a mouthful, and since it was no longer used for that purpose, most people called it Central due to its unique design. The center of the complex was a large semi-spherical hub, like a half-buried ball. Three concourses stretched out from the hub forming a three-pointed star, each ending in a launchpad abandoned centuries ago. On two sides of each launchpad, metal frames rose several hundred yards.

Early starship jump drives were rudimentary, and in addition to low gravity—which even the latest jump drives required—the first-generation jump drives required high-velocity and acceleration vectors. The tall metal frames at each launchpad were magnetic rails, used to launch early space-ships to the required acceleration and velocity values. After more sophisti-cated jump drives were developed, eliminating the need to launch from Central, the lunar facility had remained the hub of humanity's space explo-ration effort until it was modified into a military facility after the outbreak of the Korilian War.

Elena informed McCarthy that Central had provided docking instruc-tions, and the shuttle angled toward an open portal in the side of Central's hub. The shuttle passed through a shimmering life-support shield and Central's gravity generators took effect. Lara shielded her eyes from the bright spaceport lights, noting several dozen shuttles docked in the multi-level spaceport. The shuttle settled into an empty bay in the highest level, where a four-star admiral awaited: Admiral Liam Carroll, Fleet Admiral Fitzgerald's deputy fleet commander.

After the shuttle touched down and the door slid open, Lara and McCarthy stepped into the spaceport.

"Welcome to Central," Carroll announced. Turning to McCarthy, he said, "Fleet Admiral Fitzgerald has requested a meeting after the operations brief, although you probably already know that."

"Actually," McCarthy replied, "I typically don't follow my own timeline, usually only during battle or before sensitive occasions where advance knowledge could be critical. Knowing what everyone is going to say before they say it can make the day quite tedious."

"I find the prospect quite enticing," Carroll replied, "but I suppose the novelty could wear off after a while."

"Believe me," McCarthy said, "being able to foresee the future is not always a blessing."

"A blessing and a burden, I imagine. Also," Carroll added, "Regents Alperi and Xiang have requested you join them on the observation deck for a few minutes before your brief begins. I suspect the meeting will be more

The End of Time 39

of a publicity event than a strategy discussion. They're accompanied by public affairs personnel, and I'm sure they'll want a video clip of them talking with the Hero of the Korilian War."

Lara recalled that Morel Alperi and Lijuan Xiang were the two senior regents aside from the Council president, and with the president's scheduled retirement next year, both Lijuan and Alperi had begun jockeying for advantage in the pending presidential selection. News clips of them discussing the Fleet's upcoming operation with Admiral McCarthy would be excellent publicity.

McCarthy provided no reaction to Carroll's comment about how the public had dubbed him the Hero of the Korilian War—some even called him humanity's savior—leading the combined Fleet to victory against the Korilian armada during the Final Stand. During previous occasions when the moniker had been mentioned, McCarthy appeared neither impressed nor irritated with the praise, simply redirecting the conversation elsewhere.

"I'll make an appearance with them," he said.

"I won't delay you any longer," Carroll replied. "I'll see you at the brief."

Carroll departed through one spaceport exit while Lara and McCarthy left through another. They proceeded through the passageways filled with men and women hustling between compartments, making final preparations to recommence the Liberation Campaign assaults. Lara noticed how their faces brightened when Admiral McCarthy passed by, as well as the lingering looks from men toward her. She was an attractive woman, and the form-fitting blue-and-white Nexus uniform accented her body. Plus, Nexi were a rare sight; there were only six assigned to the Fleet—seven if you counted McCarthy—but he wore the Colonial Navy's burgundy-and-crimson uniform instead.

After taking the nearest elevator, they stepped onto Central's top level, its circumference lined with twenty-foot-high windows offering a 360-degree view of the lunar surface. A clear dome capped the observation deck, with the stars and Earth shining brightly through. Standing near the observation deck perimeter were Lijuan and Alperi, accompanied by an entourage of aides and security personnel, plus a public relations staffer filming the regents as they interacted with Central's personnel. Alperi spotted McCarthy and Lara and gestured for them to join the group.

The regents greeted them, then Alperi moved alongside McCarthy as the Council staffer's wrist camera followed. Not to be outmaneuvered, Lijuan stepped beside Lara, ensuring she was captured in any video used for promotional purposes.

"And here we are on Central with Admiral McCarthy," Alperi announced to the camera, "who will once again lead the combined Fleet into battle. The details are classified, of course, but the Council is confident that the Liberation Campaign will regain its momentum under his exceptional guidance."

Alperi turned to McCarthy, waiting for a response.

"That's the plan," McCarthy replied.

Lijuan draped an arm around Lara. "And for those of you who don't know who this is, let me introduce Lara Anderson, a Nexus Eight who was Admiral McCarthy's guide during the Final Stand. We owe a debt of gratitude not only to Admiral McCarthy but to Lara as well. Her guidance was instrumental during the critical battle."

Lara felt uncomfortable with the accolade but forced a smile in response.

Lijuan seemed to have sensed her discomfort, because she shifted topics. "It's an impressive sight, isn't it?" She spoke to the camera, gesturing toward one of the three concourses extending to a launch complex, framed by the Apennine Mountains in the distance. "Our exploration of the galaxy began here at Central, with the launch of the first ship with a jump drive."

"Actually," Alperi interjected, "jump drives were our second attempt at deep space exploration." He glanced at the video tech to ensure the exchange was being caught on camera. "Our first attempt was the Prometheus Project: space stations creating wormholes for instantaneous travel, controlled from Central. But the project was plagued with problems and eventually terminated. Jump drives were developed shortly afterward, and Central's three concourses and launchpads were added."

Alperi smiled.

"You're quite right about the Prometheus Project being our first *attempt*," Lijuan replied. "But as I stated, our exploration of the galaxy began with jump-drive starships launched from Central."

The back-and-forth exchange between the two regents continued, and

The End of Time 41

Lara's thoughts drifted toward McCarthy's pending departure for battle. As her eyes wandered, she spotted another Nexus Eight standing alone along the perimeter, staring through the transparent panels at one of 5th Fleet's battle groups in the distance. Lara recognized the woman as Angeline Del Rio, the 3rd Fleet guide and Lara's mentor during the hectic weeks prior to the Final Stand.

Lara excused herself to join Angeline, feeling bad about abandoning McCarthy to the two regents but figuring he'd survive. She checked her wristlet; in ten minutes they would have to depart so McCarthy could prepare for the operations brief.

Angeline greeted her with a hug, then pulled back and smiled. "It's good to see you."

"You too," Lara replied. "Waiting for the operations brief?"

Angeline nodded. "I've been putting the wait to good use, trying to invoke premonitions of the Liberation Campaign, hoping to gain a glimpse of the outcome."

Unlike Nines or Tens who could choose a specific timeline to follow into the future, Eights had occasional glimpses of the future, like peering through a foggy window with a temporary circle of clarity that quickly misted back over. Additionally, even though the premonitions could be focused on a particular event or time, the visions were random.

"I haven't had much luck for some reason," Angeline said. "And the one worthwhile vision I've had was odd. The wrong fleets were participating in the battle. Fifth Fleet had joined the Liberation Campaign, while Third Fleet was missing."

"That does seem odd," Lara replied. "Perhaps it's several weeks or months into the future, and Third Fleet has been withdrawn for an extended refit."

Angeline shrugged. "Perhaps. It still felt different for some reason, and I don't know why. But enough of my problems. How are you doing?"

"I'm doing well, all things considered. Tired, mostly. The One has added praetorian lessons to my regimen, plus I've resumed training as a fleet guide."

"I heard about Alayne's death. That makes you the first backup fleet guide. How is your training going?"

"I'm getting better," Lara replied, "although I still can't invoke visions at will. But my Rosetta Stone is developing; I can at least tell if the vision is bad news."

One of the reasons Lara had been selected as a fleet guide was that in addition to being an Eight, all fleet guides were synesthesians—a rare talent—receiving their premonitions with a common theme. Angeline was a color synesthesian; her visions always had a color scheme, with each color having a particular meaning.

Fog was the common theme in Lara's visions, although she had not yet mapped the variations in the fog to specific meanings. She had, however, determined that a vision beginning with a room full of fog or a thin layer spreading across the floor was benign, whereas fog in the shape of a weaving tendril portended danger. Lara explained to Angeline the two basic fog variations in her visions, then revealed her true concern.

"Working with Admiral McCarthy during the Final Stand was easy, since he's used to deciphering visions. But he'll have overall control of the campaign this time. If I'm called up, I'll be working with a standard fleet admiral instead of a Nexus Ten. I'll have to determine the meaning of my visions on my own, and I don't know if I can do it."

Angeline placed her hands on Lara's shoulders, offering support. "No fleet guide can decipher every vision, especially in the time available during battle. You can only do your best, relaying what you can, and don't get frustrated by the visions you can't interpret."

Her former mentor's encouraging words helped ease Lara's angst, and she was about to shift the conversation to another topic when she spotted movement above. Tendrils of fog had sprouted from the center of the clear canopy above the observation deck, spreading out along the semi-spherical enclosure.

Lara's body tensed as she studied the fog moving swiftly down the canopy sides.

"What is it?" Angeline asked.

"Tendrils."

Angeline took a deep breath and closed her eyes, concentrating. After a short moment, her eyes snapped open.

"What did you see," Lara asked.

The End of Time   43

"Red."

"Where?"

"Everywhere!"

Angeline turned toward McCarthy and shouted, "Incoming!"

The regents beside McCarthy seemed irritated by Angeline's rude interruption, but McCarthy simply stared at her. Lara was too far away to detect the cool sensation from his view, but she knew he was evaluating the nearby timelines, most likely starting with his own.

"Evacuate the observation deck!" he yelled. "Head to the defense bunkers!"

Then he tapped his wristlet, speaking rapidly as stunned Central personnel began moving toward the elevators and stairs.

Lara was about to join McCarthy when she was almost blinded by several dozen bright white flashes above the lunar base.

A shimmering defense shield appeared overhead in response, encapsulating Central within a protective dome as Central's alarm activated—alternating high and low tones accompanied by flashing red lights—followed by an announcement emanating from the observation deck speakers.

"General Quarters, General Quarters. All hands report to assigned stations."

As the light above faded, Lara looked up to a sky filled with four squadrons of Korilian warships—similar in design to Colonial Navy ships, aside from the gray exterior and numerous communication spires jutting outward from the hull. The warships were joined by a troop transport already launching surface assault vehicles, which were descending toward the lunar surface. Two Korilian carriers began launching marauders—the Korilian counterpart to Colonial single-pilot vipers.

Central's defense artillery activated—blue tyranium pulses shooting up toward the Korilian starships—while the nearest Colonial battle group also engaged, sending almost one hundred pulses toward the intruders, melting holes through every Korilian warship.

The carnage above was almost mesmerizing. Explosions rocked the enemy warships, and several starships hit by multiple pulses disintegrated in bright orange flashes—their jump drives had been damaged and imploded. In another minute, once Central's and the Colonial battle group's pulse generators recharged, there would be little left of the Korilian warships.

It's a suicide mission, Lara thought. *But for what reason?*

Lara and Angeline began moving toward the nearest observation deck exit, angling toward McCarthy and the regents and their entourage. Lara's eyes kept being drawn toward the gray warships, and she suddenly realized there was something odd about the Korilian tactics. There was no sign of defensive shields forming around their warships.

Starships had to jump with shields down, energizing them immediately after completing the jump. However, power could be diverted instead to the pulse generator, overcharging it for a single shot at twice the strength, but the effort would destroy the pulse generator.

Lara realized her assessment was correct; the Korilians had made a one-way suicide trip to Central, with the surviving warships firing a single pulse before they were destroyed. As she wondered why, she spotted the surface assault vehicles converging toward a single spot as they descended.

Seconds later, the surviving Korilian warships fired simultaneously, their red pulses impacting Central's shield in the same spot. An entire sector of the shield disappeared, leaving a hole in the lunar base's defense, toward which the Korilian assault vehicles headed.

Nearby sectors in Central's protective dome began expanding, closing the gap. Assault vehicles slipped through until the hole finally closed, clipping the last shuttle. The back of the vehicle vaporized, sending the forward section spiraling down until it plowed into the lunar surface, creating a wave of lunar dust and debris expanding outward from the impact point.

As Lara and Angeline joined McCarthy, Central's defense artillery and the Colonial battle group fired again. Several more Korilian warships disintegrated in orange flashes, with purple explosions spurting out of even more as damaged shield generators imploded.

When the blue pulses faded, not a single Korilian warship remained operational; several had been vaporized, while those that remained were darkened hulks, lit up inside by explosions throughout their compartments. However, several dozen Korilian assault vehicles were approaching the lunar surface, while five hundred marauders took station above

Central. The moon base's powerful tyranium artillery batteries were effective against large starships but wouldn't be able to take out the nimble fighters.

As Lara and the others reached the stairway, clogged with personnel evacuating the observation deck, Alperi asked McCarthy, "Are we going to a defense bunker?"

"No," McCarthy replied. "Our path will be blocked."

"By what?"

"A slayer."

Alperi's face turned pale. "They've sent a slayer?"

McCarthy fixed his gaze on the regent. "They've sent *four*."

8

McCarthy led the way to Central's main deck, which connected to the three concourses and the underground command center. Instead of heading toward the reinforced bunkers, however, he veered to his left, just before Central's outer wall was ripped open by an explosion.

Lara and the others were knocked from their feet by the pressure transient as debris blew past them. An emergency environmental shield formed over the damaged section, but that didn't stop twenty Korilian combat troops, led by a slayer, from passing through the iridescent barrier into Central's main hub. The combat Korilians and slayer wore body armor and wielded a pulse-pistol in each of their four upper limbs. Additionally, the slayer was surrounded by a shimmering energy shield. However, it was protected by only one shield, in contrast to the double-shielded slayer that had stood guard outside Elena's prison chamber on Hellios.

The Korilian combat troops were bigger than standard Korilians, while the slayer, standing twelve feet tall, was fifty percent larger, its body covered in fibrous black plates. Its head was likewise encased, its eyes protected by translucent panes. In addition to the weapons, the Korilian limb armor tapered to sharp edges, glowing bright red.

As Lara regained her feet with McCarthy and the others, terror saturated the air around her, emanating primarily from the Council regents' entourage. When McCarthy continued heading toward the nearest concourse instead of the reinforced underground bunkers, the Council entourage hesitated, then bolted toward the people flooding the bunker entrance, leaving their regents behind with the three Nexi.

Ignoring the five humans angling toward the concourse, the Korilians targeted the mass of humanity clogging the bunker entrance. The combat Korilians fired their pulse-pistols, while the slayer wielded a weapon Lara hadn't seen before—a fat, stubby assault carbine.

Instead of firing a red laser pulse, the slayer's weapon shot a bright orange burst that sped across Central's hub and enveloped a Council staffer —the public relations assistant who had been filming on the observation deck—in a hollow, orange sphere. The man shook violently as electric arcs sizzled through him, the intensity increasing until the sphere vanished in a bright flash. The man's charred, lifeless body fell to the floor.

Lara, Angeline, and both Council regents followed McCarthy into Concourse Alpha. As they ran down a large, forty-foot-wide passageway, an explosion rocked the far end of the concourse. Debris ricocheted up the corridor as smoke obscured the view, and then the smoke and debris were sucked back toward the source of the explosion, revealing another ten combat Korilians and a second slayer.

The breach in the concourse hull was sealed by an emergency environmental shield as an alarm sounded throughout the concourse, followed by Central's computer announcing in a woman's calm voice:

"Containment breach, Concourse Alpha. Isolating Concourse Alpha."

Lara glanced over her shoulder. The heavy emergency doors at the concourse entrance were slowly closing behind them. Just before the doors sealed together, two squads of armored Marines carrying assault carbines arrived, one squad engaging the Korilians in the hub while the second squad entered the concourse, advancing toward the Korilians at the far end.

The dozen Marines had decent odds of killing the standard Korilian troops, but they had no chance against a slayer. Lara had witnessed first-hand on Hellios what a slayer could do against an entire handpicked platoon of the Marine Corps' finest.

McCarthy abruptly turned into a nanotechnology lab, joined by Lara and the others, where they ducked below a panel of windows looking into the concourse's main corridor. As they hid inside, Lara rose just enough to peer through the windows.

The Marines were advancing toward the Korilians, wisely focusing on the standard combat troops; their weapons couldn't kill a slayer. Only a coordinated effort by a larger unit or heavy weapons could penetrate a slayer shield. Lara had no idea how many Marines were in Central or what kind of weapons they had. As far as she knew, only a small security detachment was posted at the lunar base.

The Korilians also advanced, with dead and injured Marines and Korilians falling as the opposing sides engaged. The slayer fired its weapon, waiting several seconds between shots for it to recharge, each time leaving a charred Marine in melted armor on the concourse floor. But the Marines were taking out the standard Korilian combat troops just as fast, and both sides dwindled until there was a single Marine facing the slayer. After another orange pulse, the Marine's smoldering remains lay on the concourse floor as the slayer passed by.

The slayer continued on, reaching the sealed concourse emergency doors, where it searched the adjoining laboratories, then began working its way back down the corridor.

As McCarthy sat on the floor with his back against the wall, staring into space, Lara felt the cool sensation from his view. Then he stood and approached the nano-lab doors, which opened to the concourse.

"We need weapons," he announced, his gaze going to the assault carbines lying beside the dead Marines.

A faint golden glow lit the nano-lab through its windows for a moment as the slayer returned to the main passageway before disappearing into another lab.

McCarthy opened the door and sprinted into the passageway, collecting three assault carbines before returning to Lara and the others huddled beneath the nano-lab windows. He handed one carbine to Angeline and one to Lara, keeping the third for himself.

"Has your praetorian training advanced to carbines yet?" he asked Lara.

Lara shook her head. "But Liza showed me how to operate one before the assault on Hellios, in case I picked one up along the way." Lara recalled the instructions provided by the Marine who had been her bodyguard during the treacherous descent into the Korilian facility on the desolate planet.

McCarthy stared into the distance for a moment, analyzing their options. While Lara waited, she wondered why McCarthy had led them into a concourse that had just been sealed from the main hub, and what his plan might entail. She searched the passageway for a solution, her eyes drawn to the large hole in the concourse where the Korilians had blasted their way inside. The environmental shield that had formed over the gap was flickering, and it suddenly disappeared.

A few seconds later, Lara heard another announcement over Central's speakers:

"Warning. Life-support failure in Concourse Alpha, main passageway."

The concourse's center corridor could no longer support human life; they could not leave the nano-lab.

They were trapped.

9

McCarthy sat silently for another moment, then tapped his wristlet. Fleet Admiral Fitzgerald, who was in Central's command bunker, appeared on the display. McCarthy provided his status, then Fitzgerald spoke.

"The good news is—we've eliminated all standard Korilian combat troops. The bad news is—we have no Marines left and four slayers remain: one in the main hub and one in each concourse. It looks like each is working its way through the compartments, killing everyone it encounters. I've ordered reinforcements with heavy weapons, but they're a ways out, plus it looks like the Korilian marauders are going to hold off reinforcements until Fleet vipers can clear a path to Central."

After providing the update, she asked McCarthy the critical question. "Will help arrive in time?"

"I don't know," he replied. "There is no firm prime timeline, which means the future is in flux. But I'll analyze the options and pick the plan that keeps us alive the longest."

"Understood," Fitzgerald replied.

After McCarthy's wristlet display went black, Lara asked, "What the hell is going on? Why would the Korilians sacrifice half a battle group to attack Central? And why commit four slayers, when they've never sent more than a single slayer to lead an entire planetary assault?"

The End of Time   51

"Good questions," McCarthy replied. "There are a number of things that don't make sense at first glance. However..." His voice trailed off.

"What is it?" Lara asked. When McCarthy didn't immediately reply, Lara added, "You know what their plan is, don't you?"

McCarthy nodded. "They're here to kill *me*."

"This is what Fitzgerald was afraid of," Lara replied. "Why she kept your abilities a secret until the Final Stand."

"The Korilians have obviously figured things out, and it also sheds light on Elena. It's clear that she didn't tell the Korilians about me, or they would have hunted me down earlier."

Alperi interrupted their conversation. "What's the plan, Admiral? How are you going to keep us safe? I needn't remind you that Lijuan and I are Council regents, and you have the utmost responsibility to safeguard our lives."

Lara almost screamed at Alperi. Did he not comprehend that the Korilians had come to kill *McCarthy*? However, his next statement revealed he had understood clearly.

"Since the Korilians are intent on killing you, perhaps we should split up. Leave Lijuan and me in a safe place while you keep the Korilians occupied."

Lara wanted to slap Alperi, who was thinking only about his safety and not of McCarthy's. Could he be so shortsighted that he didn't realize the war would be lost if McCarthy was killed?

"It's your choice, Regent," McCarthy replied. "But you'll be safer with me."

Lijuan placed a hand on McCarthy's wrist, and it seemed like she was gathering her thoughts for a moment, then spoke. "We'll stay with you, Admiral."

"Speak for yourself," Alperi snapped.

Lijuan rephrased her words. "I'll go with you, Admiral. If Alperi wants to be left behind, all by himself, that's up to him."

"Fine," Alperi said bitterly, returning his gaze to McCarthy. "But you had better be right about being safer with you."

Angeline interjected. "We can't stay here. The slayer will eventually search this lab. We can't leave, either." Angeline pointed to the control panel beside the nano-lab doors, which displayed in red letters:

WARNING – CONCOURSE LIFE-SUPPORT FAILURE – WARNING

"The ventilation system." McCarthy looked toward a square vent in the center of the lab ceiling. "We can make it to the concourse assembly bay."

"Assembly bay?"

"It's the bay at the end of each concourse, used when Central launched the first starships with jump drives. Final assembly of the starships occurred in the bay, before they were moved onto the launchpad. Ships with modern jump drives no longer need assistance from magnetic rails, so the launchpads were abandoned centuries ago, and the assembly bays were converted into warehouses."

"What do we do when we reach the assembly bay?"

"There are exposure suits we can use to exit Central, then reenter the hub and head to the command bunker. Along the way, we'll set a trap for one of the slayers."

McCarthy climbed onto a lab counter beneath the ventilation duct and removed the cover, revealing a three-foot-by-three-foot-wide opening.

"I'll go first," McCarthy announced.

He placed his assault carbine into the ventilation duct gently, to minimize the noise, then pulled himself into the shaft as quietly as possible. Lara went next, followed by Alperi and Lijuan, then Angeline.

Lara pushed her assault carbine before her as she crawled. The going was slow but straight, the ventilation duct illuminated by their wristlet displays. After passing beneath a large fan, they reached what appeared to be a dead end; the shaft was sealed by emergency levers that must have closed when the concourse lost life support.

McCarthy located a small control panel, and his hand hovered over the numeric pad for a few seconds as Lara felt the cool sensation from his view; he was analyzing every permutation of authorization codes until he found the correct one. He punched in the code, and the levers swiveled open.

A faint white glow appeared in the distance, growing brighter as they continued their trek until McCarthy came to a halt. There was the sound of grating metal as he removed the duct cover, then let it fall into the assembly

The End of Time

bay with a clank. Light flooded the ventilation duct, and McCarthy disappeared from the shaft.

Lara moved to the end of the duct, which opened into the assembly bay ten feet above the deck. She tossed McCarthy her assault carbine, then twisted around and dropped feetfirst into the assembly bay, with McCarthy partially catching her on the way down. The two regents and Angeline followed.

The assembly bay was sealed off from the concourse by emergency doors that had shut when the concourse lost life support. As McCarthy had explained, it was a warehouse now, filled with stacks of containers and construction equipment, ostensibly for periodic maintenance of Central's centuries-old exterior and interior structure.

"How do we kill the slayer?" Angeline asked.

"It won't be long before it arrives, and we'll have a surprise for it. The plan is to lure it under one of the cranes." McCarthy pointed to a ten-ton overhead crane.

"Squash it like the bug it is." Angeline grinned. "How do we lure it under the crane?"

"We're going to be the bait. We'll position ourselves at the far end of the assembly bay, and when the slayer heads toward us, it'll pass beneath the crane. But first, we need to pick up something heavy with the crane and also find something to hide behind."

McCarthy examined the spaceport, his eyes stopping on a stack of large containers.

"Regent Alperi, Regent Xiang. I need you to help Lara and Angeline move that stack of containers to the left about twenty feet, directly across from the assembly bay doors."

Alperi gave McCarthy an indignant look until Lijuan replied, "We'd be happy to help."

McCarthy headed over to the crane controls while the regents helped the two Nexi move the containers. It was obvious that cardio training wasn't part of Regent Alperi's daily routine, because he soon became winded, perspiration beading on his face. Although Lijuan strained with the effort, she fared much better.

Meanwhile, McCarthy examined the crane console, then manipulated the controls, energizing and then guiding the overhead crane toward a large shipping pallet. He lowered the hook and then guided it through a fastener on top of the pallet. A moment later, the seven-ton pallet—its weight displayed on the console—had been lifted high in the air and positioned midway across the assembly bay, bisecting a straight line between the entrance and the containers that had been restacked in their new location.

"Time to suit up," McCarthy announced. "Once the slayer blasts its way into the assembly bay, we'll lose life support in here."

He led everyone into an adjoining room, stopping alongside a rack of exposure suits. After selecting what appeared to be the proper size suit, Lara slipped into one, as did the others, with McCarthy assisting Lara with the final step: the helmet was placed over her head, then twisted into its locked position. The helmet facepiece lit up with an array of indications on one side while data scrolled down the other: air quality, hours of oxygen remaining, heart and breathing rates, blood pressure, and suit temperature.

After Lara's helmet clicked into place, there was complete silence. The others continued talking, but she heard nothing.

Once McCarthy donned his suit, he pointed to the wristlet built into the left forearm of his exposure suit, which displayed the number 12. He manipulated the controls, raising and lowering the number, then restored it to 12. Lara set her controls to 12 and suddenly heard Angeline talking.

"—here, Admiral."

"I'm here," Lara said.

A few seconds later, Lijuan and Alperi joined the communication channel.

"Let's get positioned," McCarthy said.

10

After they returned to the assembly bay, McCarthy addressed the others.

"Regents, hide behind the stack of containers you just moved. Lara and Angeline, take position in front of the containers, facing the concourse doors. When the slayer enters the assembly bay, fire at it once and then hide behind the containers. You'll have to move fast—its reaction will be quick."

As Lara and the others took their positions, McCarthy returned to the crane control booth and hid behind the control panel. Standing in front of the containers with Angeline, Lara took a deep breath and tried to quell her rising trepidation, telling herself that everything would be fine. McCarthy wouldn't have set the trap for the slayer unless it would work and everyone survived.

While they waited, the only thing Lara heard was the sound of her own breathing, and despite her best effort, her anxiety mounted with each passing second.

Several minutes later, the center of the concourse doors began glowing red, increasing in brightness until the doors exploded inward. Smoke clouded the entrance as debris ricocheted into the assembly bay. The smoke quickly cleared, and the smaller pieces of debris reversed course and tumbled back toward the shattered entrance doors as the assembly bay depressurized into the concourse passageway and out into space through the breach in the concourse hull.

The slayer stood there for a moment, waiting for the pressure transient to subside, the debris bouncing off its shimmering defense shield and down the concourse passageway.

Lara and Angeline fired their carbines, the pulses lighting up the slayer's energy shield in sizzling electrical sparks, delaying the slayer from returning fire long enough for Lara and Angeline to dash behind the containers, joining the Council regents.

Angeline positioned herself at one end of the containers, and Lara did the same, peering around the edge. As the slayer advanced toward them, it aimed its weapon at the containers, shooting orange pulses that melted three-foot-diameter pits into the container stack. A few more pulses, Lara thought, and a hole would be melted completely through the containers.

"Almost there," Lara heard McCarthy say over her exposure suit's communication circuit.

As the slayer continued toward Lara and Angeline, firing its weapon as it recharged, McCarthy peered out from behind the control console. When the slayer passed beneath the overhead crane, McCarthy pressed one of the crane controls. The heavy pallet dropped onto the Korilian, crushing it under the weight of seven tons. The slayer lay motionless as its defense shield sizzled and crackled.

Lara emerged from behind the containers and approached the pallet, kneeling down to examine the squashed slayer. But then the slayer's appendages began twitching, and it suddenly looked at her. The pallet atop the Korilian began moving upward as the slayer struggled to unpin itself.

As the slayer freed the limb holding its weapon and swung it toward Lara, McCarthy approached and fired his weapon. The pulse penetrated the slayer's weakened shield, severing the Korilian's head from its body. The pallet collapsed back onto the slayer, crushing it as the Korilian's defense shield sizzled, then dissipated.

11

"That was easy," Alperi said as he emerged from behind the containers, eyeing the dead slayer. "Let's haul the carcass off and set the trap for the next one."

"That won't work," McCarthy said. "Korilians are telepathic. The other three slayers already know what happened and will avoid any overhead cranes. We need to get out of here before another slayer shows up. One is already on its way. Follow me."

McCarthy led the group into a large air lock that opened onto the lunar surface. After entering the chamber, he shut the doors behind them. Through the viewports in the outer set of doors, the only thing visible was the barren lunar landscape. They had only an hour of faint light remaining before the moon entered its two-week-long night.

"It'll take a minute while the air lock depressurizes," McCarthy said as he manipulated the control panel.

As air hissed through ports near the top of the chamber, Lara heard Alperi's voice through her helmet. "You realize there's no such thing as the dark side of the moon?"

"What?" Lara asked. Not that she didn't know, but why would Alperi bring up trivia at a time like this? There was a nervous quaver in his voice, so perhaps this was his way of maintaining control.

"It's a common misconception that there's a dark side of the moon," he continued. "But every area of the moon experiences day and night as it revolves around the Earth. What's true is that there's a near and far side of the moon. As the moon revolves around Earth, we always see the same side —the near side."

"That's fascinating," Lijuan said sarcastically. "But I think we're more interested in seeing the far side of these air lock doors."

"Almost ready," McCarthy said. A few seconds later, the control panel indication turned green, and the air lock outer doors opened.

McCarthy and Lara stepped onto the lunar surface, followed by Alperi and Lijuan, then Angeline. The gravity decreased to the moon's one-sixth value as soon as they exited the air lock, and Lara lost her balance after her next step, her body tilting too far forward. She fell onto the lunar surface, rolling a few feet before coming to a halt. The powdery regolith clung to her exposure suit and assault carbine as she pushed herself to a sitting position.

Alperi and Lijuan took notice of Lara's mishap and maintained their balance, although they struggled at first. Angeline had no problem, however, and Lara realized she had never asked Angeline what planet she was from. It was clear that she had experience walking in lighter gravity.

McCarthy helped Lara to her feet. "Slow and easy," he said.

When Lara stood, she found the moon's surface unexpectedly firm; she had expected to sink several inches into the lunar dust, but her boots pressed into the powdery regolith only a fraction of an inch, leaving perfect impressions of her boots. In the distance, faint pinpricks of light emanated from Central's main hub over a half mile away.

McCarthy headed toward the concourse. "Stay against the hull," he said, "under the windows so we can't be seen."

Lara began to get the hang of things and was soon able to walk at an even, steady pace, keeping up with McCarthy. After a twenty-minute trek, they reached the hub.

"We're going to enter the hub through the life-support deck air lock. But it's a few levels up and not designed for personnel passage. It's used to swap fuel cells from supply transports that mate to the hub.

"There's a set of handholds on the hub's exterior that will take us to the life-support deck where we can manually open the air lock. We have to time it perfectly, though. We don't want to enter the air lock the same time one of the slayers is passing by."

McCarthy led them along the hub's perimeter until they reached a set of handholds. "We're going to get off at the eighth deck," McCarthy announced. "That's when it gets hard. We'll have to work our way left about a hundred feet to the air lock. But here are no handholds, just a six-inch-wide ledge."

After slinging his assault carbine over his shoulder, McCarthy began the climb. Lara followed his example, as did the others, and they soon reached the eighth deck. McCarthy began working his way left along the ledge, with Lara following and Alperi behind her, each carefully stepping off the rung and onto the narrow protrusion.

Fortunately, the hub curved away as it bent toward Central's apex, and Lara was able to lean against the hull as she worked her way along the ledge. Even so, the going was slow and treacherous. She lost her foothold on one occasion and barely kept her balance. After that, she gingerly put weight onto her left foot every time she moved it, ensuring it was firmly planted onto the narrow ledge each time.

They passed windows that were spaced sporadically along the perimeter of the life-support deck, until finally, only a twenty-foot-wide window remained between them and the air lock. McCarthy stopped when he reached the window edge, with its bottom starting at chest height.

"We're in a bit of a crunch," he said. "A slayer is going to come by soon, but we can't wait. I'll give everyone a heads-up just before it arrives, and we'll have to duck below the window until it passes."

McCarthy moved past the window, and Lara followed, peering inside the life-support deck as she made her way. Inside was the Atmosphere Control Room, which was unlit, but the lights were still on inside the hub, and light streamed into the room from the passageway. The machinery was still running, its green, yellow, and blue indicator lights blinking in the darkness.

When McCarthy reached the end of the window, he said, "One of the slayers will pass by in about twenty seconds. Everyone needs to duck below the window for the next minute."

As Alperi crouched down below the window, his left foot slipped off the ledge. He tried desperately to regain his balance, clawing the surface of the hub as he fell, to no avail. He tilted to the side and fell toward the lunar surface.

Lara reached out and grabbed Alperi's hand. But the weight and angle of the regent's fall pulled her off-balance. Rather than fall backward, she pushed off from the hull as she fell, reaching toward the ledge on her way down. Her hand hit the protrusion, and her grip held. Lara and Alperi swung toward the hub, and Lara felt a slight vibration in the hull as they hit. She maintained her grip on the ledge with her left hand, holding Alperi with her right.

Seconds later, a shimmering glow appeared through the window, growing in intensity.

"Stay down," McCarthy said.

"I've got that taken care of," Lara answered.

The shimmer grew stronger until it stopped just above Lara and Alperi.

"Lara," McCarthy said. "I've got some bad news. You and Alperi are doing a great job staying below the life-support deck window, but not so good with the cafeteria window."

Looking down, she noticed that Alperi was dangling in front of a window below them.

McCarthy added, "Another slayer will be entering the cafeteria soon, so you've got to pull Alperi back up to the ledge."

Lara flexed her left hand, verifying she had a firm grip on the ledge before attempting to pull Alperi back up. "It's a good thing you weigh only about thirty pounds on the moon," Lara said as she slowly pulled him up until he was able to grab onto the ledge.

"Stay there for now," McCarthy said.

The shimmer remained at the window above Lara and Alperi, and it was soon joined by a glow from the window below it. No one spoke or moved as the two slayers bracketed them. Finally, both shimmering glows receded.

"Okay," McCarthy said. "Everyone back onto the ledge."

Lijuan worked her way toward Alperi while McCarthy approached Lara, and Alperi and Lara were helped back to a standing position on the ledge. McCarthy continued his journey toward the air lock, and after a short moment to collect her thoughts and breath, Lara followed.

"Thanks for the advanced warning about Alperi's fall," Lara said sourly to McCarthy. "Aren't you supposed to be viewing the future?"

"I am," McCarthy answered, "and I knew you'd catch him and that you'd both be safe. Providing someone with advance warning of the future can sometimes change it."

Lara pondered McCarthy's response as she worked her way past the window. Viewing the future seemed straightforward, but the ramifications of revealing that future—to whom, when, and what extent—were obviously complex.

Her thoughts were cut short as she reached the life-support deck air lock, joining McCarthy inside. Both regents and Angeline entered a moment later, and McCarthy manipulated the controls, closing the air lock doors behind them.

12

While they waited for the air lock to pressurize, Lara peered through the door window into Central. A half dozen charred bodies lay strewn across the passageway floor, but there was no sign of the slayers. A moment later, the red warning sign in the air lock switched to a green LIFE SUPPORT ESTABLISHED notification. McCarthy opened the air lock doors and stepped into the passageway, where he began removing his exposure suit.

"We won't need these anymore," he whispered.

They followed McCarthy's direction, and the suits were soon removed.

McCarthy adjusted the controls on his assault carbine. "Set it to maximum," he said.

Lara recalled that while preparing to engage the slayer on Hellios, the Marine platoon had shifted their assault carbines from normal to maximum. But even at maximum power, it had taken a dozen pulses to collapse the slayer's shield. Additionally, at the most powerful setting, it took several seconds to recharge between pulses—time they might not have.

"We're going to the cargo bay," McCarthy whispered.

He led them down the passageway, passing through several corridor intersections before taking stairs down to the berthing deck. After the stairwell door opened, Lara breathed a sigh of relief. There were no slayers in sight. But her relief was short-lived as a slayer turned the corner at the far end of the passageway.

"Run!" McCarthy yelled.

He grabbed Lara and pulled her around the nearest corner, where they were joined by the others as a Korilian pulse melted a hole in the wall behind them. They sprinted down one passageway after another in an attempt to lose the slayer, but it steadily gained on them, its defense shield illuminating the corridors behind them, growing brighter at every turn.

As they ran down a long passageway, McCarthy turned abruptly into another corridor as a slayer pulse narrowly missed Angeline. But what greeted Lara next shocked her.

McCarthy had led them into a dead end!

Or at least what seemed like a dead end.

At the far end of the corridor was a set of closed doors. But there wasn't enough time to reach the end of the passageway; the slayer would turn the corner any second and be able to fire at will.

McCarthy stopped suddenly and turned, letting the other Nexi and regents pass by, then raised his carbine to his shoulder. When the slayer entered the corridor behind them, McCarthy fired.

The pulse lit up the slayer's shield, stunning the slayer for a moment, which surprised Lara. The slayer on Hellios and the one in Concourse Alpha hadn't even been fazed by a single pulse. Looking closer, she noticed electrical arcs sizzling across the slayer's shield, similar to how the slayer's shield in the assembly bay had appeared after the slayer had been crushed.

Lara realized that the shield had been damaged during the slayer's foray through Central, which meant they might have a chance. In the assembly bay, McCarthy had approached the slayer and fired from only a few feet away, the pulse passing through the shield and severing the slayer's neck. At close range, an assault carbine could penetrate a compromised slayer shield.

As the arcs dancing across the slayer's shield began to fade, Angeline pressed the *Open* command on the door control panel. They passed through the doorway into the cargo bay, McCarthy the last to enter, just before the slayer began moving forward again, firing a pulse that just missed McCarthy.

He closed the door, then blasted the door controls with his carbine.

"Stand behind me!" he said as he moved against the bulkhead a few feet from the doorway.

Seconds later, the center of the door began glowing red, the spot growing brighter and larger until an explosion ripped the door apart, sending fragments flying across the cargo bay.

When the slayer passed through the doorway, McCarthy fired his carbine. The slayer's shield lit up, but the pulse didn't penetrate it. Instead, the shield glowed even brighter, increasing in intensity until it disappeared in a bright flash that blew McCarthy off his feet. He landed on his back as the slayer slumped to the ground.

Lara ran to McCarthy, praying he was okay as she knelt down to examine him. He had a pulse. He was alive, but unconscious. As she checked his body for injuries, she noticed movement in the corner of her eye. The slayer was propping itself up with two limbs, swinging its weapon toward her and McCarthy.

Angeline fired her carbine, hitting the slayer in the chest, but the pulse didn't penetrate its armor. The slayer ignored Angeline, remaining focused on McCarthy. As Angeline's carbine recharged, the slayer's weapon steadied on the admiral.

Lara went for her carbine, slung across her shoulder, but knew she'd be too late. In another second, McCarthy would be incinerated by the slayer's pulse.

Just before the slayer pulled the trigger, Angeline stepped in front of McCarthy, absorbing the pulse. She was enveloped in an orange sphere, and her body shook violently as electric arcs sizzled through her until the sphere vanished in a bright flash. Angeline's charred, lifeless body fell to the floor.

As the slayer slowly pushed itself onto its lower limbs as its weapon recharged, Lara leveled her assault carbine at the slayer, aimed carefully at the neck seam in its armor, then pulled the trigger.

It was a good aim, and the pulse penetrated the neck seam. The slayer's body collapsed onto the floor while its head rolled a few feet before coming to a stop.

Lara's mind and body went numb as she stared at Angeline's burnt remains, unwilling to believe the Nexus Eight was dead.

Lijuan stopped beside Lara and shook her shoulders. "We don't have time for this!"

Lara recovered from the shock of Angeline's death, forcing herself into motion as Lijuan picked up McCarthy's assault carbine. Angeline's weapon was useless, turned into a molten slag of metal, leaving them with two carbines. Against an undamaged slayer shield, they had no chance.

Her eyes went to the weapon in the dead slayer's claw. She handed her carbine to Alperi and pried the weapon from the Korilian's grip. She had no idea if there was a biological or telepathic safety preventing her from firing it, so she gave it a try, pointing it across the cargo bay. The weapon was bulky and difficult to wield, built for a twelve-foot-tall slayer, but she was able to steady her aim and pulled the trigger. An orange burst vaporized a three-foot-diameter hole in a nearby container.

Lara joined Lijuan and Alperi, who were kneeling beside McCarthy, who was conscious now but struggling to regain his senses.

"Go," was the only guidance he could muster as a shimmering glow began to illuminate the corridor leading to the cargo bay.

She scanned the area, searching for a place to hide, or perhaps to identify the reason McCarthy had led them there—a shuttle transport, perhaps —but the cargo bay was filled only with several stacks of containers. Lara chose a pallet of containers farthest away, near the large, heavy doors that opened to the spaceport, and they dragged McCarthy toward them.

A slayer entered the cargo bay just as they slipped behind the containers. The regents lowered McCarthy to the ground, placing him with his back against the wall, where he sat slumped at an angle with a glazed look in his eyes.

Once they were behind the containers, Lara faced the slayer, which was advancing toward them, and fired. A pulse sped from the weapon, enveloping the slayer's spherical energy shield in another orange sphere, which dissipated in a bright flash. There was no visible harm to the slayer, but the burst stunned it, halting the Korilian's advance for a few seconds. Lijuan and Alperi joined her, firing the Marine assault carbines, but they had no effect aside from lighting up the slayer's shield in electrical arcs.

The slayer returned fire as it advanced, each orange burst melting a three-foot-diameter pit in the containers or leaving a molten imprint on the thick spaceport bulkhead behind them.

Looking around frantically, Lara assessed their predicament. They were cornered at the back of the cargo bay, with the only exit being the door into the spaceport beside them. The spaceport door was immense, over one foot thick and thirty feet high by fifty feet across, providing passage for equipment and supplies arriving from Earth. She continued firing at the slayer while McCarthy slowly recovered, struggling to sit up straight.

When Lara thought things couldn't get worse, another slayer entered the cargo bay through the molten doorway. She continued firing at the first slayer until the second was astride the first, then fired alternately at each one. But the net effect was that she was able to stun each slayer only half as often as before. The Korilians kept advancing toward them.

Lara's gaze shifted desperately between the slayers, McCarthy, and the spaceport door. Then she noticed the green Atmosphere indication was lit on the door control panel, indicating the spaceport atmosphere was capable of supporting human life.

"We're going into the spaceport!" she yelled as she moved to the control panel, still protected behind the containers.

When Lara reached the control panel, the ghostly image of another Korilian—a type she hadn't seen before—appeared through the foggy observation window. The Korilian's shadow bobbed back and forth, with numerous antennas protruding from its bulbous head. Lara froze, realizing they were trapped.

The large spaceport door lifted slowly upward as the Korilian tried to gain access to the cargo bay. Lara frantically punched the control panel, trying to stop the heavy metal door from opening. The door halted after rising a few inches, and Lara saw the Korilian's shadow through the opening on the cargo bay floor. Lara decided to smash the control panel, hoping to prevent the Korilian from raising the spaceport door.

As she lifted the heavy weapon, preparing to smash the panel, McCarthy spoke.

"No!" he said, finally alert. "Open the door!"

Lara couldn't believe what she was hearing. McCarthy had directed her

The End of Time 67

to open the spaceport door with another Korilian on the other side, only a few feet away.

"Are you crazy?" she shouted. "There's—"

"Open the damn door!"

Lara turned and glanced at the two advancing slayers, who were only twenty feet away now. She finally acquiesced, pressing the *Open Bay Door* icon on the control panel.

As the spaceport door slowly rose, dozens of shadows were cast across the cargo bay floor. When the door reached shoulder height, Lara finally realized why McCarthy wanted her to open the door. Stretched across the opening was a platoon of Marines. Across from her stood the supposed additional *Korilian*, who was a Marine wearing an exposure suit with a bulbous helmet and several antennas attached to communications equipment.

The Marines were arranged across the spaceport opening in two rows: one on their knees with a second row standing behind them. Each Marine, brandishing an assault carbine, fired on the slayers. Their defense shields lit up from the Marine onslaught, with blue pulses peppering their shields, plus an occasional orange burst as Lara joined in. But while the slayers' advance had been halted, none of the shots penetrated their defense shields.

Both slayers turned their weapons onto the Marine detachment. The Marines stood their ground, but every few seconds, as the slayer weapons recharged, a Marine was reduced to a smoldering carcass. Lara's initial elation was replaced with despair, as almost a third of the Marine platoon lay incinerated on the spaceport floor, while the Marine weapons had no noticeable effect on the slayers.

As Lara began to panic, she noticed three teams of Marines running toward them from a shuttle in the spaceport, carrying heavy equipment. They reached the other Marines and started setting up behind the two rows, each team attaching a large weapon to a four-pronged support stand. The weapon was similar in design to the assault carbines the Marines carried, only much larger; so large that it took two Marines to hoist the device into place.

The slayers noticed the activity and focused their attack on the Marines in front of the heavy weapons. They were able to break through the human shield in front of one team, vaporizing the heavy weapon. But the other two weapon teams completed their setup, inserting a six-inch-diameter cartridge into each weapon. The gunners were tapped on the shoulder, and the heavy weapons recoiled as both gunners fired almost simultaneously.

Each slayer's defense shield lit up in a bright white flash. The light slowly subsided, and to Lara's dismay, both slayers were still standing.

But then she realized their shimmering defense shields were gone.

That fact wasn't lost on the Marines as they continued firing at the slayers, their carbine pulses blowing chunks from the Korilians' armor encasing their bodies, driving them backward as the heavy weapon teams reloaded. The gunners were tapped on the shoulder again, and they aimed and fired, obliterating the slayers in two brilliant explosions.

13

In the cargo bay the following day, Lara stood in a line beside McCarthy and five other Nexus Eights—the remaining fleet guides—plus Dewan Channing, the Deinde Eight, as a Nexus honor guard prepared to load Angeline's coffin into one of the transport ships. Nearby, the bodies of over four hundred other men and women who had been killed during the Korilian rampage were being loaded onto ships with much less fanfare, forklifts moving the coffins into the cargo holds.

Also joining them was Admiral Natalia Goergen, in command of 3rd Fleet, who had entered battle with Angeline by her side for over a decade. Aside from McCarthy, Goergen was the most accomplished fleet commander, and Angeline had no doubt been a critical element of her success; Angeline's experience had dwarfed that of the other fleet guides.

The Fleet would sorely miss Angeline, as would Lara. Angeline had been her mentor during the frantic weeks before the Final Stand, training her to assist McCarthy in the short time available. Angeline had been the only guide Lara had been comfortable talking with; the only one near her age. Of the five guides beside her today, all were still teenagers, while Lara had just turned thirty. Not that they weren't capable—the Nexus House trained them well—but there was a hardness to the younger guides, a single-minded sense of purpose. Lara found it hard to relate to them, while Angeline had been like the sister she had never had.

Lara reflected on her discussion with Angeline on the observation deck before the Korilian warships appeared over Central. Angeline had commented about how her vision of the Liberation Campaign felt different. Lara now knew why. It was because Angeline had viewed a future where she was no longer alive. A future after she had stepped in front of the Korilian pulse, sacrificing her life to save McCarthy's. And Lara's.

When the Nexus honor guard lifted Angeline's casket onto a hover-cart, which moved slowly toward the awaiting shuttle, McCarthy reached over and took Lara's hand in his. Lara was unable to hold back the tears as she watched Angeline's body travel up the ramp into the transport's cargo hold. Her thoughts then turned to McCarthy.

She could easily lose him, too. He was about to take command of the Liberation Campaign. During battle, the Korilians focused on destroying the Colonial Fleet command ships. Each time they had lost a Nexus guide, the fleet admiral had usually been killed as well. Three years ago, McCarthy had barely survived when Regina was killed at Ritalis, and now that the Korilians were aware of his abilities, he was in more danger than ever.

As the cargo ramp slowly rose, sealing Angeline inside the transport, Lara's thoughts drifted to the previous day. After the Marines killed the last two slayers, she had slumped to the deck, her back against the wall, her hands shaking uncontrollably. If that was what it was like being a praetorian, defending the Nexus House in close combat, she wasn't cut out for it.

Lara's wristlet vibrated, but she was in no mood to check messages. Admiral Goergen's wristlet also vibrated, and after reading the message, she turned to Lara.

"I look forward to working with you," Goergen said, "as my new guide."

14

In Central's operations center, standing before a twenty-by-twenty-foot data fusion table, Fleet Admiral Nanci Fitzgerald was joined by Lara and McCarthy on one side and Regents Morel Alperi and Lijuan Xiang on the other as they viewed a holographic image of Central.

"How could this have happened?" Alperi asked Fitzgerald.

"The Korilians obviously knew we were assembling for a brief at Central, giving them the opportunity to deliver a devastating blow, killing most of our fleet leadership if the attack had been successful. That means they had a reconnaissance probe surveilling the increased activity as personnel traveled to Central. We examined all nearby asteroids and found nothing. That meant the probe was somewhere on the moon itself."

Fitzgerald turned to one of the screens on the front wall, displaying video of the lunar surface. "After scrutinizing our sensor data, we detected faint jump waves in the vicinity of the Apennine Mountains. A few minutes ago, we located a Korilian probe in a deep ravine between two mountain peaks. The Korilians have been sending mobile probes into the ravine so their jump waves were concealed, then they climbed atop the ridge to spy on Central."

Fitzgerald activated a video clip showing a Colonial Defense Force drone flying above the mountain terrain. It detected a probe climbing the steep incline and destroyed it with a laser pulse.

"As far as we can tell, there are no more Korilian probes within surveillance distance of Earth or Central. That's the good news."

Fitzgerald waved away the holographic representation of Central. After a few taps on the fusion display, holographic images formed of the ten planetary systems where Colonial Defense Force ground troops were stranded. Fleet reconnaissance probes were jumping into each planet's orbit to obtain periodic updates, with the Korilians destroying the probes as soon as they were detected.

"The bad news is—intel reported that the Korilians have fielded another battle group at the front line, bringing their total strength to sixteen battle groups, equivalent to our four Liberation Campaign fleets. If Korilian warship quantities continue increasing at this pace, it won't be long before the Korilians regain the advantage, even with McCarthy in direct command of Liberation Campaign forces.

"We're building four more starship construction yards, but even when those become operational, we will have closed only half of the gap between our warship construction rate and the Korilians'. Building another four yards will take five years. We don't have five more years."

There was silence after Fitzgerald pointed out the critical issue. She waited a moment, letting the gravity of the situation sink in, before continuing.

"If there's one lesson we can learn from the Korilian assault on Central, it's that we need to be more daring. Had the Korilian attack succeeded, killing our Fleet leadership and especially Admiral McCarthy, it would have changed the outcome of the war in a single stroke. We need something comparable—a bold change in strategy."

She turned to McCarthy. "Do you have any ideas?"

"There are two viable options," McCarthy replied. "The first is to commit a fifth fleet to the Liberation Campaign, which would give us a twenty-five percent advantage. If I'm given direct command of all five fleets, we should be able to move forward again on a broad front."

"Absolutely not!" Alperi interjected. "Did you already forget what just happened? A surprise attack on Central, which could just have easily been

The End of Time

a surprise attack on Earth! We cannot afford to relinquish one of Earth's defense fleets."

"Even if we assign one of the two defense fleets to the Liberation Campaign," Fitzgerald replied, "it would take the equivalent of four Korilian fleets to penetrate Earth's defenses and destroy our construction yards before the other fleets return to assist."

"I must point out," Alperi replied, "that the Korilians now have four fleets positioned at the front line, and who knows how many more warships in reserve."

"If the Korilians attempt a surprise attack with all four fleets, we'd have advance notice," Fitzgerald insisted. "Concealing four dozen starships en route to Central isn't terribly challenging, but we'd notice the disappearance of the entire Korilian armada and be able to respond appropriately. A surprise attack on Earth is an unlikely scenario."

"*An unlikely scenario.*" Alperi repeated Fitzgerald's words. "That's not a gamble worth taking. The Council will not agree to stripping Earth of one of its defense fleets."

Fitzgerald turned to Lijuan, seeking her input.

"I'm afraid Alperi is correct," Lijuan said. "The Council will never agree to this."

It appeared that McCarthy's first proposal had no chance of approval. "What's the second option?" Fitzgerald asked.

McCarthy answered, "Although the Korilians have significantly rebuilt their fleet, it's still only two-thirds as large as ours. However, along the front line, the Korilians can muster equal forces because we have two fleets tied down defending Earth from a surprise attack. This is our Achilles' heel we need to address.

"If we can locate and attack the Korilian home world, even if it's with a single fleet—just to get their attention—we can establish equal footing, with both sides forced to tie down assets defending their home planets. That would reduce the Korilian forces opposing the Liberation Campaign, likely to the equivalent of only two fleets, creating a two-to-one advantage on our side.

"If we then change our strategy from regaining colonies to penetrating the Korilian Empire at the fastest rate possible, we might be able to reach the Korilian home world and destroy it, or perhaps enough of their construction yards along the way, forcing the Korilians to sue for peace."

"It's a sound proposal," Fitzgerald commented. "But we don't know where the Korilian home world is. Our efforts have come up empty. We don't even have the faintest clue on where to focus our reconnaissance probe searches."

"You have a valid point," McCarthy replied. "It's a problem we need to solve."

15

In the north wing of Domus Praesidium, Rhea Sidener sat behind her desk talking with Noah Ronan about measures to improve the security of the Nexus House, and in particular, that of Jon McCarthy. She was in the middle of a sentence when her wristlet vibrated, overriding the *Do Not Disturb* setting she had set for her meeting. She tapped her wristlet, and a supervisor in the Nexus intelligence center appeared on the wristlet's display.

"We have a critical naviganti alert," the supervisor reported, referring to the level-nine Nexi on watch in the intelligence center.

"What's the issue?" Rhea asked.

"The Council is holding an emergency meeting."

"The topic?"

"Elena," the supervisor replied.

Rhea decided to follow a regent's timeline to learn the details quickly, choosing Regent Alperi. It took only a few seconds to realize an intervention was required.

Rhea addressed Ronan as she stood. "We'll continue our discussion later."

After entering the Nexus communication center, Rhea stopped beside the senior supervisor. "Hack into the Council meeting," she directed, "and prepare for my hologram projection."

"Yes, One," the supervisor replied. "But I must point out that if you project into their meeting, they'll discover that we've broken their encryption and have been monitoring their communications."

"Do it," Rhea ordered.

Rhea entered a thirty-foot-diameter chamber, stepping onto a small circular platform. The communications supervisor's voice came across the chamber's speakers a moment later.

"We're ready."

Rhea tapped her wristlet, and twelve holograms appeared, evenly spaced along the chamber circumference. The white-robed regents were evenly split between men and women, with each of the three senior members—Council President Portner, Alperi, and Lijuan—holding a staff in one hand.

When Rhea joined the conference, Alperi was speaking: "I don't care about *one* woman!" He pounded his staff on the chamber floor. "We should interrogate—"

He cut his oratory short when he noticed The One's hologram appear in their midst.

Alperi turned toward Rhea. "What are you doing here? How did you gain access to this conference?"

Rhea replied, "I understand the topic of today's meeting involves the well-being of a Nexus. Ergo, my presence."

"You were not invited," Alperi said. "Leave this conference at once."

Rhea directed her response to the Council's senior member. "President Portner, I request your authorization to participate in this meeting."

Before Portner responded, Lijuan interjected. "President Portner, I think it's acceptable for the Nexus One to participate in this critical meeting. After all, Elena is one of the most capable and valuable members of the Nexus House."

Alperi shot Lijuan a vicious glare as Portner considered Rhea's request.

"Of course, Rhea," Portner replied. "You may participate. Your insight is always welcome."

Rhea nodded her appreciation, then turned to Alperi. "I understand you plan to interrogate Elena?"

Lijuan answered instead of Alperi. "Interrogate might be too strong a word. What Alperi meant to say is that we want to talk with Elena and learn what she knows."

Alperi replied, "I choose my words carefully, Lijuan, and it would be prudent to pay closer attention to them. I said interrogate, and that's what I meant."

Lijuan's expression hardened. "You don't have the authority to dictate how we proceed. This is an issue for the entire Council to decide. What might happen to Elena could affect the outcome of the war."

Alperi offered Lijuan a look of disdain, then turned to Portner. "Perhaps we should play the transmission now."

Portner concurred, then Alperi tapped his wristlet, and a hologram appeared in the center of the conference chamber. It was an image of Elena Kapadia in her Army uniform, standing in an underground command center. She appeared to be only nineteen or twenty years old, which would have placed her on Darian 3 shortly before it fell to the Korilians.

Alperi tapped his wristlet again, and the hologram came to life.

Elena's image shook occasionally, accompanied by the rumble of nearby explosions.

"*This is Major Elena Kapadia, attached to the last operational Third Army Group headquarters. This will be our last transmission. Whoever receives this message, forward it to the Colonial Council—they will understand. It is of the utmost importance. Billions of lives are at stake. In eighteen years, the war will turn against us again, but I have found a way to end the war. You must destroy the Korilian complex on the fourth planet in the Hellios system. Then you must send a strike force to the Korilian home world.*"

There was a loud rumble, and the hologram froze.

After a short silence to let the regents digest Elena's message, Alperi spoke.

"As you can see, Elena predicted the war would turn against us again and had critical information regarding how to defeat the Korilians, and that was *before* she spent eighteen years on Hellios, working with the Korilians for much of that time. It's likely that Elena has gained vast knowledge that would be valuable to the Colonial Defense Force—she may even know the location of the Korilian home world. That would give us the advantage we need to sustain the Liberation Campaign, by forcing the Korilians to tie down forces defending their home planet, or even win the war outright by destroying their starship construction yards.

"Unfortunately, we don't know what Elena knows, because she isn't talking. She refuses to answer questions about what she learned during her time on Darian and Hellios."

"I do not dispute that Elena likely has knowledge of significant value," Lijuan replied. "The issue is the process by which we obtain it. Elena's physicians believe that forcing her to discuss potentially traumatic issues before she is ready could have severe consequences to her mental health."

Alperi asserted, "You have a narrow and warped perspective, Lijuan. You're concerned about the consequences to *Elena*, when her failure to disclose what she knows could have severe consequences for *humanity*. It is an age-old and rather simple dilemma—the fate of one versus the fate of many. Elena must reveal what she knows, and if she refuses, we should obtain it by force if necessary. There are drugs and procedures that can extract every bit of relevant information we desire."

"Extract it?" Lijuan asked. "At what cost? Elena's mental state is precarious, and the best course for her well-being is to give her the time she needs to recover."

"Time is a commodity we don't have much of," Alperi replied. "The longer it takes to learn what Elena knows, the more this war tilts back into the Korilians' favor. We have no idea how long it will take for Elena to come around on her own, and we can't afford to wait for however long that is."

"Your proposal goes too far," Lijuan said. "We should not authorize a procedure that could destroy her mind. Elena has rights."

Alperi pounded his staff on the floor. "She has whatever rights we say she has! We've watched the Korilians slaughter our people for three decades, driving us to the brink of extinction. But we survived. We destroyed their armada during the Final Stand and have steadily retaken our colonies. I'm not embarrassed to say I've enjoyed the last few years. Three years of payback for three decades of slaughter. But the war is

The End of Time 79

turning against us again, and we must take whatever action is required to maintain the advantage."

"I agree that we must extract what Elena knows. But we should do so in as compassionate a manner as possible, a way with less potential for harm."

"You ask for compassion?" Alperi asked. "This woman viewed for the Korilians! She's responsible for the deaths of millions, and you think she deserves compassion? She deserves to be executed for *treason!*"

Rhea intervened. "That is enough!"

"Enough?" Alperi asked. "Perhaps it is *not* enough. Perhaps you share the blame, Rhea. For inadequately training Elena, for delivering a faulty product to the Colonial Defense Force—a woman so easily broken."

Rhea's expression hardened as she stared at Alperi's hologram. "Be thankful you are not in my physical presence. I would show you how easy it is to break someone. You would be groveling at my feet, begging me to end your life, offering me *anything* to do so quickly."

Rhea let her words sink in before continuing. "Let me be clear, Regent Alperi. If any harm befalls Elena due to the Council's decision today, you will be the first person I visit."

"Are you threatening a regent!"

"Call it what you will. But I prefer to consider it my duty to educate you on the consequences of your decision."

Alperi surveyed the other eleven Council members. "Are we to stand for this—a regent being openly threatened?"

Council President Portner intervened. "The Nexus One hasn't threatened anyone. I'm sure her example of what might happen to you is a figure of speech. There would be severe consequences for harming a regent, even to an organization as valuable as the Nexus House."

Portner stared at Rhea, who stared back.

After an uncomfortable moment of silence, Portner continued. "The matter before us today is clear. Do we authorize the extraction of Elena's knowledge against her will and with the potential for permanent damage to her mind, or do we let Elena reveal what she knows at whatever timetable she is comfortable with?"

Portner turned to the other regents. "If I have adequately summarized the issue, is there a motion to proceed to a vote?"

"I so motion," Alperi replied.

"I second the motion," another regent added.

Portner announced, "Vote *extract* to authorize the extraction of relevant knowledge without Elena Kapadia's consent and at peril to her health, or *defer* to allow Elena to divulge what she knows at her own pace."

He turned to Alperi, who voted *extract*.

Additional regents voted, and by the time Lijuan's turn came, there were six votes to extract and four to defer. However, if she and Portner voted to defer, the motion would end in a tie and would not be approved.

"*Defer*," Lijuan announced, then turned to Portner, who would cast the deciding vote.

Portner held Lijuan in his eyes for a moment before speaking.

"I consider myself a compassionate man, and I abhor what might happen to Elena during forcible extraction. However, I have a responsibility to do what's best for humanity. I vote to *extract*."

Portner focused on Rhea and appeared ready to announce the Council's decision when Rhea interjected.

"I motion to amend."

Alperi replied, "You cannot make a motion, Rhea. You are not a regent."

"Perhaps you'd like to hear my proposal, and a regent would be kind enough to motion for me."

"Go ahead," Portner said. "What is your proposed amendment?"

"I propose a twenty-four-hour delay in executing the extraction order, and that the extraction be cancelled if Elena provides satisfactory information—as determined by the Council—within that time frame."

"I so motion," Lijuan announced.

"Does anyone second the motion?" Portner asked.

The motion was seconded by Salma Zaph, the Fringe Worlds regent.

The Council voted again, and the motion passed.

Portner announced to Rhea, "You have twenty-four hours to obtain satisfactory information about the location of the Korilian home planet. If Elena refuses to cooperate, we will extract the knowledge we desire, regardless of the potential harm.

"Do you have any questions?" he asked.

Without answering, Rhea tapped her wristlet and the twelve holograms disappeared, then she stepped from the hologram platform. After exiting the conference chamber, she tapped her wristlet again, establishing a communication link with McCarthy.

16

McCarthy's shuttle slowed its descent through the atmosphere, angling toward the Ural Mountains. Seated beside him in the Nexus shuttle he had named *Elena*, Lara watched the descent as she held his hand. McCarthy and Lara had departed Central, and he was headed to Colonial Navy headquarters in Brussels, taking a detour to drop Lara off at Domus Praesidium to resume her fleet guide training, which had taken on added urgency now that she had been assigned to 3rd Fleet. In two weeks, 3rd Fleet would join three other fleets as they recommenced the Liberation Campaign.

She had big shoes to fill, replacing Angeline, and already felt inadequate. Her visions were still random and difficult to interpret in tactical terms, providing information a fleet admiral would find useful in battle.

As they pierced the clouds, McCarthy's wristlet vibrated. He answered, and an image of the Nexus One appeared.

Rhea spoke first. "The Council has authorized a forcible data extraction from Elena."

"You can't be serious," McCarthy replied. "You know what that often does to the person, much less someone in Elena's condition."

"Fortunately, the Council has delayed the extraction for twenty-four hours, giving us the chance to obtain the desired information. If the Council is satisfied, they'll cancel the extraction order."

The End of Time   83

"What do they want?"

"The location of the Korilian home world or whatever information Elena has that could lead us to it."

Before McCarthy could reply, Rhea added, "Go to Elena. Convince her to reveal everything she knows that might be helpful."

The One's image faded from McCarthy's wristlet, and he gave new orders to his shuttle.

"*Elena*, take us to Sint-Pieters."

The shuttle veered toward Belgium.

During the transit, McCarthy probed Lara for advice. Prior to becoming a Nexus, Lara had been a grief counselor for ten years, consoling the families of those killed in the war, helping them deal with the sorrow, anger, and depression as they transitioned through the various stages of grief. Elena's situation wasn't exactly the same, but she was undoubtedly dealing with similar emotions: guilt from aiding the Korilians, anger at being abandoned on Darian and Hellios, and depression due to her uncertain future. She might never leave Sint-Pieters Sanitorium.

When their shuttle landed, they were met by Elijah Guptah, who escorted Lara and McCarthy inside the facility. They stopped in a glass-walled lobby adjacent to a circular open-sky garden atrium, its circumference lined with cherry and beech trees and flowering shrubs.

Elena was sitting on a bench, wearing a sundress and a wide-brimmed hat to protect her pale skin from the sun's rays. At the moment, however, she had her face tilted to the sky, her eyes closed, soaking in the sun's warmth. She had spent eighteen years in her underground prison chamber on Hellios and hadn't seen the sun for almost two decades.

An armed guard approached, holding a carbine.

"As before," Guptah said to McCarthy, "you will be monitored by a sentry with his weapon set on stun, should Elena turn violent."

McCarthy acknowledged Guptah's comment, then entered the atrium, leaving the guard, Lara, and Guptah in the glass-walled lobby. Elena's face was still tilted skyward, her eyes shut, but he felt the cold sensation from her view as he stopped beside her.

"Hi, Jon," she said. "I've been expecting you."

Elena's view halted as she opened her eyes. She turned toward him, then patted the bench beside her.

McCarthy joined her, examining her more closely. "You look much better."

"I feel better. I think I'm finally accepting the fact that I'm really back on Earth."

"I'm glad," McCarthy replied. "It's good to see you returning to your old self."

Elena smiled.

McCarthy considered viewing alternate futures, examining various conversations that would guide Elena to the topic they needed to discuss, but decided otherwise. Elena would detect his view and potentially conclude that he wanted to manipulate their conversation. While that was true, it was better if she wasn't aware. He decided to let the conversation take its natural course.

"How are things going with your therapy?"

"I'm making progress," she replied. "The hard part is processing everything that's happened in the last twenty years. Everything I've done. Trying to work through the guilt. I'm responsible for the deaths of millions of men and women, and I can never be absolved of that sin."

McCarthy took her hand in his. "You did what you could to prevent it. You even tried to kill yourself. You would have succeeded if your body hadn't healed itself."

"I tell myself the same thing. Try to convince myself there was nothing more I could have done." After a short pause, she asked, "Do you know what my worst sin was?"

When McCarthy offered no answer, she said, "Did you ever wonder why Korilian strategy was so straightforward during the first half of the war, overwhelming us with brute force rather than surprise? Then how much better their strategy became after Darian 3 fell?"

"We noticed," McCarthy replied, "that their strategy became more complex over time. You had something to do with that?"

Elena nodded. "I taught them to lie. I taught them how to incorporate deceit into their war plans. They didn't understand the concept at first. I suppose it has something to do with them being telepathic and unable to deceive each other, but they eventually grasped the concept.

"But enough about the Korilians," she said. "What have you been up to for the last twenty years, aside from engaging in Fleet battles? I got a short glimpse the last time you were here, but only a few months into the past. I'm sorry for not asking for permission first."

Although a Nine or Ten could follow someone's line into the past without asking, it was House policy not to do so without that person's approval; others could view your most sensitive and private moments. As a result, doing so was authorized only for official reasons. That hadn't stopped Elena during their previous visit, but she seemed more stable today and conscious of the rules Nexi were expected to abide by.

She glanced at McCarthy's left hand, searching for a ring. "Did you ever get married?"

McCarthy shook his head. "Almost. I fell in love with a woman named Teresa, but her starship was destroyed while we were engaged."

"It must have been difficult for you," Elena said. "And difficult now, to relive those memories." Then her face brightened. "I have an idea. Let me finish following your line into the past. Let me catch up. All the way back to the day we left Domus Praesidium."

McCarthy hesitated, realizing Elena would be able to view his intimate relationships with Teresa and Lara. Considering Elena's feelings for him, that might not be a good idea.

"There are things that might be painful," he replied. "My relationships with other women, for example."

"I realize that. But it would mean a lot to me. Knowing that I'm special enough to let me view your past—all the details."

McCarthy evaluated the pros and cons of letting Elena follow his line into the past, unable to determine whether it would be helpful or harmful. However, gaining Elena's trust and making her feel cared about seemed crucial, and letting her view his past would certainly help gain her trust. Whether it would help her feel cared about was unclear. During his last visit, Elena had revealed that she was in love with him, and letting her learn the details of his relationships with Teresa and Lara would be risky.

Even if he said no, there was the chance she would disregard Nexus protocol and view his past without asking. He would have achieved nothing aside from giving Elena the impression he didn't care enough about her to share the intimate details of his life.

He decided to grant Elena's request.

McCarthy nodded his approval, and Elena began following his line, staring at him with a glazed look as she sped through his past. During Nexus views of the past or future, information was gleaned at a far faster pace than real time, and it took Elena only a half hour to complete the twenty-year journey into the past. Tears formed in her eyes as she viewed, and McCarthy wasn't sure if they were tears of sorrow or joy.

Her eyes finally cleared, and she turned away, wiping the tears from her face. After a while, she turned back to McCarthy. "Thank you. I can't tell you how much this means to me. There is so much to process..."

"But enough small talk," she said. "You didn't stop by just to chat and share your memories. I know why you're here."

"Can you help?" McCarthy asked. "I need enough information to convince the Council to cancel the extraction order. You need to reveal everything you know about the location of the Korilian home world, plus anything else that might help us win the war."

Elena replied, "For the first two years I fought on Darian 3, I spent almost every waking moment searching for a way to defend against the next Korilian assault, a way to win the next battle, how to defeat the Korilian campaign. But when the Korilian victory on Darian 3 became certain, I became desperate and searched for a way to end the war. There were a few lines that held promise," she said. "In one of my views, I made it to a planet in the Vormak system. Into a terraforming facility similar to the ones the Korilians built on Hellios 4."

"What did you find there?"

"A control center with an unencrypted database."

Unencrypted? McCarthy keyed on the revelation.

The few Korilian warships the Colonial Navy had captured had encrypted databases, preventing the extraction of critical information. But

The End of Time

if they could gain access to a complete, unencrypted database, they should be able to access—

"A map," McCarthy said. "A map showing the location of the Korilian home world."

"I remember looking at it in my view," Elena said, "not understanding its significance. Not understanding why my search to end the war would lead to a simple map."

"Do you know where the Korilian home world is?"

She shook her head. "The map was too complex, with millions of star systems and no reference point I could identify. But there were thousands of navigation routes, and there was one planet through which every route passed."

McCarthy announced the obvious. "The Korilian home world."

"I believe so," Elena replied.

"Is there anything else? Anything that might help us win the war?"

"Maybe. I need to think through some things to determine if it will help."

"You must reveal what you know, Elena. The Council's order was clear."

"I have viewed Rhea's meeting with the Council. They directed her to obtain all information that would be *helpful*. I do not yet know if this issue is relevant, and I don't want to clutter your mind with distractions."

"Potentially helpful information would not be a distraction."

Elena looked around the atrium, at Guptah standing in the lobby. "I may never get out of here, locked away forever. There are issues that need to be resolved, and I cannot predict their outcomes. In the meantime, let me help. I *need* to help. If I find anything useful in what I sort through, I promise I'll let you know."

McCarthy considered her proposal, then nodded.

"Thank you," she said, "for giving me the opportunity to start paying my debt for the harm I caused while aiding the Korilians." She leaned toward McCarthy, then kissed him on the cheek.

Elena glanced at Lara, staring at them through a glass panel. "I see you brought *it* with you."

McCarthy followed Elena's eyes. "You mean Lara?" He turned back to

Elena, noting she had called Lara *it* on Hellios and a few days ago during his last visit. "Why do you call her *it*?"

"Because it has no line."

McCarthy reflected on Elena's response; on the many nights he had thought about the same issue. About Lara—*the One with no line.*

McCarthy's eyes went to Lara; she was staring at him and Elena through the glass wall.

"It has no line," Elena reiterated. "Don't you find that alarming?"

"I find it intriguing that I can't predict her future. With Lara, I can be a normal person, unable to predict her reactions ahead of time and not be tempted to manipulate her."

"You're a fool, Jon." Elena's voice took on an ominous tone. "Every living thing has a line. You. Me. The trees. Even the blades of grass at our feet. Some lines are narrow and almost imperceptible, but everything alive has a line." She glanced at Lara again. "*It* does not."

"What are you suggesting?" McCarthy asked.

Elena's eyes narrowed. "I don't know what it is yet, but I do know it's dangerous. And that if it's not careful, it will destroy us all."

McCarthy pulled back from Elena. "What do you think she's going to do?"

"I don't know," Elena replied. "It's just a feeling..."

Elena gazed into the distance, lost in her thoughts for a while, then her eyes widened.

Her head snapped toward McCarthy. "You let it fall in love with you, and you never told it?"

McCarthy realized Elena had gleaned more than he had expected while viewing his past; she had learned what he'd been withholding from Lara.

"I could never find the right time."

"Before your first kiss would have been appropriate."

There was a short silence between them, then Elena said, "Let me tell it."

There was excitement in her voice, giddy anticipation. This wasn't the Elena he once knew. He was staring at someone who would enjoy the revelation, deriving pleasure from Lara's pain.

"No. It's my responsibility."

The End of Time 89

"Then let me be there when you tell it. I want to see its reaction." She draped her arms around McCarthy's neck and rested her chin on the edge of his shoulder, staring at him.

McCarthy didn't respond, and after a while, she released him and pulled back.

"You should go now, Jon. I need some time alone." Elena laughed softly. "Eighteen years in isolation, and now I need time for myself."

She paused, then added, "I'm not well. I'm broken in a way that can never be fixed. But I do want to heal, if you know what I mean."

She closed her eyes and tilted her face toward the sun.

"No," she said, "you don't know what I mean. Thank you for stopping by, Jon."

McCarthy watched her closely as she sat there, her face turned to the sky, the slight rise and fall of her chest. He leaned over and kissed her on the cheek, then left the atrium, the lobby's glass doors opening and then closing behind him.

As McCarthy approached Lara, Elena's words echoed in his mind.

You haven't told her.

It was an issue he'd been avoiding, one that Elena had painfully reminded him of. But this wasn't the right time. He wondered if there ever would be.

When he reached Lara, she said, "In all my years of counseling, I've never felt anything like it, especially from this distance. Elena is incredibly unstable, struggling to hold everything together, on the verge of a violent mental disintegration."

McCarthy glanced at Elena, still sitting on the bench. Her lips were moving; she was talking to herself. He couldn't fault her. For eighteen years, there had been no one else to talk to.

His focus shifted from Elena to Lara's reflection in the glass panel, and he recalled Elena's warning.

If it's not careful, it will destroy us all.

17

Lara sat beside the Nexus pilot as her shuttle rose from the Domus Praesidium spaceport, headed to Brussels for the brief at Fleet command headquarters. The message directing her attendance had provided no details, but Lara figured it had something to do with the reconnaissance probes sent to the Vormak system, searching for the Korilian facility Elena had mentioned. What Lara hadn't yet figured out was why her presence had been requested at the brief, since she was now the 3rd Fleet guide, destined to resume the Liberation Campaign in a few days.

After descending through the clouds above Brussels, the shuttle touched down on a landing pad atop the Colonial Navy headquarters building, where a Fleet aide awaited her arrival. He escorted her to a conference room filled with two dozen Navy and Marine Corps officers.

She scanned the room for familiar faces, spotting McCarthy. She moved toward him and was about to strike up a conversation when Fleet Admiral Fitzgerald entered the conference room. Everyone took their seats, with the conference table lined with a Marine Corps general and several admirals, including McCarthy and Admiral Natalia Goergen, the 3rd Fleet commander. Lara settled into a chair along the room's perimeter behind McCarthy, joining several other Navy and Marine Corps officers as Fitzgerald began the brief.

The End of Time 91

"As most of you know, we've sent reconnaissance probes to the Vormak system, searching for the Korilian facility Elena Kapadia mentioned to Admiral McCarthy. Elena was correct. On the fourth planet in the system, there is indeed a Korilian facility. It appears to predate the start of the Korilian War, which provides hope that the databases within the complex are unencrypted. Additionally, there are no Korilian warships in orbit, plus no indication of ground troops housed nearby."

Fitzgerald tapped her wristlet, and a hologram of the planet appeared, rotating slowly above the conference room table. Another tap and the hologram zoomed in on a complex on the planet's surface.

"The facility appears to be a control station for eighty terraforming units on the planet. We don't know how many Korilians are inside the facility or what type, but it's a relatively small facility, only one-tenth as large as the one on Hellios, so we don't expect a large contingent of Korilians, and hopefully no combat troops."

Fitzgerald then announced what Lara had deduced after noticing that both she and Admiral Goergen had been invited to attend the brief. "I plan to send Third Fleet, accompanied by a Marine brigade, to the Vormak system, tasked with obtaining a map showing the location of the Korilian home planet."

There were no comments from those in attendance, so Fitzgerald turned the brief over to Captain Tom Wears, who provided additional details about the Vormak system and the pending operation.

After Wears finished, Fitzgerald took over again.

"For a mission this far from the other five fleets, with no hope of reinforcements, it's critical that Third Fleet remain undetected while entering and returning from Korilian territory. Admiral McCarthy will accompany Third Fleet, doing his best to select jump points that will keep the fleet concealed during its approach and evade Korilian pursuit during its return to Colonial territory. In addition, I intend to keep the Korilians focused on other issues and their warships tied down. I will recommence the Liberation Campaign with four fleets as currently planned, plus send Third Fleet to Vormak."

There were murmurs in the audience; the Council's edict on keeping two Earth defense fleets in orbit was clear. Fitzgerald raised her hand, silencing the discussion.

"Vormak is twenty jumps inside the Korilian Empire—fifty jumps from Earth—but we'll be traveling through the Telemantic vortex on the way, which will reduce the journey by twenty-five jumps."

Lara recalled that Telemantic was one of two hyper-jump vortexes in the Colonies, with Telemantic in the path toward the Korilian Empire and the Gideon vortex on the opposite side of the Colonies, where jumps of up to twenty-five times the normal distance were possible.

"So, we're talking about a four-week round-trip mission. That's what I'll be asking for: a reduction to one Earth defense fleet for four weeks. A four-week gamble that could obtain the information we need to end this war."

She turned to McCarthy. "Will the Council agree?"

Lara felt McCarthy's view as he followed timelines into the future, viewing the outcome of Fitzgerald's proposal.

McCarthy nodded. "The Council will agree."

"I'll petition the Council this afternoon," Fitzgerald replied, then turned to Admiral Goergen. "I understand Third Fleet has completed refit and is fully operational?"

"Yes, Admiral," Goergen replied.

"Commence the transit to Vormak once the Liberation Campaign counterassault begins."

18

On the eightieth floor of the Fleet headquarters building, in a suite provided to admirals and dignitaries spending the night in Brussels, Lara stepped from the bathroom wearing a plunging-neckline blue satin dress with a cutout exposing her toned stomach and slender waist. There wasn't much covering the front of her body; only the parts men wanted to see most. McCarthy realized that Lara had planned ahead, hoping to spend time with him after today's brief, packing a tantalizing outfit for dinner.

Their dinner reservation wasn't for another hour, so she joined McCarthy on a balcony terrace overlooking the city. After he handed her a glass of wine, she stood against the railing and took a sip, enjoying the view: the multicolor lights illuminating the city, the hundred-foot-tall holograms advertising products, the stream of hover-cars weaving through the city's congested air routes, and the mass of pedestrians below.

They had been talking for a few minutes, and Lara had just mentioned how the scene reminded her of her apartment on Ritalis—the one she had shared with her husband, Gary, before he had been killed in battle—when she fell quiet, then turned suddenly toward McCarthy and searched his eyes.

"What is it?" he asked.

"After Gary's death, I thought I'd never love another man again. For three years, I was consumed with grief."

McCarthy recalled the details of her husband's death. He was a Fleet officer who had been killed in the Tindal star system. McCarthy had been there, had participated in the desperate battle.

Lara laughed uncomfortably. "I felt like a joke—a grief counselor who couldn't deal with her own anguish. But then I met you and found the one person who could replace Gary."

McCarthy caressed Lara's cheek. "I felt the same way after Teresa died. Her loss was devastating, and I swore not to fall in love with another woman until after the war was over. But then I met you."

Lara smiled briefly, then looked away, and he could sense emotion gathering in her chest. When she turned back to him, her eyes were brimming with tears.

"I'm afraid, Jon. I don't want to lose you."

McCarthy didn't respond as he wrestled with the one demon that threatened their relationship. The issue Elena had so easily discerned.

Lara must have misinterpreted his silence. "I know that you and Elena are close. I'm afraid of what might develop between you, now that she's back."

He hadn't shared what Elena revealed during his first visit at the sanitorium: that she was in love with him. But Lara had apparently picked up on it after they visited Elena a few days ago, either because she was an empath or by deducing Elena's feelings from watching their interactions.

McCarthy wrapped his arms around Lara and pulled her close. "You have nothing to worry about," he said.

"Your connection with her is so strong. I can sense it."

"You're not wrong," McCarthy replied. "I have a strong bond with Elena, and I'd do almost anything for her. But I'm not in love with her. I'm in love with *you*."

Lara rested her cheek against his chest for a moment, then pulled back and wiped the tears from her eyes. She took another sip of wine and gazed over the city, lost in her thoughts for a while, and her body gradually relaxed.

The End of Time   95

Then she wrapped her arms around him and looked up with a devilish smile.

"Why don't we delay dinner. We can have dessert first."

McCarthy grinned. "An excellent suggestion." He leaned in for a kiss, his right hand finding the zipper on the back of her dress, which he unzipped at a tantalizingly slow pace.

19

Mountain peaks in the distance cast long shadows across the North China Plain as Lijuan Xiang's Council transport glided high above the homeland of her ancestors, headed toward her villa for the weekend. At least that was what others had been led to believe. Her true destination was Domus Salus, the last Corvad House compound. It had been several years since her last visit; she limited her trips to minimize the potential that Nexi would discover Domus Salus and raze it to the ground as they had done to the main Corvad stronghold, Domus Valens, three decades ago.

Lijuan followed several timelines into the future, viewing the outcome of her pending visit, searching for changes in Nexi patterns that would indicate her true destination had been detected via electronic surveillance. She had put safeguards in place, however, and there was no indication in her view that her detour would be discovered.

The other issue was the Nexus ability to follow someone's timeline, delving into their past and future. Such scrutiny would potentially detect her visits to Domus Salus, revealing that not only had a Corvad compound survived, but that she was a Corvad Ten. However, Lijuan was uniquely suited to address that issue.

In addition to having the powers of charm and suggestion, she was a timeline blocker and view shifter. It was because of that ability that she had

The End of Time

been selected to lead the cadre of Corvad personnel at Domus Salus, spirited away just before the Nexus assault destroyed Domus Valens. Lijuan had been christened the savior of their House. But she had also been responsible for its near destruction, and that guilt haunted her to this day.

Thirty-three years ago, when she was still a teenager, she had passed the Test and become a Corvad Ten. Her talent had developed soon afterward, and a formidable talent it was, one that was highly valued and had been mastered by only one other Corvad in the three-millennium existence of her House. Not only could she block timelines from being viewed, she could also alter the views of Nines and Tens, fabricating fake timelines into the future.

Under the tutelage of the Corvad Primus Talentum, responsible for developing emerging talents, she had experimented with her new ability, attempting to determine if she could fool the three Nexus Placidia Tens.

The Nexus response had been swift and unexpected; the Corvads clearly didn't have an appreciation for what their attack on Domus Praesidium five hundred years ago had done to the Nexus psyche.

Five centuries ago, the views of the Nexus Placidia Tens had been blocked, a precursor to a Corvad assault that had destroyed the Nexus Codex. Thirty-three years ago, when Lijuan altered the views of the three Nexus Tens, the Nexi had somehow detected what she had done and reacted harshly. The Nexi incorrectly concluded that the Corvads were about to initiate another assault and had decided to strike first, launching an attack on Domus Valens.

In three thousand years, no one had penetrated Domus Valens's defense. To attempt to do so was tantamount to suicide, committing a major house's full military might, including its entire praetorian legion to the effort. Even if successful, there would be few praetorians and scant military equipment remaining, insufficient to fend off even a minor house assault.

The Nexi had taken the gamble and prevailed, and the Nexus One and her coalition of minor houses had somehow kept the Corvad-aligned minor houses at bay. The Nexus One had then decreed the House War was over, and the three-thousand-year conflict had faded into memory.

Not exactly.

The Corvad House had survived, and it was only a matter of time before it regained sufficient strength to strike back, delivering a blow that would reduce the Nexus House to smoldering ruins. The prediction was recorded in the Corvad Apocalypsis.

Thirty-four years after the fall of Domus Valens, Domus Praesidium will in turn be destroyed and the Nexus House vanquished.

It had been thirty-three years thus far.

Only a week ago, their premier protégé, Gavin Vaus, had finally passed the *carcerem cellula*—the level-ten Test—and been certified, the first new Corvad Ten in thirty-three years. Additionally, his talent had begun to emerge.

The pieces were starting to come together, but it wasn't yet clear how Lijuan would orchestrate the destruction of the Nexus House. The Nexi were powerful and numerous—over ten thousand in Domus Praesidium and another seventy thousand spread throughout the public, hidden in government bureaucracies, financial institutions, and military organizations to ensure Nexus influence, wealth, and safety. Only a few hundred Corvads had escaped the slaughter at Domus Valens, and three decades later, there were only five thousand Corvads. However, Lijuan had focused her House's efforts on developing praetorians, which numbered almost two hundred.

Lijuan's thoughts shifted back to her journey aboard the shuttle. She had already taken precautions to prevent her trip to Domus Salus from being discovered by the prescient Nexi, altering her timeline so that any Nexi probing her past or future would not discover she was a Corvad or the existence of Domus Salus. That left the technical details to address.

Her shuttle approached the Taihang Mountains, where Lijuan would fool any attempt to electronically track her transit to Domus Salus. The terrain rose toward her shuttle as foothills climbed toward the mountains, and the transport was soon weaving through deep valleys between mountain peaks. Up ahead was a unique section of the mountain range, a large overhang suspended over a section of the mountain that had collapsed beneath it. Hovering beneath the overhang was an identical shuttle, waiting to swap places.

Lijuan buckled herself into her seat as the pilot, a Corvad Four, disengaged the autopilot, taking manual control of the shuttle. When they passed beneath the overhang, the pilot deactivated the transport's identification beacon and engaged the reverse thrusters, throwing Lijuan against her seat restraints as the shuttle slowed. At the same time, the decoy shuttle activated its beacon and accelerated, emerging from beneath the overhang at the same speed at which Lijuan's shuttle had arrived.

Lijuan's shuttle waited beneath the overhang for an hour until night arrived, then resumed its journey with its interior lights extinguished. Following another hour-long trek through the Taihang Mountains, they arrived at Domus Salus, entering a deep recess in the mountain face.

After the shuttle landed in the primitive spaceport, Lijuan emerged and was greeted by Nero Conde, her Primus Nine.

Conde bowed his head in respect. "Welcome back to Domus Salus, Princeps."

In one hand, Conde held a jewelry box, which he opened, revealing the princeps's ring, containing the Corvad House seal. She would normally have dispensed with the formality of donning the princeps's ring for the short visit, but the pending encounter dictated the accoutrement. She took the ring and slid it onto her finger.

Conde escorted Lijuan into Domus Salus, past thick metal doors that slid slowly open, then guided Lijuan toward Gavin Vaus.

"How is his talent progressing?" Lijuan asked.

"He's made significant strides, but the Primus Talentum advises patience. He is not yet ready to engage in battle, plus we do not yet have sufficient strength to prevail against the Nexus House. We need more praetorians."

"Considering the outcome on Darian 3, we need more *capable* praetorians," Lijuan said. "It was an even-odds engagement, yet we lost all ten praetorians, including our Deinde Nine, while the Nexi lost only two."

"They were led by Ronan, their Primus Nine."

"Would the outcome have been different had you led the assault?"

Conde didn't respond.

"I make my point. We need better praetorians, trained to the same standard as before, when our praetorians were equal to the Nexi's."

"I need better candidates. Better raw material. The Nexi have first pick, selecting the cream of the crop to induct and train. They recruit openly, while we're forced to slink in the shadows, hiding our existence. I get to sift through the rejects, looking for potential the Nexi overlooked."

"I cannot improve the pool of candidates," Lijuan replied. "You will have to train them better."

"We don't have adequate training facilities in this decrepit domus."

"Domus Salus has kept us hidden and safe for three decades. It will have to do until we reclaim Domus Valens. In the meantime, do your job."

"I am doing my best. But there are limits to what I can accomplish considering the constraints."

"I don't want to hear excuses, Nero. I am aware of the challenges. Your task is to overcome them."

Conde's jaw muscles twitched as he endured Lijuan's admonishment. Then he bowed his head slightly. "Yes, Princeps."

They arrived outside the chamber where Vaus was training, stopping to watch through a one-way electronic wall. Vaus was training with the Corvad Primus Talentum, responsible for developing talents. Vaus closed his eyes and placed a hand on the shoulder of a stone statue. After a few seconds, the statue crumbled into pieces.

Vaus had developed the power of disintegration, the ability to turn nonliving objects to dust. However, as impressive as his talent was, its uses were limited. He could clear obstacles from their path, disintegrating security doors, for example, or reduce an opponent's body armor to powder. However, even if he dissolved the armor, he'd still be facing a Nexus praetorian and would not survive long. Vaus was a gangly teenager, and although he would fill out as he matured, it was unlikely he would become skilled enough to defeat even the average Nexus praetorian. He needed to develop his talent further.

The Primus Talentum was working with him, hoping Vaus was capable of the ultimate disintegration talent—the ability to dissolve living things.

Accompanied by Conde—for good reason—Lijuan entered the training chamber, ostensibly to congratulate Vaus on achieving level ten and developing a rare and devastating talent. But more important, she aimed to secure his allegiance. Unlike the Nexi, only a single Corvad could rule the House. Vaus was now a Ten, as was Lijuan, and his talent was superior to hers: she had the powers of charm and suggestion and was also a timeline blocker and view shifter, talents even rarer than disintegration, but not as valuable in combat. If Vaus challenged her, he would have the advantage.

Fortunately, Lijuan was a Placidia Ten, able to view without creating turbulence, which meant she was superior to Vaus and could not be challenged. However, that hadn't stopped previous Corvad Tens from disregarding protocol, using their talents in ruthless and sometimes successful attempts to rule the Corvad House.

Vaus and the Primus Talentum turned to greet her when she entered, and Lijuan stopped with Conde at her side, far enough from Vaus so Conde could intervene if he attempted to touch her, just in case Vaus had secretly developed the ability to disintegrate living matter. She had viewed the pending encounter and had confirmed Conde would remain loyal, but Vaus's reaction was unknown. When two Tens interacted in sensitive matters, the prime timeline typically dissolved, as it had in this case.

"Congratulations, Gavin. You have achieved a rare feat, becoming the first new Corvad Ten in over three decades. The Corvad House welcomes your valuable view."

"Thank you, Princeps," Vaus replied.

There was no slight bow of his head, as was customary when first speaking to the princeps. He was now a Ten and had chosen to address her as his equal. Lijuan ignored the transgression.

"Your talent has also developed quite nicely, and according to the Primus Talentum, you have not yet reached your full potential."

"One can only hope."

There was a moment of strained silence, then Lijuan spoke. "You know why I am here."

"I do," was the response.

"You are now a Ten, as I am. But as a Placidia Ten, I rule the House. Which makes you the Primus Ten." She extended her hand, the one with the Corvad House ring. "As it has been done throughout the ages, swear allegiance to your princeps."

Vaus fixed his gaze on her for a long moment, and a deep chill seeped into her body.

Then he knelt on one knee, bowing his head slightly. "Lead, and your Ten will follow."

Lijuan's view suddenly cleared. For the foreseeable future, Vaus would not challenge her.

The tension in her body eased. "Rise."

After Vaus rose to his feet, she said, "Your allegiance will be rewarded."

She departed the training chamber, Conde at her side, leaving Vaus to continue his training with the Primus Talentum.

Lijuan had accomplished the main goal of her trip, but obtaining Vaus's allegiance wasn't the only reason she had visited Domus Salus. Squirreled away in her 120-floor Council headquarters building, her view was limited, and she was faced with difficult decisions. The Corvad Apocalypsis predicted the Corvads would prevail over the Nexi in only a year's time, and Lijuan had no idea how. At the moment, the Nexi were superior to the Corvads in every way, except one—Corvads had a superior view.

Nexi deliberately hindered their analysis of the future, excluding emotion from their views. Corvads, on the other hand, harnessed emotion, using it to propel their view through the mist of uncertainty. The stronger the emotion, the stronger the view and the longer it held before dissolving.

Lijuan, like all Corvad Tens, fed on various emotions, but the strongest ones were the negative emotions: hatred, rage, jealousy, and fear. And there was no stronger emotion than the terror a person experienced when faced with certain death.

She turned to Conde. "Is the view chamber ready?"

"Yes, Princeps."

Lijuan followed Conde to the chamber entrance, where she examined the meager accoutrements: several hooks on the wall for her clothes, a nearby shower and towel for afterward, and a weapon. She followed her timeline a moment into the future; inside the chamber was a naked man of Russian ancestry, standing with his hands and feet bound to a vertical post behind him.

She removed her white Council robe and stripped naked, then entered the chamber, the door closing behind her with a heavy clank. Under normal circumstances, the arrival of a nude attractive woman would have elicited a sexual response from the man. Instead, his eyes widened in fear upon spotting a dagger in Lijuan's hand.

Exactly as planned.

Lijuan approached at a measured pace, letting the man's apprehension build.

"Let me go," he said, his voice quavering. "I'll do anything you want."

She said nothing as she stopped before him, then caressed one shoulder with the flat side of her cold dagger. As she moved it slowly down his chest, she rotated the blade and sliced a shallow cut into his breast.

The man cried out in pain, then reiterated his plea. "I'll do anything you want!"

Lijuan stepped closer. "I know you will. But the only thing I want is for you to die."

The man stared at her, perhaps comprehending what was about to happen, but not understanding why.

"You know you're going to die, don't you?"

The man shook his head. "No. Please don't!"

She brought the knife to his neck, then flicked another shallow cut through his skin.

"I'm going to cut you deeper and deeper, until I slice through your carotid artery. Once you start bleeding out, your life will end in a few minutes."

"I don't understand," the man whimpered. "Why are you doing this to me?"

"You don't have to understand why. You just have to understand what's going to happen."

Lijuan cut into his neck again, deeper this time.

The man began struggling against his bonds, trying to break free.

She sliced into his neck again, then whispered in his ear, "Almost there. The next slice will sever your artery. If you believe in God, say your prayer now, and quickly."

Lijuan stepped back slightly so she could fully grasp the terror in his eyes, then placed the knife edge into the cut. She began viewing, following her line into the future, opening dozens of alternate timelines postulating different actions and plans she could put into motion.

"Time's up," she said, then cut deeply into the man's neck, slicing through his artery.

Blood gushed from the wound, pulsing in rhythm to the man's heartbeat. Some of his blood coated her arm, shoulder, and chest as the man struggled, sending spurts of blood in various directions.

She closed her eyes and let the man's terror flow through her, harnessing the emotion to propel her view faster and more strongly through the future, analyzing one line, then another, and another, branching some alternate lines into alternates of their own, her view branching like a tree sprouting from the ground, its trunk splitting into more and more branches as it grew upward.

After a short while, the man's terror began to fade; he was losing consciousness. But she had already abandoned the lines that hadn't been fruitful, focusing on those that were.

As the man's fear ebbed away with his life, Lijuan's views dissolved into a gray mist.

But she had analyzed enough potential futures to identify a few lines that held promise. She couldn't be certain of some outcomes, because several lines interacted with Nexus Nines and Tens; timelines that interacted with those who could view and change them were always difficult to predict with certainty.

After her views faded and her thoughts returned to the present, her gaze focused on the man before her. His head had sagged forward, his eyes frozen open, and his skin—where it wasn't coated in blood—had turned pasty white.

Lijuan left the chamber, then stepped beneath the showerhead and turned on the water, rinsing the blood from her blade and body. As she watched the blood collect at her feet and swirl down the drain, she sorted through what she had learned.

The revelations had been stunning; the plot itself, as well as the tools she would wield to destroy the Nexus House. Lijuan smiled as she recalled a proverb written several millennia ago, which had proven true countless times.

Heaven has no rage like love to hatred turned, nor hell a fury like a woman scorned.

The End of Time

She now knew what needed to be done.

20

Following her supposed weekend stay at her vacation villa, Lijuan continued west toward Belgium, her shuttle descending toward a landing pad at Sint-Pieters Sanitorium. Along the way, she reviewed Elena Kapadia's file, including video of McCarthy's two visits. Elena's interactions with McCarthy confirmed what Lijuan had learned during her emotion-fueled view at Domus Salus; Elena was in love with her childhood friend.

Waiting beside the shuttle pad when her transport landed was Dr. Elijah Guptah, who escorted Lijuan to Elena. The Nexus Ten spent most of her time in the atrium, Guptah explained as they stopped in a glass-walled lobby providing a view of the circular, tree-lined garden. An armed guard joined them in case Elena assaulted the Council regent.

Elena was sitting on a bench as she had during her last visit with McCarthy, but this time in the shade of a cherry tree along the perimeter rather than in the center of the atrium. To Lijuan's surprise, Elena no longer wore a sundress; she wore a Nexus blue-and-white jumpsuit with ten white stripes around each upper arm. This was something Lijuan hadn't seen in her view at Domus Salus. However, she had been following dozens of alternate lines simultaneously and had sped through them quickly. Elena's attire might not have been a detail that registered.

Before entering the atrium, Lijuan took precautions. She was about to engage a Nexus Ten who'd be able to follow her line into the future or past, back to the weekend she had just spent at Domus Salus. Lijuan altered her timeline, removing any evidence of her trip to Domus Salus.

When Lijuan entered the atrium, Elena noticed the entrance of the white-robed woman, her eyes watching the Council regent as she approached and stopped before her.

"May I join you?" Lijuan asked.

Elena nodded, her eyes still studying her. Lijuan felt the chill from Elena's view, probing her line as she sat beside her.

"I'm Council Regent Lijuan Xiang, Director of Material. I helped authorize the mission to Hellios, and I wanted to check in on you. See how you're doing."

There was no response from Elena; she just stared at her.

Attempting to break the ice, Lijuan said, "I see you've shifted into your Nexus uniform. I'm curious as to why you did so, considering that technically, you're still an Army officer."

Elena shrugged. "I like the colors?"

She hadn't really answered Lijuan's question, but at least she had responded.

"On behalf of the Council, I want to extend our thanks for everything you've done to support the war effort."

A pained expression appeared on Elena's face. "For everything I've done?"

"You've dedicated over half of your life—twenty years—to defeating the Korilians."

"I'm not sure you understand," Elena replied, "...about everything I've done."

"I *do* understand, and you have nothing to feel guilty about. You did the best you could, and that's all anyone can ask."

"It wasn't good enough. I should have tried harder..."

Elena turned away, and Lijuan felt emotions building inside the Nexus Ten.

Everything is proceeding as planned, Lijuan thought. Elena had reacted as expected once Lijuan broached the sensitive issue, about how she had betrayed humanity by viewing for the Korilians. But that wasn't the goal of today's visit; it was merely a means to an end. A way to prepare Elena for the suggestion she would plant in her mind.

Before proceeding, Lijuan decided to use her Touch and look into Elena's mind to ensure she was ready for the suggestion. She placed her hand on Elena's, purportedly to offer support, and searched her thoughts.

Lijuan almost recoiled at the turmoil—the thoughts and emotions swirling inside Elena's mind. Most disturbing of all was a scene of Elena restrained in her prison chamber on Hellios. It took a lot to turn a Corvad Ten's stomach, considering the ritual employed for emotion-fueled views, but a chill went down Lijuan's spine as she watched the Korilians flay the flesh from Elena's body, down to bare bones on her arms and legs. The Korilians waited for Elena to regenerate her flesh, then they flayed her again, and again, and again. Although Elena could heal herself, she wasn't immune to the pain. Eventually, her will—and her mind itself—had snapped.

Elena's turbulent thoughts and emotions were so disorienting that Lijuan became nauseated. She removed her hand from Elena's and did her best to hide her physical reaction.

Lara had been right during her visit to the sanitorium with McCarthy, warning him that Elena was struggling to hold things together, her mind on the brink of a violent disintegration.

Perfect.

As her stomach settled, Lijuan focused on what she had learned during her brief Touch, discerning which issues could be used to her advantage. That Elena was in love with McCarthy was obvious, but also complicated. Simmering beneath Elena's calm demeanor was a decades-long anger and hatred, a result of her belief that she had been abandoned on Hellios. Elena was struggling to convince herself that her conclusion had been incorrect, that McCarthy hadn't received her message from Darian 3 until a few months ago.

Lijuan prepared to use her power of suggestion to plant an idea in Elena's mind, then touched her hand again.

"You realize that McCarthy doesn't love you. That he never will."

Elena cocked her head slightly to the side, her eyes focusing on Lijuan in a way they hadn't before. "How would you know?"

The End of Time · 109

Lijuan withdrew her hand. Something had gone wrong. The suggestion hadn't taken hold.

Elena stared at her, waiting for a response. She had taken Lijuan's statement at face value rather than the suggestion it was meant to be. Lijuan backpedaled mentally, evaluating how to continue the conversation, finally latching onto a plan.

"It's just my supposition. A woman's intuition." She leaned closer to Elena. "Would a man who loved you let you rot on Hellios for eighteen years?"

"He didn't know I was there," Elena replied, although Lijuan detected uncertainty in her voice.

It's working. Elena's confidence in McCarthy can be shattered.

"Would a man who loved you let you waste the rest of your life away in this sanitorium?"

"He's trying to get me out of here."

"There has been no request from the Nexus House for your release. I fear that they believe you are a burden to them now. An asset easily discarded now that you're defective. It wouldn't surprise me if they locked you away forever, like one of their Lost Ones, deemed permanently insane."

Lijuan felt an emotional crack in the woman across from her, watched various emotions play across Elena's face. Lijuan had hit on a tender issue and she had to work fast, before the woman's emotional state disintegrated.

"But I believe in you," Lijuan said. "I know you can help."

Elena searched Lijuan's eyes for a moment before she replied. "You do?"

During the trip to Sint-Pieters, Lijuan had watched the final few minutes of Elena and McCarthy's last encounter and knew how desperate Elena was to help, to make amends for what she had done.

"Of course you can help," Lijuan replied. "You're intelligent and talented. You're a Nexus Ten, after all, and you're a healer and drainer. You can put those talents to good use, against those who deserve it."

Had Elena not resisted Lijuan's earlier attempt to plant a suggestion in her mind, Lijuan would have explained exactly how Elena could put her ability to drain a person's life force to good use. Hopefully, the verbal suggestion, although subtle, would take hold.

"I think you've recovered enough to leave this place," Lijuan said, "to help us defeat the Korilians. I have an idea."

Lijuan provided the details, explaining her plan to Elena.

When she finished, Elena stared at her, giving no indication as to whether she thought the plan was a good idea or not, or whether she was willing to assist in the manner desired.

"Is that something you'd like to do?" Lijuan asked, hoping for a positive response.

After a long moment, Elena slowly nodded.

"Excellent," Lijuan replied. "I'll talk with Dr. Guptah. I'm sure he'll agree that you're healthy enough to be released."

Lijuan left Elena on the bench beneath the cherry tree, rejoining Guptah in the atrium lobby. Before discussing the critical issue with Guptah, she glanced at Elena, who was staring into the distance, talking to herself.

She turned to Guptah. "It appears that Elena has made significant progress. She'll be released soon?"

"Not likely," Guptah replied. "She's still unstable, and probably will remain so until we work through a few significant issues."

Lijuan touched Guptah's hand, planting a suggestion. "Elena has made tremendous progress. I think she's well enough to leave now."

Guptah stared at Lijuan as he reevaluated the situation. "You're quite right," he finally said. "Elena has made tremendous progress. I think she's well enough to be released. I'll begin the processing now."

21

On the south coast of France, near Côte d'Azur, the orange sky was smeared with streaks of purple and red as Lijuan Xiang's shuttle descended toward its destination. Morel Alperi's residence was a six-story building constructed in an inverted format; each higher floor was larger than the one below it, with the top level overhanging the rest of the building on all four sides.

The rooftop complex contained a shuttle landing pad and garden, although the garden, filled with grass and trees as well as decorative flowers and manicured hedges, was more like a park, complete with gazebos dotting the open areas. Along one side of the rooftop was a large infinity pool, its water spilling over the edge onto the base of a cliff two hundred feet below. The pool was bordered by a flagstone patio on both sides and a sand beach on the end, each lined with lounge chairs and shade canopies.

After Lijuan's shuttle landed, she emerged from her transport as Alperi put down his drink and rose from a poolside table.

"Welcome, Lijuan. I'm glad you finally accepted my invitation." He strode toward her wearing sandals and a loose-fitting white robe exposing a good portion of his hairy chest.

Lijuan was similarly attired, taking advantage of the warm weather. She was wearing a white robe lined with gold fringe along the hems, with a plunging neckline chosen to provide an ample view of her breasts. A sash was tied around her waist, accentuating her slim figure, and a slit was cut in her robe all the way up to her left hip, exposing a long, lean leg.

"I've been meaning to join you," Lijuan lied as she approached him. "But something always seems to come up that requires my attention."

"I'm glad you were able to find the time," he said as his eyes roamed over her body. "Can I get you a drink?"

Lijuan contemplated what she was in the mood for, and considering who had fueled her emotion-laden view over the weekend, made an appropriate request.

"A White Russian."

Alperi snapped his fingers at a servant hovering nearby, who approached and took Lijuan's order, while Alperi requested another gin and tonic.

Lijuan joined him at the table, and as they waited for their drinks, she took in Alperi's opulent residence, one of a half dozen homes he had built for himself since becoming the director of Personnel. As director of Material, Lijuan had frequently been approached by military construction representatives offering enormous bribes, and she suspected that Alperi, who controlled every human's fate—their job assignment upon reaching the age of sixteen—had been similarly enticed.

The drinks arrived as Lijuan complimented Alperi on his residence.

"I designed it myself," he replied. "Just a few sketches, though, outlining my vision."

"It's beautiful," Lijuan said as she sipped her drink. "I especially like the pool."

"It's too bad you didn't bring a swimsuit with you. It's a bit warm today, and we could have cooled off in the water."

"Who needs a swimsuit?" Lijuan said as she stood, loosening the sash around her waist. She tossed it on the table and pulled her robe from her shoulders, letting it fall to her feet.

"Care to join me?" she asked as she slipped off her panties and sandals, then sauntered toward the pool.

Alperi quickly disrobed and followed her.

Lijuan stepped slowly into the pool, letting Alperi savor her body as she sank into the cool water, the sun's golden rays reflecting off the water's surface. She leaned back against a side of the pool, stretching her arms out along the edge, letting Alperi's eyes devour her.

He moved across the pool toward her, stopping an arm's length away. Then he leaned forward and placed his hands on the ledge, an arm on each side of her, brushing against her breasts.

His gaze suddenly hardened. "What do you want, Lijuan?"

She feigned surprise at his question.

Alperi added, "That you traveled here rather than hologrammed me says much. Or have you finally succumbed to my charm and wish to bed me?"

"There *is* something I want. How long I stay and how we entertain ourselves—I haven't yet decided."

"I assume my answer to your request will influence your decision?"

Lijuan smiled. "Of course."

"I'm intrigued."

She rested her forearms on his shoulders. "It's about Elena. I stopped by Sint-Pieters today and discussed her condition with her physicians. She's doing remarkably well, and they're processing her for discharge."

"I see," Alperi replied. "And as the director of Personnel, I control Elena's tasking."

Lijuan nodded. "Even though she's a Nexus, she was handed over to the Council twenty years ago, and you still determine her assignments."

"What task do you have in mind?"

Lijuan moved toward Alperi, pressing her naked body against his as she whispered in his ear.

"Your request has merit," Alperi replied as Lijuan pulled back. After considering the issue for a moment, he agreed. "I don't see why not. I'll have her new assignment transmitted tonight. In a few hours, however..."

He grinned as he ran his hands down Lijuan's sides, resting them on her hips. Then his smile faded, and his voice took on a stern tone.

"What do you *really* want, Lijuan? You didn't come all this way to ask for a task reassignment."

"Actually, I did," she said, then offered a mischievous smile. "And now, I think I'll stay awhile."

She caressed the sides of his face as she planted a suggestion. "When I leave tonight, you won't recall the details of our conversation; that I asked you to change Elena's tasking. Instead, it was your idea. Understand?"

Alperi nodded slowly.

Lijuan offered a kiss, which Alperi hungrily reciprocated.

22

"Impressive, isn't it?" Lijuan asked.

Regent Lijuan Xiang, the Colonial Council's director of Material, responsible for building new starships, stood on a skywalk overlooking Assembly Shipyard Eight in Earth's low orbit. Beside her stood Fleet Admiral Nanci Fitzgerald, Admiral McCarthy, and Lara. Before them sprawled a vast industrial complex, ten assembly lines abreast, each stretching for miles into the distance.

Lijuan explained, "Each shipyard simultaneously builds over a hundred starships, assembling the smaller components built on Earth. A new warship rolls off one of our assembly lines every fourteen hours. I shudder to think of the ramifications if anything happened to our yards. It'd take a decade to reconstitute the industrial capacity we have today.

"Our timing is fortunate," she said as a new battleship undocked and fired its stern thrusters.

It emerged slowly from the assembly yard, and its bow thrusters fired, gradually turning it away from Earth, then its main engines ignited for the first time. As the starship approached the shimmering defense shield enveloping Earth, a sector disappeared, allowing the new warship to continue its outbound transit.

"We've reduced the shakedown cruise to a few days," Lijuan said as they watched the battleship accelerate away from the construction yard, beginning an unmanned voyage on an automated test run and its first jump.

Jump drives were fickle, and the slightest flaw in their construction could result in the starship's implosion, leaving just enough left of the immense warship to fit in the palm of one's hand. As a result, a starship's first jump was unmanned.

The assembly yard lost no time, as the next ship in line was slowly moved toward the final assembly station the battleship had just vacated.

Morel Alperi entered the skywalk with Council President David Portner.

"President Portner," Fitzgerald said, "I'm pleased you were able to join us."

"Thank you for the invitation, Nanci. It's not often that my duties allow me such luxury. Admiral McCarthy, it's good to see you again."

Turning to Lara, he said, "Miss Anderson, it's a pleasure to finally meet you. I have heard much about you."

"All good, I hope," Lara replied.

"Of course. Morel and Lijuan have kept me abreast of your valuable assistance."

Portner looked out from the skywalk at the vast assembly yard. "I must say you're doing an admirable job, Lijuan. The logistics required to support our defense forces is a daunting task."

"It is, but I have an exceptional staff. They deserve all the credit."

"You have also done well, Morel," Portner said. "The war has been an enormous drain on our personnel, and allocating our people optimally is not an easy job. Manning four more assembly yards and the facilities on Earth fabricating the necessary components will add to the burden, but we have no choice. We must increase our starship construction rate."

Portner turned to Fitzgerald. "However, despite how admirable a job Lijuan and Alperi are doing, we didn't come here to discuss starship production. I understand that *Trafalgar* will be arriving momentarily?"

"It is," Fitzgerald replied as she checked her wristlet. "In another minute."

Their gaze shifted from one side of the skywalk to the other, staring away from Earth, until a white flash illuminated the darkness. The light

The End of Time 117

faded, revealing a cargo ship that had just completed a jump. It rested motionless, just outside the planet's protective shield.

"Shall we?" Fitzgerald asked.

"By all means," Portner replied.

Fitzgerald escorted the group to the assembly yard spaceport, where they boarded an executive Fleet transport. Several minutes later, after departing the assembly yard spaceport, they entered another spaceport, this one inside the massive cargo ship *Trafalgar*. Upon exiting the shuttle, the group was greeted by the ship's captain, standing by to escort them to the cargo hold.

"Have you seen one of these Korilian objects before?" Portner asked Lara.

"No, Regent," she replied.

"Please, call me David," he said, then held his elbow out. "If you please. It's not often that I get escorted by a beautiful woman. It seems that Morel never assigns the attractive ones to my staff."

Alperi replied, "I believe the real problem is that your eyesight is failing, David."

"That is most likely true," Portner replied.

Lara wrapped her arm around Portner's, guiding him through the ship's passageways.

"None of us has seen one of these Korilian obelisks in person, I think," Fitzgerald said. "This is the first one transported back to Earth."

"It is," Portner affirmed. "The Korilians leave a marker on every planet they've occupied, placing it after exterminating all humans. Each marker is identical, with the same inscription. We were reluctant to bring any of them back at first. But we've analyzed them extensively, and there's nothing to be concerned about. Just plain obsidian."

They stopped before a sealed cargo hold guarded by two Marines.

"Open the hold," Fitzgerald ordered.

One of the Marines entered an access code into a security panel, and the doors slid open. White vapor billowed out, slowly dissipating as Lara felt the chill from McCarthy's view. She glanced at him, looking for reassurance that they were safe, and after observing no reaction on his face, concluded they were.

Lights flickered on as they entered the hold, growing brighter until the object before them was fully illuminated. It was a black obelisk, about a hundred feet tall and ten feet wide at the bottom, lying on one side. Fiery red symbols were etched into the marker's base.

"What do they say?" Lara asked.

Portner replied, "It's difficult to translate Korilian to English, but our best estimate is that it says, *Time will stop for you*. Most experts think it's a wordy way of expressing the Korilians' intent to exterminate humanity, with a more succinct translation being—*We will end you*.

"There's another word at the end," he added, "but there's disagreement on how it translates. Most linguists believe it translates to *also*. But that doesn't make much sense. The other faction believes it means *soon*, which is more consistent within the context."

Alperi interjected, "The linguists can deliberate over the exact translation, but I don't think there's any debate over what the inscription means. The Korilians have been slaughtering us for three decades."

"I don't think there's any doubt on their intent," Portner agreed. "I'm afraid it's going to have to be them or us."

Lara stared at the inscription on the obelisk, curious about the odd choice of words. As she studied the Korilian symbols, fog began to spread outward from beneath the obelisk, coating the deck as it expanded toward the cargo hold bulkheads. She checked McCarthy and the others, who appeared not to notice the fog, and concluded she was having a vision.

The Korilian symbols on the obelisk began melting, the red color oozing outward as the symbols dissolved. The red substance then began to coagulate into different patterns, and Lara realized they were taking the form of English letters.

Lara could almost make out the words, but the letters were unstable. The meaning of the Korilian symbols teetered on the edge of her mind like words on the tip of her tongue, knowing what she wanted to say but unable to find the words to express herself. Then the letters morphed back to their original form again: red Korilian symbols on the base of the obelisk.

McCarthy looked at her as she stared at the object, realizing she'd had a vision.

"What did you see?"

The End of Time 119

"I almost had it. The symbols were being translated into English."

"You saw what?" Portner asked.

"She had a vision," McCarthy explained, then addressed Lara. "Try again. Try to invoke the vision this time."

Lara looked at the obelisk and concentrated, using a technique that Dewan Channing, the Deinde Eight, had taught her before the Final Stand. She imagined she was standing in the cargo hold, alone, unable to see through a thick mist that surrounded her. A small swirling hole appeared in the fog, tunneling outward until the Korilian obelisk appeared. On the object's base, the red letters began to melt and run together, transforming into English again. But they failed to stabilize long enough for Lara to read them before they returned to the static Korilian symbols.

"They morph back into Korilian symbols too quickly."

"That's quite all right, Lara," Portner said. "We don't need your talent to translate them. We already know what they mean."

"I suppose you're right," Lara said.

Still, she wanted to try again. This time she closed her eyes and waited. She saw the Korilian symbols in her mind. They grew larger and began to pulse, the red letters turning brighter by the second. Then she felt it. A foreign and yet familiar feeling at the same time.

She now knew what they'd been missing.

Lara opened her eyes. "Your linguists are being too literal. These Korilian symbols impart not just meaning. They convey emotion as well."

"What emotion is that?" Portner asked.

Lara shuddered as the emotion faded from her mind.

"Intense hatred."

"Like I said," Portner replied, "they'll stop at nothing until they slaughter us all."

But there was something else. Embedded within the hatred was an emotion more specific, but Lara couldn't put her finger on it—an emotion crucial to understanding the Korilians and their maniacal obsession with exterminating humankind.

They examined the object for a while longer until Fitzgerald announced, "It's time. I need to return to the Fleet command center, and Admiral McCarthy and Lara need to proceed to the Third Fleet command ship. The Liberation Campaign is about to recommence, distracting the Korilians while Third Fleet travels to the Vormak system."

They departed the cargo hold, and Lara looked back at the obelisk. As the doors closed, sealing the object inside again, she realized she had discovered something crucial; that understanding the emotion embedded in these obelisks was far more important than deciphering the words.

23

In the underground Fleet command center, Fleet Admiral Fitzgerald took her seat in the center of the last tiered row. With her console situated higher than the others, she overlooked the personnel stretched before her, busy at their consoles as they discussed issues over their headsets, their gazes shifting between the computer screens before them and the large displays blanketing the front wall.

All four Liberation Campaign fleets were in a jump hold, each two jumps away from their rendezvous point. Each fleet had taken a different route toward its destination, with all four fleets within striking distance of three planetary systems where Colonial Defense Force armies were stranded, keeping the Korilians guessing. In a few minutes, however, Fitzgerald's plan would become clear—with all four fleets rendezvousing in the Antares system.

Despite her display of confidence, Fitzgerald was nervous. They were about to engage the Korilians at even odds, and in the thirty-three-year history of the war, the Fleet had never defeated the Korilians without a thirty percent advantage unless McCarthy had been in direct command. That had been the plan until a few days ago, when McCarthy had been reassigned to assist 3rd Fleet in its critical mission to Vormak, one that would hopefully help end the war soon.

In McCarthy's absence, Fitzgerald had modified the goals for this Liberation Campaign assault: keep the Korilians focused on the ten frontline worlds where Colonial forces were engaged, while minimizing Fleet losses. The Liberation Campaign fleets would temporarily overwhelm the Korilian battle groups in the Antares system before the other Korilian battle groups arrived, long enough to establish a jump corridor for resupply ships and to evacuate the seriously wounded.

Fitzgerald was nervous for another reason, however. This was 5th Fleet's first offensive operation since the Final Stand, when each fleet had been reduced to barely one third of its original strength and 2nd Fleet had been annihilated. Over the last three years, all six fleets had been restored to full strength, but 5th and 6th Fleets had been retained in Earth's orbit as a defensive measure, in case the Korilians launched a surprise attack on humanity's home world. As a result, 5th and 6th Fleets lacked experience. Offensive operations required more tactical prowess than defense, and Fitzgerald wondered how 5th Fleet would fare relative to the three more experienced Liberation Campaign fleets.

The red digital clock on the center display counted down toward zero, marking the time when all four fleets would complete their hold, ready for the double jump to Antares.

The clock reached zero and stopped, and a hush fell over the command center as the personnel awaited Fitzgerald's order.

She examined the strength of the Korilian armada one final time, reported by reconnaissance probes sent to the ten frontline systems and those nearby. After convincing herself that the Antares assault would succeed with minimal losses, hopefully followed by successful resupply missions in the other nine star systems, she gave the order.

"Commence the assault on Antares."

24

In Earth's high orbit, Lara and McCarthy were aboard *Surveillant*, the 3rd Fleet command ship, monitoring the assault in the Antares system. Seated in her fleet guide chair beside Admiral Goergen, with McCarthy standing beside them, Lara watched the battle unfold on the displays. Over the previous few days, as the Liberation Campaign fleets converged toward their potential targets, the Korilians had repositioned their ships in response, with five battle groups in each of the three target systems, leaving one group in reserve.

The five Korilian battle groups at Antares had withdrawn upon the arrival of the four Colonial fleets. They were just now returning, this time accompanied by eleven other battle groups. The four Liberation Campaign fleets had established a protective jump corridor within a spinning cylinder with a closed top, designed to rotate fresh ships into the path of the Korilian onslaught, which was attempting to bore a hole in the side of the protective shield.

Inside the jump corridor, resupply was proceeding smoothly, but the effort to keep ten million troops supplied for another two months was enormous. Hundreds of cargo ships were transferring material to smaller transports, which descended to the planet's surface. The lower section of the

Fleet's protective cylinder was busy suppressing Korilian artillery batteries targeting the supply ships, blue pulses raining down upon the planet.

With all sixteen Korilian battle groups committed to Antares and the Korilian military command focused on the battle, Admiral Goergen decided to commence the transit to Vormak.

"To all Third Fleet ships, prepare to jump at time two-one-four."

A moment later, the operations officer announced, "All ships report ready for the jump."

"Jump at the mark," Goergen ordered.

The operations officer relayed the order, and five deep tones reverberated throughout the command ship, followed by the computer's female voice over the ship's intercom.

"One minute to the jump."

The time counted down, and Lara prepared herself for the nauseating effect of the jump. But her thoughts were interrupted by the communications supervisor.

"Admiral," he announced. "We've received a Council directive to delay the jump. There's an incoming Council shuttle."

Goergen cocked her head at the unusual order, her eyes going to the clock.

Thirty seconds remaining.

The situation was highly irregular; the Council rarely interceded directly in Fleet operations. However, she could not disregard a Council directive.

"Hold the jump," Goergen ordered. "Relay to the fleet."

After the order went out, the communications supervisor announced, "Incoming message. Commanding officer eyes only."

While Goergen checked her wristlet, reading the directive, Lara felt the chill from McCarthy's view as he probed the future. His gaze shot toward Goergen, whose eyes met his.

"Can you shed light on this issue?" Goergen asked.

McCarthy didn't respond. Instead, Lara felt the chill from his view intensify.

"I have no advice to offer at the moment," he said. McCarthy was extraordinarily good at controlling his emotions, but the concern in his voice was unmistakable.

Goergen replied, "I don't like last-minute changes in plans, especially when it involves issues I don't fully understand." She rose from her chair. "My quarters," she said to McCarthy, her tone making it clear it was not a request. Although both were four-star admirals, Goergen was senior and this was her fleet.

Both admirals left the bridge without another word.

McCarthy and Goergen returned to the command bridge a few minutes later, neither admiral revealing what they had discussed.

The communications supervisor announced, "The Council transport has docked."

"Provide an escort to the bridge," Goergen directed.

The admiral was quiet as she studied the displays, reporting the status of her fleet and the battle at Antares, but Lara could tell she was stewing.

Goergen turned to McCarthy. "This is your department. Make sure nothing imperils the success of this mission."

The elevator doors opened, and a lieutenant entered the bridge, escorting a woman who stopped before the two admirals and Lara.

"Admiral Goergen," the woman said. "I've been directed to accompany you on this mission for reasons that should be obvious. I will do my best to assist."

She turned to McCarthy. "Hello, Jon."

"Welcome aboard, Elena," he said. "I look forward to working with you."

Lara was stunned at his casual response. This scenario was a disaster waiting to happen.

Elena shifted her gaze to Lara for a moment before returning her attention to McCarthy.

"I see you brought *it* with you. Be sure to keep your pet on a leash so it doesn't bite anyone."

25

"If she calls me *it* one more time, I'm gonna flatten her!"

After the jump, while 3rd Fleet waited for the physical effects of the jump to dissipate before continuing its transit, Lara and McCarthy had retreated to their quarters aboard *Surveillant*.

McCarthy was about to respond to Lara's outburst when his wristlet vibrated, indicating a priority message. He tapped is wristlet, and the Nexus One appeared on the display.

"You requested I contact you," she said, "about Elena's assignment to Third Fleet, I presume."

"Why wasn't I given advanced notice?" McCarthy asked. "You have an entire intelligence department monitoring critical timelines and events."

"Elena's assignment was unexpected. Our last analysis indicated she'd be at Sint-Pieters for at least a year. There was a sudden alteration in her timeline."

"I need guidance," McCarthy said. "Her line is difficult to follow, and I have trouble determining specifics; I see hazy glimpses of her future, which are hard to piece together and easily taken out of context." He paused for a moment. "I need to know if she's dangerous."

"It's difficult to say," Rhea answered, "considering Elena's propensity to drain and without fully understanding what might trigger her to do so. I also have difficulty following her line. One issue to consider is that Elena is a line blocker. Our inability to follow her line may be a deliberate move on her part instead of the mental instability we suspect."

McCarthy considered Rhea's words. Elena was the first Nexus ever to become a line blocker, a talent heretofore considered a Corvad ability only.

"There are many things to consider," Rhea added. "First and foremost, I think we should consider Elena's recovery incomplete, regardless of the asinine physicians at Sint-Pieters who authorized her release, as well as Regent Alperi, who decided to assign her to Third Fleet. In that regard, you should consider this mission part of Elena's therapy. I have no doubt that she is haunted by the assistance she provided to the Korilians, and perhaps this is an opportunity for her to make amends. Let her help in whatever way she can."

"Let her help?" Lara shouted.

McCarthy held up his hand, requesting Lara's silence, then responded to The One's comment. "I must admit that her condition improved significantly between my two visits, but I still have concerns."

"Sometimes we see demons where there are none," Rhea replied. "My recommendation is—treat Elena as a friend and ally until she proves otherwise."

"I understand," McCarthy said, then Rhea's image faded from his wristlet.

"I don't care what Rhea says," Lara interjected. "Elena is dangerous! There's no telling what's going to set her off or what she'll do when she loses it."

"We have reason to be concerned," McCarthy agreed, "but there are several issues to consider, and Rhea has a point. Elena would probably benefit tremendously from helping us end the Korilian War. Plus, I can't turn my back on her after everything she's been through. She deserves our support until she proves otherwise."

"I don't want Elena on this ship!"

"You're overreacting, Lara."

"Overreacting?" Lara shouted as her face turned red. "I'll show you overreacting!" She grabbed a drink container on the desk and flung it across the room at him.

McCarthy didn't flinch as it sailed over one shoulder and smashed into the bulkhead behind him.

"You *really* need to improve your aim," he said calmly.

Lara clenched both hands into fists as she searched for another object to hurl at him.

"You care more about her than me!" Her temper exploded, and McCarthy ducked just in time as an electronic tablet spun across the room, narrowly missing his head before shattering against the bulkhead. "First you name your shuttle after your precious *Elena*! And now you're more concerned about her feelings than mine!"

"That's enough!" McCarthy shouted.

Lara felt his anger surge across the room. During the entire time she'd known him, he had lost control of his emotions only once before—three years ago aboard the Fleet hospital ship *Mercy*, when she had pushed him too far. She paused for a moment, collecting her thoughts.

McCarthy's anger subsided, and he approached her, then took her in his arms.

"You have nothing to worry about. How many times do I have to tell you? You don't have to worry about us, or about Elena. I'll talk to her. See how she's doing and what she's thinking. If I have any doubt about our safety or her impact on the mission, I'll have Admiral Goergen remove her from *Surveillant* and sequestered until we return to Earth." Lara looked up at him as he asked, "Will that do?"

She nodded. "It'll do...for now."

26

Standing at the door to Elena's quarters, McCarthy pressed the talk icon on the adjacent panel. The door opened before he had a chance to speak, followed by Elena's voice emanating from the speaker.

"Of course, you can come in."

McCarthy entered what had been the executive officer's stateroom until earlier this evening, vacated upon Elena's assignment to *Surveillant*. She was sitting on the edge of the bed, and it appeared she was preparing to go to sleep, although she had stripped the blanket from the bed, scrunching it into a corner of the stateroom. Her eyes followed McCarthy as he approached and sat beside her.

"I see you've been released from Sint-Pieters. A complete recovery, then?"

Elena shook her head. "I wouldn't say that. Apparently, the psychiatric definition of *sufficiently recovered* has wide latitude."

"Still working through some issues?"

"That's an understatement." Elena forced a smile, then added, "But participating in this mission should be helpful."

She took his hand in hers. "Just being here, with you..." Her voice trailed off.

After a while, she asked, "Do you remember what you told me after my Test?"

McCarthy recalled Elena's *carcerem cellula*, a final exam a Nexus must pass before being certified as a Ten. It was a frightening ordeal, since failure resulted in one's mind being trapped in an alternate reality, permanently insane.

During her Test, Elena had followed the prime timeline farther than she had been allowed before and had seen the future, one in which humanity was exterminated.

"*We have to do something*," Elena had said. "*We have to guide the Prime into the right line. Please tell me we can do that. Tell me we'll be able to change the future.*"

McCarthy had replied, "*We'll try, Elena. We'll try together.*"

His thoughts returned to the present. "I remember," he said.

Somehow, they had succeeded, at least temporarily. They had turned back the Korilians at the Final Stand.

"It hasn't turned out like I imagined," Elena said, "but here we are, working together again. *It* being here doesn't help, though."

McCarthy had been searching for a segue to discuss the two items on his agenda tonight, and Elena had provided an opportunity to address the first.

"Can you do me a favor and stop calling Lara *it*?"

"Sure. Would you prefer I call it Lara?"

"If it's not too much of an effort."

"It's quite an effort. But for you, Jon—anything."

There was silence for a moment before Elena spoke again. "Speaking of —Lara—have you told her your secret?" Then she offered a mischievous smile. "If you don't, maybe I will."

"I don't see the humor in the situation."

"I find it quite entertaining. I just want to be there when you tell her."

"That's not going to happen."

Elena squeezed his hand. "Don't spoil all the fun."

"I'm concerned, Elena. Concerned that you would enjoy the pain endured by another. This isn't like you."

Elena pulled back, her face crestfallen at his rebuke.

The End of Time

Her features suddenly hardened. "This isn't like me? You have no idea what I'm like now. I'm not the sixteen-year-old girl who left Domus Praesidium. Do you know what three years of daily combat does to someone? What eighteen years imprisoned on Hellios did to me?"

She leaned toward McCarthy. "You're right, Jon. You *should* be concerned."

McCarthy was keenly aware that Elena still held his hand, that she could drain his life force if desired. He would have to act quickly if he felt the sensation.

However, it wasn't his safety he was worried about. It was Lara's. That Elena considered Lara a competitor was obvious. What wasn't clear was what Elena was willing to do about it.

Lara was a delicate issue between them, one that needed to be carefully managed. He had a plan, but didn't know if it would work.

"The first time I visited you in Sint-Pieters, you said you loved me."

"Of course," Elena said. "We're meant to be together."

"Then there's something you need to know."

She took his hand in both of hers. "What is it?"

"You need to understand how hurt I'd be if anything happened to Lara. And that I could never forgive whoever harmed her."

Elena's body stiffened, and McCarthy noticed uncertainty and concern in her expression as she processed his words. He had painted her into a corner. Eliminating Lara was the only way Elena could have the type of relationship with him that she desired, but if she harmed Lara, he'd never forgive her, destroying that possibility. McCarthy had trapped Elena inside a classic catch-22 paradox.

She pulled her hands from McCarthy's as the emotions faded from her face. Then she slowly nodded before dropping her eyes to the floor.

"I understand."

Elena looked away, and McCarthy sensed emotion building inside her again. He reached up and gently turned her face toward him, her eyes locking onto his. "I want you to know how much you mean to me. I *do* love you, and will do almost anything for you. I want us to be as close as we were at the Praesidium."

"Like brother and sister?" Elena asked, disappointment evident in her tone.

Before McCarthy could respond, she turned her head away again. Her complexion turned flush, and he sensed rage building inside her. He moved directly in front of her, his face only a foot away.

"I've seen what you've been contemplating, glimpses of what you might do. You *must* maintain control. I need to be able to trust you."

His words failed to have effect. The reddish hue of her skin kept deepening, and her breathing turned rapid and shallow.

McCarthy cupped her face in his hands. "Breathe deeply," he said. "In and out. Remember what they taught us in Domus Praesidium. How to manage our emotions. Let them flow through you and around you, like a wave breaking upon the shore, fading as it flows past until there is nothing left except the calm, receding water."

She took a deep breath and let it out, then placed her hands atop his shoulders and closed her eyes. After a few more deep breaths, the color began to fade from her face and her breathing slowed. Then she pulled him toward her.

McCarthy let her hug him. She buried her face in his neck, like she had after her Test. Tears began to flow, soaking into his uniform as she trembled. He held her close until the tremors ceased.

Elena pulled back, wiping the tears away.

"Thank you," she said. Then she stared into the distance for a while before speaking again.

"I will do as you've asked."

27

Lara and McCarthy entered the officers' wardroom for dinner, joining eleven others awaiting their arrival. Admiral Goergen stood at one end of the table, with five vice admirals lining one side: Goergen's deputy fleet commander and her four battle group commanders.

As Goergen made the introductions, Lara realized that 3rd Fleet's battle groups were named after mythical weapons: King Arthur's *Excalibur*, Thor's hammer *Mjölnir*, Shiva's trident *Trishula*, and the legendary Japanese blade *Kusanagi*.

Goergen finished with, "I believe you're already familiar with Vice Admiral Nesrine Rajhi, in command of the Excalibur battle group."

Upon spotting Vice Admiral Rajhi, Lara's mood soured. Three years ago during the Final Stand, Lara's relationship with Rajhi had gotten off to a rocky start after Rajhi disobeyed a direct order from McCarthy, and Lara held a pulse-pistol to her head, forcing her to comply. During the retreat from Hellios a few months ago, Rajhi made it clear that she wasn't the forgiving type, directing Lara to not speak to her again unless she had something important to say.

Rajhi was difficult to deal with, but Lara had to admit the woman was fearless. She had volunteered to lead the suicidal cruiser mission at Hellios, during which over half of her task force was destroyed.

Lara smiled and greeted Rajhi, but the vice admiral offered no response as she stared at Lara with dark eyes.

On the other side of the table stood four Marines whom Lara hadn't seen since the assault on Hellios: Major Drew Harkins, head of the handpicked platoon that had accompanied McCarthy and Lara into the Korilian facility, the two squad leaders—Sergeant Majors Narra Geisinger and Ed Jankowski—plus Sergeant Liza Kalinin, a six-foot-tall Russian redhead who had been Lara's bodyguard. Despite everything they had gone through on Hellios, Lara brightened upon seeing the four Marines.

The Hellios mission was supposed to have been a quick in-and-out insertion taking less than a day, its goal to access a Korilian intelligence center and download its artificial intelligence algorithms. However, unbeknownst to the assault participants, Elena had survived Darian 3 and had been coerced into aiding the Korilians. With Elena's help, the Korilians had set a trap for 2nd Fleet in orbit and the almost one million ground troops assigned to the assault.

The 3rd Marine Expeditionary Force, holding the perimeter around the Korilian facility, had lost four hundred thousand troops during the onslaught, and of the ten thousand Marines that entered the Korilian complex, only four survived—the Marines at the table. During the escape from the facility, Liza had almost killed Elena for what she had done, stopped only by McCarthy's intervention.

Lara and McCarthy took places at the table beside the Marines, opposite the vice admirals and a civilian whom Goergen hadn't yet introduced.

"Devin Anjul," Admiral Goergen announced, "from Special Intelligence Division."

Anjul greeted the two senior admirals. "Admiral Goergen, Admiral McCarthy, it's a pleasure to join you this evening." Addressing McCarthy, he added, "I'll accompany the ground forces into the Korilian facility and assist in downloading whatever databases we find."

Goergen and the others took their seats at the table, which was covered by a white tablecloth and place settings of fine china, silver cutlery, and crystal glasses. They were served by two attendants dressed in spotless white uniforms, each with a napkin draped over one forearm, who filled

The End of Time   135

their glasses with water and wine, delivered baskets of warm dinner rolls, then served the dinner's first course.

As soup was being served, the wardroom door whisked open, and they were joined by another guest. Elena stopped behind the chair at the end of the table, across from Goergen.

"Request to join the mess."

Goergen nodded. "Please do."

Liza's eyes locked onto Elena, then the Marine stood, throwing her napkin on the table.

"I've lost my appetite."

"Sit down, Sergeant," Harkins commanded. "If you're going to eat in the officers' mess, you need to act like one."

Liza instead turned to Admiral Goergen. "By your leave, ma'am," she said, requesting permission to leave the table.

"No," Goergen said sternly. "Take your seat, Marine."

Liza's eyes shifted between Harkins, Elena, and Goergen, then she settled into her seat, her eyes boring into Elena.

Meanwhile, Elena ignored the Marine, staring at Lara instead. The tension in the air was palpable, with Lara noting that it followed a bizarre pattern: Liza and Elena; Elena and Lara; Lara and Rajhi.

The attendants continued serving, and despite the obvious tension, or perhaps because of it, the conversation stayed light and enjoyable. Lara enjoyed the stories told by Goergen and her admirals, and she found herself laughing on several occasions. After the dessert dishes were cleared, Goergen gestured to the lead culinary specialist.

"The Penfolds," she said.

The man returned with a large liquor bottle inside a wood case with a glass face. Goergen slid the glass up and retrieved the bottle, turning the label for others to see.

"A rare bottle of Great-Great-Grandfather's tawny port. Bottled from port aged in casks for over a century. I've been looking for an occasion to share this bottle, and considering the length of our journey, far from reinforcements should we become outmatched, it seems like an appropriate time. I would hate for it to go to waste."

After drinks were poured, Lara and the others took a sip of the potent liquor, and it wasn't long before McCarthy and Goergen began ruminating about their early years in the Colonial Navy. Lara's attention was particularly captured by a story McCarthy was telling.

"...on the planet Gideon for R and R between battles." He turned to Lara, explaining the term R and R. "Rest and Recuperation, although the crews tend to interpret R and R as Refreshments and Recreation." Addressing the rest of the table again, he continued, "On Gideon, like many planets, there was a forbidden zone for sailors and officers on liberty—typically an area of ill-repute—which of course meant it was the first place we went. I was a wet-behind-the-ears ensign back then, trying to catch up with my running mate," he pointed to Goergen, "who was the chief engineer on the battleship *Tulaga* with me. Fleet Admiral Fitzgerald—Captain Fitzgerald at the time—had assigned me to a senior running mate to provide more mature guidance and keep me out of trouble while on liberty.

"Natalia had gotten a head start that night, and I tracked her to a bar with a sordid reputation." He looked around. "Before I continue, does everyone know what a deplin is?"

There were several headshakes, so McCarthy explained. "A deplin is an animal native to the planet Canopus, a Fringe World that's a few centuries behind most others in development. Needless to say, their entertainment options are less sophisticated than the norm, with one of them being the timed riding of wild deplins, with the winner being whoever stays on the longest.

"So, I walk into this hole-in-the-wall bar, and what do I see?" He paused for effect. "Natalia Goergen on the back of another officer on his hands and knees, her legs scissored around his waist, pulling his head back with a fistful of hair while she's leaning back and whipping his ass like a wild deplin with her other hand. The man was none too pleased, and it didn't help that he turned out to be our fleet commander's aide."

There was laughter around the table. "Are you making this up?" Lara asked.

"I'm afraid not," Goergen replied. "That one cost me a month in hack. It's amazing I got promoted to captain."

"I'm amazed she got promoted to admiral," McCarthy added. "A little too much fun for her own good on occasion."

The End of Time 137

"There's no such thing as too much fun," Goergen replied.

"What about Stennis 4?"

Goergen stared at him with a blank expression. "I don't know what you're talking about."

She maintained a straight face for a few seconds, then burst out laughing.

McCarthy grinned from ear to ear. "I have to admit. As Natalia's running mate, I learned a lot about what to do—and what not to do. I wonder if that was Fitzgerald's plan all along."

"Unfortunately," Goergen said, her voice taking on a serious tone, "there'll be no R and R during this mission. Fifty jumps round trip, and that's if we head directly back to Earth after reaching Vormak. If we find a lead and continue on, we could be in for a much longer journey."

"Too bad the Prometheus Project failed," Anjul said. "We could've made the entire journey to Vormak in an instant if the portals had worked. Folding time and space in larger intervals is a significant challenge, but we'll eventually figure it out. In the meantime, we'll have to find a way to pass the time while we lurch toward our destination." His eyes went to the empty bottle of tawny port.

Dinner finally ended, and the Marines requested permission to depart, followed by the vice admirals, then Anjul and Elena, leaving McCarthy and Lara at the table with Goergen.

McCarthy turned to Lara. "I have a few things to discuss with Natalia. If you want to return to our quarters, I'll join you soon."

Lara decided to leave, taking the opportunity to track down Liza and the other three Marines. They had saved her life on Hellios, and she had never thanked them, going separate ways after rejoining 2nd Fleet. She brought up a diagram of *Surveillant* on her wristlet, identifying the quarters assigned to the Marine detachment. After working her way through the starship, she arrived at a nearby recreation room. She stopped at the doorway and peered inside, hoping to spot Liza and the two sergeant majors, or perhaps Major Harkins.

There were three dozen enlisted Marines inside, playing hologames projected from their wristlets or just drinking and talking. A Marine near the door spotted Lara spying on them.

"Can I help you?" he asked.

Lara stepped inside. "I'm looking for Sergeant Kalinin. Do you know where she is?"

The Marine turned toward the back. "Hey, Liza," he called out, "there's a Nexus Eight here to see you."

Liza rose from a table near the back and approached Lara. When she stopped before her, Lara was flooded with emotion: the difficult journey into the depths of the Korilian facility, fighting their way past a double-shielded slayer that decimated their platoon, plus the harrowing escape as they were pursued by combat Korilians.

Lara hugged the six-foot Russian, holding her close for a moment.

Liza seemed surprised by the affection, unsure of how to react.

"Hey, ladies," the Marine said, "can you take it outside? We have children in here."

Lara released Liza and stepped back, laughing at the Marine's comment. Technically, he was correct. By the look of things, not one of the three dozen Marines had reached the age of twenty, with some as young as sixteen. Even Liza, who had more Korilian kills than any Marine or soldier thus far in the war, was only nineteen. Major Harkins had explained why during their transit to Hellios.

For five years before the Final Stand, in an attempt to slow the Korilian advance toward Earth while the Colonial Defense Force built up the Fleet, they had saturated their remaining colonized planets with ground troops. By the time the Korilians reached Earth, the Army and Marine Corps ranks were depleted aside from a handful of veterans and millions of teenagers fresh out of boot camp. But the last three years had been different. With the Korilian armada retreating and Fleet warships in orbit providing fire support, they had consistently defeated the Korilian ground troops, gaining valuable experience.

Lara and Liza stepped into the corridor where it was quieter. They talked for a few minutes, Lara catching up on what Liza, Geisinger, Jankowski, and Harkins had been up to since Hellios, learning that there had been no combat. They had been busy rebuilding the 3rd Marine Expeditionary Force. Marine Corps Command had decided to keep the 3rd MEF as its premier assault corps, pulling in the most experienced and capable Marines from other units. Liza's ten-thousand-strong brigade, which had been wiped out on Hellios, had already been rebuilt.

21st Division, 1st Brigade wasn't yet combat-ready, as they still had to learn how to operate as a unit, transformed from a group of experienced strangers into a cohesive entity. 21st Division's 2nd Brigade had been assigned to the mission to Vormak instead.

Like during the assault on Hellios, Major Harkins would lead a hand-picked platoon guarding McCarthy and Lara if they descended to the planet's surface. As before, Liza would be Lara's bodyguard. When the topic of Elena came up, Liza was understandably upset.

"I don't understand why she's here. After what she did, she should be in prison."

Lara found herself unexpectedly coming to Elena's defense. "You don't know the whole story. Everything she's been through."

"I know enough," Liza said, "to not trust her."

"Well, there's that," Lara agreed. "But Elena deserves a chance to make amends for what she's done."

"There are some things that cannot be atoned for."

"Just give her a chance," Lara implored, noting the irony of her words. "Elena needs to help; it's part of her therapy. At least that's what Admiral McCarthy believes, and I trust his insight. I presume you do as well?"

Liza slowly nodded.

After their conversation ended, Lara hugged Liza goodbye, then checked her wristlet for directions to officer berthing. She followed the directional dot and arrow guiding her through *Surveillant*'s passageways. When she finally reached senior officer berthing, she turned the final corner, surprised to find Elena standing in the way.

Elena grabbed her by the neck and slammed her against the corridor bulkhead, pinning her against the wall. Lara tried to wrest Elena's hand away, but her strength quickly faded; she felt Elena's cold grip draining the life force from her body. When she no longer had the strength to resist, her hands falling lifelessly to her sides, Elena stopped draining.

"Precious Lara," Elena said with a snarl. "There's nothing more annoying than a woman who doesn't deserve a good man's affection."

Lara replied, "There's nothing more annoying than a jealous woman who can't let go."

Elena moved closer to Lara, her face only inches away. "You'll *never* be a Ten and will *never* be worthy of him. *I* am his true love, and *nothing* can change that. You're just a temporary distraction, a shiny new object with no line to follow. Just a pretty girl he'll eventually become tired of. And I'll be there when he tosses you aside."

Elena added, "Until then, enjoy your time together."

Warmth flowed from Elena's hand back into Lara's body, and her strength returned. Elena released her grip and stepped back as Lara rubbed her neck, searching for a response. Then she cleared her throat and stepped toward the Nexus Ten.

"I *will* enjoy my time with Jon. And know this. If anything happens to me and you end up together, the woman he'll be thinking of as he takes you in his arms will always be *me*."

"Well then," Elena replied, then smiled. "At least your conviction is firm, however deranged it may be."

"Deranged!" Lara repeated. "Have you looked in the mirror lately?"

Elena's smile faded, her voice taking on an ominous tone. "You *really* should be more careful. It's unwise to call a crazy person deranged."

Lara was temporarily at a loss for words. Elena had a point.

McCarthy turned the corner at the end of the corridor, concern appearing on his face after spotting them separated by only a few inches.

"Hi, Jon," Elena said as she smiled and took a step back. "Lara and I were having an interesting conversation about the future. She has a fascinating perspective—it's got me thinking."

"About what?" McCarthy asked.

"Nothing important. Just girl talk. I'll see you in the morning." She turned and headed down the passageway.

When she disappeared into her stateroom, Lara vented her frustration. "That bitch!"

28

In the Korilian command center, Pracep Mrayev rested on all six limbs as he studied the sensor data, evaluating the human assault at Antares and subsequent operations. The human strategy had become clear: establish secure jump corridors to resupply their ground forces stranded on the ten frontline planets. They would be successful to a large degree. It took time for Mrayev's forces to react once the human fleet committed to a particular assault. However, the humans were being forced to disengage earlier each time as the potential attack points dwindled. When there was only one planet left to resupply, the next human assault would be easy to predict and Mrayev's battle groups would be ready.

But what then? Mrayev was receiving replacement starships at a faster rate than the human fleet, plus his ships were inflicting greater casualties. It wouldn't be long before the humans would no longer be able to establish a secure jump corridor in any of the ten systems, regardless of the surprise factor. They would soon have one hundred million troops—or what was left of them—stranded without resupply, which made no sense. What was the human long-term plan?

A two-foot-tall hologram appeared above Mrayev's display. *Pracep Mrayev*, the supervisor began. *We successfully placed a reconnaissance probe in*

Earth's solar system long enough for a complete planetary revolution. There is only one human fleet in Earth's orbit.

Mrayev contemplated the unexpected news. For the first time since the war began, the humans had reduced Earth's defense from two fleets to one. His first thought went to the dilemma he had just been evaluating—what was the human long-term plan? It seemed they had finally committed a fifth fleet to their assaults. That would give the humans a temporary advantage. But even more important, an opportunity for Mrayev.

He conveyed a thought to his control console, and another hologram appeared above it, this one of Krajik, his executive assistant.

After explaining his plan, he thought to Krajik, *I will request an audience with the Rhysh. Your presence will be instrumental.*

I understand, Pracep. During our meeting, I will influence the members as best possible.

Both holograms disappeared, and Mrayev's thoughts focused on the unknown location of the missing human fleet. The humans were masters at deception, and there was no guarantee the fleet was on its way to the front line. What else might the humans be contemplating?

Mrayev conveyed a thought to his sensor supervisor.

Find the missing human fleet.

29

The Korilian transport descended from orbit, piercing the nitrogen-rich clouds in the darkness. Angling west, the shuttle halted its descent just above the cities and industrial facilities that formed a complete skin over the planet's surface. Inside the transport, Pracep Mrayev, commanding all fleet and ground forces allocated to the war against the humans, sat beside his executive assistant, Krajik, as they prepared to brief the Rhysh, the ruling body representing the twenty-one original Korilian planets that had formed the Empire eons ago.

After the transport settled onto the landing pad, Mrayev and Krajik lumbered into the ancient Leruk, built untold millennia ago. When they reached the Rhysh, passing through the chamber opening, Mrayev felt fortunate that his aide was Krajik, a rare royalty-combat crossbreed. The Rhysh had grown impatient with the duration of the human war, and Mrayev needed to propose a plan to annihilate the humans quickly. With Krajik at his side, the Rhysh would be more lenient regarding his failures and more receptive to his proposal.

The two Korilians entered a dimly lit chamber, illuminated by twenty-one globes hovering above and evenly spaced behind a curved, semicircular table behind which the twenty-one members of the Rhysh sat. Within the globes, each representing one of the original Korilian inner worlds, burned a replica of the planet's sun, each slightly different in color than the others. A twenty-first globe, larger than the rest and residing in the center of the other twenty, was dark, its sun extinguished. In the center of the curved table, in front of the darkened globe, sat Khvik, the oldest member of the Rhysh and the only Korilian still alive from the Time of Freezing.

Mrayev and Krajik stepped onto a stone dais, their figures illuminated by a dim blue light from above, and faced the ruling body of the Korilian Empire.

Members of the Rhysh, I humbly stand before you, at your service.

Khvik wasted no time, administering the expected admonishment.

It has been thirty-three years, Khvik reminded Mrayev, *and we have not yet defeated the humans. Even more concerning is that three years ago we were on the brink of victory, but they annihilated your armada instead. Since then, they have steadily pushed forward, reclaiming their lost planets.*

Mrayev replied, *The temporary advantage the humans gained after our defeat in Earth's solar system has been nullified. The human advance has been halted, and we are on the verge of recommencing our assault on the human colonies and eventually Earth itself.*

The humans have regained much of the territory lost during the war, Khvik said. *We cannot wait another thirty years to conclude this campaign. Over the last three years, we doubled your replacement warships to more quickly stabilize your situation, at significant impact to Pracep Meorbi's campaign. You must bring a quick conclusion to the human war.*

Korem, second in seniority on the Rhysh, spoke. *It was foolish to start a war against the humans while the primary war remained undecided.*

Khvik slammed a claw on the table, his razor-sharp talons gouging the stone surface. *Our honor demanded it!* His response was infused with centuries-old rage.

I do not question the action, Korem replied, *only the timing. We should have concluded one war before beginning another.*

Were we supposed to do nothing, ignoring the human transgression while letting them expand into our territory?

Action was warranted, Korem agreed. *But outright war should have been delayed.*

Kovar, representing the inner world closest to Meorbi's campaign,

The End of Time

spoke next. *Debating the decisions of the past gains nothing. We must address the situation today. Pracep Mrayev has requested an audience to present a proposal.*

Conceding that Kovar was correct, Khvik directed Mrayev to begin. Mrayev provided the necessary background information before revealing his plan.

At the beginning of the war, we did not know where the human home planet was, so we worked our way inward, annihilating the humans as we advanced. We now know where their home planet is and, more important, that the human industrial complex is centralized on Earth, as opposed to distributed like ours—all of their starship construction facilities are in Earth's orbit. If we destroy their construction yards, the human colonies and Earth will fall quickly.

Unfortunately, Earth is heavily defended, with the humans maintaining two fleets in orbit, augmented by formidable defense stations that project a protective energy shield around the entire planet and its orbiting construction yards. However, reconnaissance probes have detected a critical change in the human war strategy. One of the two fleets normally held in Earth's orbit has departed, undoubtedly to join the four fleets at the front line.

With sufficient forces, I can overwhelm the remaining human fleet and defense stations and destroy the human starship construction facilities before the other five fleets arrive to assist. We will bring a swift end to the war against the humans.

Khvik asked, *What of the two humans who can foresee the future? How will you catch the humans by surprise?*

Mrayev turned to Krajik, who explained. *We learned much from the human named Elena. The prescient humans are not omniscient. They perceive the future only in narrow timelines they evaluate. If we keep them focused on events of our choosing, we can catch them by surprise. For example, prior to our attack on the human lunar base, we had repelled the human planetary assaults, stranding ten armies on the abandoned planets. Their thoughts were focused on analyzing this predicament, and they failed to detect our surprise attack.*

Mrayev added, *If the humans discover our plan, I will cancel the assault.*

Khvik then pointed out the critical flaw in Mrayev's plan. *A successful attack on Earth will require additional forces. Where do you plan to obtain these warships?*

From Meorbi's campaign.

Mrayev was bombarded by a cacophony of thoughts from the Rhysh members, with the predominate emotions being surprise and concern.

After the thoughts ebbed, Khvik spoke. *We should not make this decision without consulting both praceps. The benefit of Mrayev's proposal is clear, but the risk is not. We must fully understand this risk before approving or disapproving Mrayev's request.*

The Rhysh members conferred, agreeing to summon Pracep Meorbi for consultation. A moment later, his hologram appeared on the stone dais beside Mrayev.

Members of the Rhysh, Meorbi said, *I humbly stand before you, at your service.*

After Khvik explained Mrayev's plan, Meorbi asked the critical question —How many warships did Mrayev require?

It will take sixteen battle groups to overwhelm a human fleet and penetrate the planet's orbiting defense stations. I can pull four battle groups from the front line without creating suspicion, which means I need twelve more battle groups.

Twelve hundred warships!

Only for the time it takes to make the journey to Earth, defeat the human fleet and orbiting defense stations, and destroy the starship construction yards.

That is not an easy task, Meorbi replied. *Earth's defenses are formidable. Even if you succeed, the casualties will be heavy. Many of my warships will not survive the assault.*

This is true, Mrayev replied. *But without replacement warships, the humans will be quickly defeated, and I will be able to transfer your surviving warships, plus my entire armada, to you. Additionally, instead of replacement warships being split between our campaigns, you will receive them all. You will soon have the assets required for victory.*

Meorbi considered Mrayev's proposal, then addressed the Rhysh. *For the last three years, half of my replacement warships have been redirected to Mrayev's campaign, leaving my forces stretched thin. I cannot hold the line after losing an additional twelve battle groups.*

Khvik asked, *If Mrayev is successful and ends the war against the humans quickly, what will be the impact to your campaign in the meantime?*

I cannot predict with certainty without knowing how long before Mrayev's

The End of Time 147

battle groups will be transferred to my campaign. With your permission, I will confer with Pracep Mrayev.

After Khvik conveyed his approval, Meorbi and Mrayev shared their thoughts, analyzing the time required to vanquish the human fleet if it received no replacement warships.

When the two praceps finished their analysis, Meorbi addressed the Rhysh. *I cannot guarantee the safety of all inner worlds with so many battle groups withdrawn for the assault on Earth. However, there is much territory to be lost before the inner worlds are threatened, and it is likely that I can delay the advance long enough for Mrayev's battle groups to arrive. I will then have sufficient forces to halt the advance and shift to offensive operations.*

After surveying the other Rhysh members, Khvik determined they were ready to vote. One by one, each conveyed its decision.

Khvik addressed the two praceps. *Mrayev's request is approved. Twelve battle groups will be transferred to the human campaign for a direct assault on Earth.*

30

"Man Battle Stations."

As the shipwide announcement echoed on *Surveillant*'s command bridge, Lara sat tensely beside Admiral Goergen while McCarthy and Elena stood nearby. After the computerized announcement faded from the starship's speakers, the general alarm followed: a deep tone that repeated every second.

3rd Fleet had just completed a twelve-hour hold in the Seobin star system and was preparing for the double jump to Vormak. They were now deep in Korilian territory and over two weeks away from the nearest reinforcements—the four fleets engaged in the Liberation Campaign. Fortunately, it looked like the Liberation Campaign assaults had kept the Korilians' attention focused on the front line; no Korilian reconnaissance probes had been encountered thus far. Or perhaps it had just been McCarthy's skill, ensuring 3rd Fleet avoided detection as they approached Vormak.

Upon reaching Seobin, Goergen had ordered a final survey of the target planetary system, sending reconnaissance probes to the far sides of Vormak 4's moons to conceal their jump waves, then maneuvering the probes for a clear look at the planet's surface and any starship activity.

There were no starships in orbit or elsewhere in the star system, nor did

The End of Time 149

the probes detect the departure or arrival of any communication pods. Apparently, whatever the Korilians were doing on Vormak 4 didn't require frequent transmissions. It appeared that the conclusion from their original reconnaissance was correct; the Korilians were simply terraforming the planet, which took decades or maybe even centuries.

Lara focused on the operations officer's display as he reported Battle Stations were manned throughout the fleet, then announced that all 3rd Fleet starships and the Marine troop transport were ready for the double jump to Vormak.

Goergen surveyed the command bridge displays, then gave the order.

"All ships, jump at the mark."

The operations officer entered the command into his console, and five deep tones resounded throughout the ship, followed by the computer's voice over speakers.

"One minute to the jump."

When the countdown reached zero, Lara's vision went black as she tumbled into a spiraling hole.

Her vision cleared a few seconds later as *Surveillant* materialized in the Lysinto star system, where the starships waited the two minutes it took to recharge their jump drives, before simultaneously making the second jump. When 3rd Fleet arrived in the Vormak system, Lara fought through the turbulent, swirling sensation from the double jump, listening to the urgent reports from *Surveillant's* crew.

"Shields are up!"

Lara felt a tingle as the starship's shields formed. A glance at the nearest control console showed the command ship in the center of a sphere of twelve battleships, their shields melded together to form a protective outer bubble, augmenting the command ship's own shields.

"No Korilian warships in this system!"

As the bridge's spinning slowed, Lara studied the sensor displays. Everything was as expected. There were no Korilian warships or communication pods to worry about.

Goergen waited while her warships scanned the planet's surface, searching for Korilian ground troops or air-assault artillery batteries. No defensive facilities or troop barracks were noted, nor any threats to the surface assault vehicles that would transport the Marines to the planet's surface.

Thus far, things could not have gone more smoothly.

Admiral Goergen turned to Lara. "Any sign of trouble?"

Lara tried to summon a vision, but none came; only a growing sense of inadequacy—and jealousy. She was the 3rd Fleet guide but had offered no useful guidance during their journey, with Goergen relying on McCarthy's and Elena's guidance instead. Lara's hands had clenched into fists on more than one occasion as McCarthy conferred with Elena before recommending the next jump point. With two Nexus Tens aboard, Lara was a useless third wheel.

After attempting to invoke a premonition and failing, she informed Admiral Goergen, "I have no guidance to offer."

Goergen turned to McCarthy and Elena, who confirmed what seemed apparent. Although the views of both Nexus Tens dissolved a few hours into the future, there were no immediate threats.

Admiral Goergen pressed one of the controls on her chair, and a holographic image of a Marine Corps officer appeared.

"Colonel Quinto. Commence the ground assault."

31

Time passed slowly as Lara monitored the ground assault on *Surveillant*'s displays, even though it wasn't much of an assault. 3rd Fleet's reconnaissance had been thorough and correct; there were no Korilian ground troops nearby or any defense artillery batteries. The one hundred surface assault vehicles had landed without incident, depositing 2nd Brigade's ten thousand Marines onto the planet's surface. Even upon blowing ten entrances into the exterior wall of the facility, there had been no detectable Korilian response.

After the Marines entered the facility, there had been sporadic encounters with Korilians, but no organized resistance or combat troops—just the domestic variant. Even so, the standard Korilian was quite deadly. During their journey through the facility on Hellios, Lara had watched civilian-equivalent Korilians slay several of the handpicked and fully armored Marines assigned to accompany Lara and McCarthy into the complex.

Casualties on Vormak were few thus far, but the progress was slow. Although the complex was one-tenth the size of the one on Hellios, it went down at least ten levels—over ten square miles in area—and not even the first level had been fully explored. Additionally, the closed portals at corridor and shaft intersections failed to respond to the codes that had opened portals at other Korilian facilities, forcing the Marines to blast their way through with explosives, which on several occasions damaged equipment in adjacent chambers. The last thing they wanted was to destroy the unencrypted database they had been sent to obtain.

The slow progress was disconcerting because both McCarthy's and Elena's views dissolved at the same point in time, which was rapidly approaching. Contrary to McCarthy's expectation as the assault progressed, the window into the future wasn't advancing.

3rd Fleet and its Marine detachment were safe for now, but soon, neither Nexus Ten would be able to provide prescient guidance. Speed was also critical in case Korilian Fleet command had somehow been informed of 3rd Fleet's arrival in the Vormak system and there were warships nearby. With Colonial reinforcements two weeks away, 3rd Fleet couldn't risk getting bogged down in a battle against a superior force.

McCarthy turned to Admiral Goergen. "We need to search the facility faster. I recommend you send me into the complex. I can determine the database location and identify the most expeditious route, as well as open the corridor and shaft portals without explosives."

After considering the proposal, Goergen agreed.

"I'd like to take Lara with me," McCarthy added. "My view on Hellios was impaired, and Lara's visions were helpful. She might be able to assist again."

Goergen tapped her display, and a hologram of Major Harkins appeared. "Your platoon will accompany Admiral McCarthy and Lara into the complex. How long until you are ready?"

"We're ready now. If you send Admiral McCarthy and Miss Anderson to the armory, I'll get them suited up."

After Harkins's hologram disappeared, Elena spoke. "I'll accompany Admiral McCarthy as well."

When Goergen, McCarthy, and Lara turned to Elena, she explained. "Have you forgotten my defensive talent regarding the Korilians? McCarthy is the Fleet's most valuable asset, and it'd be wise to protect him as best possible."

Lara recalled what Elena had done on Hellios. During their escape from the underground facility, they had been trapped in a corridor by a dozen combat Korilians on both sides, with only four of the twenty-five

The End of Time 153

Marines in their platoon still alive. Elena had somehow tapped into the Korilian telepathic abilities, and the Korilians had dropped to the floor, writhing in pain until they ceased moving. It had been a draining effort, Elena had explained, something she could do only once every few hours, but it had saved their lives.

Lara felt the chill from McCarthy's view, then he spoke to Goergen. "Elena would be a welcome addition."

Goergen agreed, and the trio headed to the armory, which was stocked to outfit the company of one hundred Marines assigned to defend *Surveillant*. Like all fleet warships, *Surveillant* carried a detachment of Marines to repel boarders, should the Korilians attempt to board a disabled ship during battle and harvest its weapon and shield technology.

At the armory, two Marines awaited them. Both were wearing body armor, holding a helmet under one arm. One Marine was a man whom Lara hadn't met before—Sergeant Troy Dansing, based on his name tag—who accompanied McCarthy into an outfitting room. The other Marine was Liza.

Lara's instinct immediately registered danger. Having Liza assist Lara made sense—she would be her bodyguard again—but Harkins hadn't known that Elena was accompanying them. Putting Liza in direct contact with Elena was a recipe for disaster.

Once inside the fitting room, Liza announced that she would help the two Nexi select and don their armor.

Offering a look of disdain, Elena replied, "I don't need assistance. I've probably worn body armor more times than you have."

Liza muttered, "You probably don't know your right boot from your left."

Elena's head snapped toward the Marine. "You have something to say to me?"

"Armor has advanced quite a bit in the last two decades," Liza answered. "Of course, you wouldn't know that. You were too busy helping the Korilians, cozy as a bug in that hole we should have left you in."

Elena swiveled toward Liza, her face turning red as her eyes blazed with anger. She grabbed Liza by the neck, as she had done with Lara in the corridor outside their stateroom, and the Marine's face began to pale.

Liza tried to wrest Elena's hand from her neck. When she failed, she used her body armor's strength augmentation to crush Elena's hand. Elena cried out in pain as shards of bone jutted through her flesh and blood flowed down her arm, but she simply switched hands as the first one healed. As on Hellios, Lara watched in amazement as Elena's bones rejoined and flesh grew over them.

After failing to pull Elena's hands from her neck, Liza punched her instead, her armored fist slicing into Elena's face, down to the bone. The blow didn't faze Elena, and her wound quickly healed, so Liza grabbed Elena's face with an armored hand. Her fingers wrapped around both cheeks, sinking into Elena's flesh as she attempted to crush the Nexus Ten's skull.

"Stop it!" Lara screamed.

She tried to pry the two women apart as Elena's cheekbones and jaw collapsed under the pressure of Liza's grip.

"Sergeant Kalinin, release Elena at once! That is an order!"

Lara wasn't in Liza's chain of command or even in the military, but it was worth a shot.

As directed, Liza released Elena.

Turning to the Nexus Ten, Lara spoke in a stern tone, focusing on Elena's eyes instead of the bloody pulp of flesh and bones beneath them. "Let Liza go. You've made your point."

Elena released Liza and stepped back, then dropped to a kneeling position. Gurgling sounds of pain escaped her mangled mouth as her face reformed. Although Elena could heal herself, she wasn't immune to the pain.

As Liza stood above Elena, she said, "Attacking someone wearing armor was a pretty stupid move."

After her face finished healing, Elena stood, her eyes still filled with anger. "Just keep your thoughts about me to yourself. Are we clear on that?"

"Whatever," Liza replied.

The two women locked eyes for a moment, then Liza turned to Lara. "Let's get you armored up."

Liza checked the display built into the left forearm of her suit and pulled up the desired information, then announced, "Request suit for Lara Anderson, serial number 150158."

The End of Time

The fitting room walls were lined from floor to ceiling with equipment bins, which repositioned upon Liza's request, offering the sizes per Lara's laser-fitting on *Artemis V*, the troop transport they had ridden to Hellios. The bins along a single row lit up in a soft blue glow.

Lara stripped down to her panties and retrieved her equipment, then donned her undergarments: a micromesh full-body exposure suit, socks, and thin gloves. As before, Liza assisted with attaching the armor components, beginning with the heavy boots, working her way up, each segment automatically attaching to the adjacent ones when placed in proximity.

After Lara retrieved her equipment, Elena called out, "Major Elena Kapadia, serial number 214344."

The bins repositioned, and Elena retrieved her gear, tossing it into a pile on the deck.

When Elena requested her suit, Liza cocked her head, scrutinizing Elena more closely. She watched Elena deftly don her suit, finishing before Lara even had her leg armor on.

"Corps or Army?" Liza asked, referring to Elena's announcement that she was a major.

"Army."

"Which unit?"

Lara suddenly realized that no one had explained Elena's background to Liza. Like McCarthy, Elena's psychic talents had been kept secret while assisting on Darian 3, lest the Korilians learn of her ability from captured soldiers or other intelligence and target her during battle. Only a select few had known of Elena's abilities.

On Hellios, they had stumbled across Elena by accident, and the only thing obvious to Liza was that Elena was a Nexus who had been captured by the Korilians.

"Third Army Group," Elena answered.

"Where did you serve?"

"Darian 3. My first cozy little hellhole."

Liza's eyes narrowed. "Third Army group was annihilated on Darian 3."

"Everyone but me."

Liza fell silent for a moment, digesting what she had learned as she fastened additional armor components around Lara.

"I've heard stories about Darian," Liza said. "Was it as bad as they say?"

"Worse."

Elena provided the basics—what most people knew—explaining that Darian 3 was supposed to have been humankind's Stalingrad, a reference to Russia's heroic battle against the German 6th Army on the bank of the Volga River during World War II. After ten years of steady retreat from the advancing Korilians, ceding planet after planet, Darian 3 would be the war's turning point. The Colonial Defense Force had assigned an entire army group: ten armies, each with ten million troops. But the one hundred million soldiers had just been the starter kit.

"We were ordered to hold the planet at all costs, and I have to admit we were given the support we needed until the supply corridor collapsed. But I don't think anyone outside the highest levels of the Colonial Defense Force knew the true toll. The Korilians went all in as well, and the combat was brutal. To keep Third Army replenished, we received four million replacements a week for five years."

"You lost four million a *week*? You would have chewed through an entire Marine Expeditionary Force in less than two days."

"Until the reinforcements stopped arriving, we battled the Korilians on all five continents, and the casualties were horrific. The average life span of a combat infantryman after landing on Darian 3 was twenty-five days."

Lara had heard some of the details from McCarthy. Assignment to Darian 3 was considered a death sentence; now she knew why.

"I was sent to Darian 3 to defeat the Korilians. I would help win the campaign, regardless of the odds."

Even through Elena's suit speaker, Lara detected the bitterness in her voice.

"But all I did was keep the meat-grinder running. Sending two hundred million soldiers to Darian 3 each year was a strain on our manpower, consuming almost every Army recruit. But the Korilian reinforcements seemed endless. We held solid defensive positions and inflicted four times as many casualties as we received, but they just kept coming."

Lara reflected on Elena's words. They knew very little about the Korilian Empire, had no idea how many worlds it encompassed or how

The End of Time

populous it was. On Darian 3, the Korilians had lost almost a billion troops a year and hadn't flinched.

Liza finished assembling Lara's armor—aside from donning the helmet—and although the suit was made of a composite material, tougher and lighter than metal, it was still heavy and the joints stiff. Lara could barely move across the floor.

"Your left forearm," Liza reminded her.

Lara recalled Liza's previous instructions and tapped two indentations on her armored wrist, activating her suit. She felt the armored segments adjust slightly, and when she moved her arm, little effort was needed, as if she were wearing nothing at all.

"Keep your suit on neutral," Liza said. "That will allow you to move as if you were wearing normal clothes. Although a suit can augment your strength and speed, it takes a bit of training to learn how to handle it."

Lara retrieved her helmet, which was split open along a seam that ran from the temple down to the neck on both sides, slid it onto her head, then tapped the helmet by her left ear twice. The helmet slowly closed, then sealed itself to the armored neck seam. The helmet facepiece lit up with a display of armored suit settings and life-support information on one side and data scrolling down the other.

Liza explained the life-support indications again: air quality, hours of oxygen remaining, heart and breathing rates, blood pressure, and suit temperature, then refreshed Lara on settings that could be changed by talking to the suit, such as strength, reflex, and speed; low light, infrared, and magnified vision; and augmented hearing. A refresher on communication channels followed, plus an explanation of the information available: a map that displayed the location of all Marines in their unit, and numerous other data feeds Lara could tap into.

The three women emerged from the fitting room to find McCarthy waiting with the first Marine, plus Devin Anjul from Special Intelligence Division. Anjul had a backpack strapped to his armored suit, which Lara presumed carried the computer he needed to download the data from the Korilian database.

They were about to move on when McCarthy noticed the fresh blood on Liza's armored glove. Lara felt a chill from his view, then he stepped close to Elena. He spoke to her at low volume through his helmet speaker, but Lara was able to overhear the conversation.

"Do I have to view *every* minute of your life to ensure you don't get into trouble?"

"You can do whatever you want," Elena replied. "I didn't ask for your help, nor do I want it. I can take care of myself. I did for eighteen years, or have you forgotten?"

Not having a comeback to Elena's dig, McCarthy simply said, "Just do me a favor and control yourself on Vormak 4."

. "For you, Jon, anything," Elena replied, although Lara wasn't sure whether she was being facetious or sincere.

McCarthy turned to Liza. "We're ready for the next stop."

As Liza led them toward the weapon stowage racks, McCarthy tapped Lara on her helmet, then showed her his wrist display, set to communication channel twelve. Lara selected the channel, which McCarthy had set to secure person-to-person communication between them.

"I'm sorry about what happened in there," McCarthy said. "I should have viewed the moment I saw Liza."

"It's not your fault. Both Elena and Liza share the blame. Hopefully, they got it out of their system."

"Perhaps it was for the best," McCarthy said, "considering how Elena fared against Liza. There are a lot of things Elena needs to work through, starting with learning to control herself."

"Why don't we ship her back to Earth until she does?"

"Two reasons," McCarthy replied. "The first is that we can't override the Council's decision—they've assigned Elena to this mission. The second reason is that despite Elena's shortcomings, I still believe she's an asset."

They stopped beside a weapon rack where each Marine selected a pulse-pistol and carbine. Similar to their preparation for the assault on Hellios, neither Lara nor McCarthy were provided with weapons.

Elena, however, selected a pulse-pistol and examined its controls, then placed it into its holster. Neither Liza nor Dansing objected.

Still communicating with McCarthy via the private channel, Lara said, "You can't be serious, letting Elena arm herself."

"It's not my call. From a Nexus House perspective, both Elena and I are

The End of Time 159

Tens, and I have no governance over her. Only Major Harkins can make that decision, and technically, Elena outranks him. They're both majors, but Elena is far senior, promoted to major decades before Harkins. However, I suspect Elena is pretty handy with a pulse-pistol."

"*However*," Lara repeated sarcastically, "I suspect Elena is pretty *dangerous* with a pulse-pistol."

"She can't hurt you with a single shot while you're wearing armor. Only a point-blank shot directly into a seam can penetrate your suit."

Elena flashed a hand signal, and the two Marines turned toward McCarthy and Lara.

"The gig's up," McCarthy said. "Elena knows we're on a private communication channel. Shift to channel one."

After shifting channels, Elena's voice emanated from her helmet speaker. "If you two lovebirds could refrain from planning your next date until we return from Vormak, that would be appreciated."

"We already have our next date planned," McCarthy replied. "We were discussing the wisdom of letting you arm yourself."

Lara was shocked at McCarthy's admission, but Elena gave no hint of her feelings on the matter. She simply replied, "*You* don't need to worry."

However, "*you*" was a bit vague. Did she mean McCarthy and Lara, or just McCarthy?

Liza led the way to *Surveillant's* spaceport, where their surface assault vehicle awaited, its rear ramp lowered to the deck. The rest of the platoon was already inside, with most of the one hundred seats vacant. The inside of the SAV was otherwise bare, aside from a weapon stowage rack beside each seat for the assault carbines and a bank of green lights at the rear of the vehicle above the ramp opening.

Shortly after they took their seats at the back of Jankowski's and Geisinger's squads, a low rumble emanated from the back of the SAV as the ramp rose. Light inside the vehicle faded until the ramp closed with a heavy clank, enveloping the platoon in darkness. Thin strips of blue light flicked on above each seat and on the deck, then lights at the rear of the SAV turned from green to yellow.

Liza touched a control button on Lara's armrest. Curved flaps in her seat rotated inward and clamped themselves around Lara's waist and head, holding her firmly in place. Liza then tapped the controls on the left forearm of Lara's suit, shifting life support to the suit's internal resources. Dansing did the same for McCarthy and Anjul.

The lights above the ramp turned solid red, and a few seconds later, the SAV's engines ignited. The vehicle rose slowly from the deck, then Lara felt a tingle as they traveled through the spaceport life-support shield and descended toward Vormak 4.

32

The first part of the transit aboard the SAV was smooth, with no indication the assault vehicle was moving. Lara felt light, as if she were floating in her seat, then remembered the SAV didn't have the gravity generators she took for granted on the Fleet warships and troop transports. The smooth transit was short-lived, however, as she felt tremors in the SAV's deck. Then the vehicle began pitching and bucking as it plummeted through the planet's atmosphere.

The volatile descent subsided, and the red lights above the ramp began blinking yellow. Liza pressed a control on Lara's armrest, and the restraints around her head and waist retracted. Dansing did the same for McCarthy and Anjul, and the Marines retrieved their carbines from their stows. Lara felt a sudden thud, then the SAV was still. The lights at the rear of the vehicle turned green, and the ramp lowered quickly onto the planet's surface.

Major Harkins was the first down the ramp, followed by Jankowski and Geisinger, who led the two squads from the SAV. Unlike the cold and stark landscape on Hellios, a misty environment filled with purple-green plants greeted them. They had landed in a small clearing beside several other SAVs, with the Korilian facility rising in the distance above the vegetation.

Lara checked the data on the left side of her helmet display, reporting the environmental conditions. The temperature was just over a hundred degrees and the air unbreathable long-term. Although no harmful bacteria or viruses were detected, the oxygen concentration was too low and carbon dioxide too high, although it would suffice for a few minutes in an emergency.

Harkins led the platoon, with the two squads walking in parallel columns along a path cut through the plants by previous Marines. The vegetation was neither bushes nor trees—mostly pulpy branches that splayed outward from their trunks—but some of the varieties rose a hundred feet toward the reddish-purple sky.

They emerged from the vegetation into an open expanse containing the Korilian facility. Perforating the complex's exterior every few hundred feet were large black holes where the 2nd Brigade's ten battalions of Marines had blasted their way in.

As they approached the nearest opening, Elena's voice came across Lara's helmet speaker. "I'll view from here on."

Elena's announcement took Lara by surprise. Two Nexus Nines or Tens couldn't view in proximity to each other or their views would intermingle and dissolve, but Lara had expected McCarthy to view. Lara began to object, but Elena cut her off.

"One ground battle on Hellios and you two think you're experts," she said with disdain. "I fought for three years on Darian 3. I'm viewing—end of discussion."

Lara turned to McCarthy, walking beside her, hoping he'd intervene, but he replied, "Agreed."

Elena turned to Lara. "If you'd like to help with your visions, why don't you be a good bird dog and point the way?"

As Lara considered possible retorts, Elena added, "Better yet, just stay out of the way."

Elena moved to the front of the platoon, taking station beside Major Harkins, while McCarthy and Lara remained at the back with Sergeant Dansing and Liza behind them. The two columns of Marines traveled into the nearest ragged opening, swallowed by the darkness. As they entered the Korilian facility, Lara's suit automatically shifted to low-light vision, and the rest of the platoon reappeared.

The End of Time

They were in a twenty-foot-wide corridor with the walls, ceiling, and floor constructed of black fibers woven tightly together. There weren't any distinct joints where the walls met the floor or ceiling—the fibers simply curved up from the floor to create the walls and then inward at the top to form the ceiling. A faint blue light leaked through the wall fibers, and a magenta illumination pulsed through the ceiling—four flashes followed by a few seconds of darkness. A low throbbing sound accompanied each magenta pulse as the sequence of light and sound repeated continuously. Lara recalled from her journey through the complex on Hellios that the lights and sound were an alarm system.

At the front of the platoon, Harkins issued an order, and two Marines launched tiny reconnaissance probes from their utility belts. The drones flew down the corridor, and two small video screens appeared on the right side of Lara's visor, relaying the probe images.

The platoon began moving again, with both columns walking on separate sides of the passageway, passing through portals that had been blown open with explosives. At some of the intersections, they traveled past several dead Korilians plus injured Marines being tended to by medics. Most of the Marines were missing arms or legs, their detached limbs lying nearby or already strapped to the Marines' body armor. After three decades of battling Korilians, reattaching limbs had become a common procedure.

Harkins led them deeper into the facility, through several more blasted-open portals, until Elena intervened at one intersection, directing the platoon down a specific corridor. After a long trek, they arrived at a closed portal, the wall fibers meeting in the center. Elena stopped beside a set of colored symbols embedded in the wall and touched them in a specific sequence. The wall fibers wriggled as if they were alive, moving like the tentacles of a hidden organism, pulling back to create an opening.

The platoon stepped into a large four-corridor intersection with the other three portals closed, plus an additional closed portal in the center of the floor.

"Down to the seventh level," Elena announced.

Four Marines stepped forward and took up firing positions in a circle, pointing their carbines at the floor where the fibers converged. Elena pressed several colored symbols on the wall, and the fibers wriggled back, creating a dark opening. Harkins activated his helmet spotlight, illuminating the shaft as Elena pressed two more colored symbols. Five more portals opened, providing passage to the seventh level.

A display appeared on the side of Lara's visor, showing the progress made on the seventh level underground. The Marine brigade had a foothold on the first ten levels, assigning one battalion to explore each. However, the battalion on the seventh level had descended via another shaft halfway across the complex, leaving much unexplored territory between them.

The two drones, which had been hovering in the intersection above the Marines, dove down the shaft, and Lara watched the videos as the reconnaissance probes made the journey. The corridor portals at each level were closed, and the probes waited on the seventh level.

"All clear," Harkins reported.

The four Marines standing beside the shaft shouldered their carbines, then retrieved a rappel-pistol from their utility belts. A spike protruded from the muzzle of each device, which the Marines pointed at the ceiling. The spikes shot from the pistols, embedding themselves in the fibers. Attached to each spike was a thin strand leading back to the pistol.

"Saddle up," Harkins ordered.

The Marines assembled into four lines, then the first Marine in each line, holding the rappel-pistol, jumped through the opening and disappeared into the darkness. The remaining Marines, in sets of four, attached themselves to the thin line with two hooks from their utility belts, wrapping the lines around their waists, then followed the first set. Soon only three Marines remained—Harkins, Liza, and Dansing—along with Lara, McCarthy, Elena, and Anjul. The three Marines likewise attached themselves to the thin strands, as did Elena.

"Put your arms around my neck," Liza said to Lara, "and hold tight."

Lara wrapped her arms around the Marine as McCarthy paired up with Dansing and Harkins took Anjul. The three pairs, plus Elena, leaned back over the opening and pushed off from the edge, descending through the Korilian complex.

They rappelled to the seventh level, landing in another large intersection with five closed portals: four corridors, plus the floor. The Marines had formed a circle facing outward with their carbines in case any of the portals opened suddenly, revealing Korilians waiting to attack. The first four Marines pressed a button on each rappel-pistol, retracting the spike edges, and each rappel line snaked back into its pistol until the spike re-mated with the barrel.

Harkins turned to Elena, but she just stood there. As they waited for direction, Lara felt the chill from her view, even through her body armor.

"Bad news," Elena said. "My view dissolves in less than two minutes." She turned to McCarthy, and Lara felt Elena's view cease and McCarthy's begin.

After a short while, he reported the same. "One minute into the future is all I've got."

"That's a bad sign," Elena announced as she turned to Harkins. "Recommend double line formation."

Harkins gave the order, and the Marines organized into two circles, the first row kneeling and the second one standing, both facing outward, with Anjul and the three Nexi in the middle, along with Harkins, Liza, and Dansing.

"Stay away from the center," Elena ordered. "The Korilians can open any portal, including the one in the floor."

Elena resumed viewing, then announced, "Fifteen seconds to view dissolution."

As the seconds counted down, fog began seeping through the fibers of one of the corridor portals. Lara realized she was having a vision, but as she attempted to decipher whether the fog was showing her the way, as it had on Hellios, or warning her to stay away from that corridor, the passageway portals opened.

All four corridors were filled with Korilians—the smaller eight-foot-tall, four-hundred-pound domestic version, but deadly nonetheless—standing three abreast in each passageway, who surged toward the Marine formation.

Harkins issued a command, and his platoon opened fire on the advancing Korilians. Lara listened to a continuous stream of orders and reports as the Marines coordinated their fire. The lead Korilians advanced to within a few feet of the formation, but the platoon never wavered. Each corridor stacked up with dead Korilians, one row high, then two rows high, with additional Korilians clambering over the pile toward them.

The floor portal in the center of the intersection suddenly opened, revealing the level below filled with more Korilians, with four of them already climbing to the seventh level. When the Korilians had surged toward the Marine formation from all four corridors, Lara must have taken an unconscious step backward. When the floor portal opened, she lost her balance, falling backward into the shaft. The nearest of the four climbing Korilians swung at her as she fell, connecting solidly with two of its razor-sharp limbs.

Fortunately, neither blow hit one of the body armor seams. She remained in one piece, but took a fierce blow in the chest that slammed her against the wall on the eighth level, and a second blow that cracked her helmet visor. Dazed, she slumped to the floor as four Korilians on the eighth level turned toward her.

Through spidery cracks in her helmet visor, she spotted Elena land in the center of the intersection. The four Korilians suddenly fell to the ground, writhing in pain, their limbs flailing about. A few seconds later, they lay still.

Elena must have done what she did on Hellios 4, somehow incapacitating them. But she could do this only once every few hours, and more Korilians were streaming toward them from two of the passageways.

Liza and Dansing dropped through the opening above, joining Lara and Elena in the eighth-floor intersection, blasting the approaching Korilians while Elena rushed toward Lara.

Elena grabbed Lara's hand and dragged her toward the nearest vacant corridor while Liza and Dansing formed up behind them. Despite taking out two approaching Korilians, the Marines were soon faced with four more, and neither Marine was able to avoid eight swinging limbs.

Dansing was hit at the waist, directly in the hip seam, and Lara watched in horror as the Marine was sliced in half. Liza took two blows, one to her chest and another to her shoulder. She was knocked sideways, rolling head over heels, but steadied up into a kneeling position where she took out the two nearest Korilians with expertly placed head shots.

Unfortunately, Liza was cut off from Lara and Elena by two more Korilians, with a third surging toward Elena and Lara, swinging toward Lara's outstretched arm as Elena dragged her from the intersection. Elena fired her pulse-pistol, dropping the Korilian to the floor. After dragging Lara into the corridor, Elena moved back toward the intersection to assist Liza.

With two more Korilians converging on Liza and two more speeding toward Lara and Elena, Lara heard Liza's voice over her helmet communication system.

"Leave me!"

Elena didn't hesitate, pressing the multicolored symbols. The portal fibers quickly grew toward the center, sealing the two Nexi in the otherwise vacant corridor. Then she fired a pulse at the portal controls, fusing the multicolored symbols together.

As Lara lay on the corridor floor, slowly coming to her senses, she smelled an odd odor and had trouble breathing; she wasn't getting enough oxygen. Red alarms flashed along one side of her helmet visor. Her suit oxygen level was dropping and carbon dioxide rising. Then she noticed that in addition to the spidery cracks, a gouge had penetrated her visor. Vormak 4's atmosphere, which could sustain human life for only a few minutes, was seeping into her suit.

Elena pulled Lara into a sitting position with her back against the wall, then to Lara's surprise, pressed the control on the side of Lara's helmet. It split open, and Elena removed it.

Lara's body armor life-support shield automatically energized, forming a barrier between the suit and Vormak 4's atmosphere. The air quality improved, and Lara was soon breathing normally, although she felt a tinge of nausea. Then she remembered Liza explaining why humans couldn't wear full-body defense shields. The shield intensity required to stop a pulse wreaked havoc on human physiology. Anyone wearing a full-body defense shield would be on their hands and knees within seconds, puking. The environmental shield was much weaker, but Lara still felt its effect.

She tried to stand but was still too dazed due to the dual Korilian blows, combined with breathing Vormak 4's toxic air for a while. There was a scrambling sound down the corridor, and Lara spotted another Korilian charging down the passageway toward them. Elena raised her pistol toward the Korilian, but instead of firing, backed away toward the closed portal.

As the Korilian sped toward them, Lara turned back toward Elena to ask what she was waiting for, then noticed the pulse-pistol was aimed at her. There was a wicked smile on Elena's face as the Korilian approached.

Lara pushed herself to her feet, frantically assessing her options, selecting the only one that came to mind. When the Korilian reached her, she would dive out of the way, hoping the Korilian focused instead on the human with the weapon. The Korilian seemed to have other plans, its eyes aimed toward her instead, apparently noticing that Lara was missing her helmet.

An easy kill.

There was no way to avoid four swinging limbs, each with a razor-sharp edge that would slice through her neck with ease. She'd have to make the best of it, curling into a ball. But even with forearms protecting her neck, one direct hit would slice through everything.

Just before the Korilian reached Lara, Elena adjusted her aim and fired, hitting the Korilian between the eyes, dropping it to the floor, where it lay motionless.

"You're welcome," Elena said.

Lara debated whether she should thank Elena or scream at her, then opted for neither. Elena was toying with her, and she wasn't going to let the demented bitch get to her.

Elena approached Lara, then asked a question. "Didn't it concern you that McCarthy's view dissolved partway into our journey through this facility?"

"It did," Lara conceded, "but we had to work through the same issue on Hellios."

"Do you recall what the issue was?" Elena asked. "Why McCarthy's view dissolved?"

Lara searched her memory, recalling Elena's explanation after they found her on Hellios. She'd been working with the Korilians, helping them set a trap for 2nd Fleet and the 3rd MEF. Elena had explained one of the talents she had developed—she was a line blocker.

As Lara wondered why Elena had brought up the subject, it dawned on her. McCarthy's and Elena's views on Vormak 4 hadn't dissolved due to

The End of Time 169

volatility. Elena had blocked McCarthy's view again and lied about her own being blocked.

But why?

As she considered the answer to that question, Elena raised her pulse-pistol, aiming it at Lara's head. Lara took a step back, hitting the corridor wall. A caldron of heat ignited inside her, like it had on Darian 3. The heat spread quickly throughout her body, radiating out toward her hands.

Elena pushed her pulse-pistol through Lara's life-support shield, pressing the muzzle against Lara's forehead. "I can sense what you're doing," Elena said, "and I recommend you stop. I can squeeze the trigger in a split second."

McCarthy and Ronan had felt Lara's power on Darian 3, and Elena must have felt it now as well.

The heat inside Lara stopped building but remained intense. Her skin felt so hot that she was convinced she could burn anything she touched. However, aside from her helmet, she still wore body armor, including gloves. She had no idea about what she was capable of or whether it would work through the armor.

"What do you want?" Lara asked.

Elena didn't answer. As she stood there, Lara noticed indecision in the Nexus Ten's eyes.

When Elena spoke again, the tone and cadence of her voice was different, as if someone else was speaking. *"What are you waiting for?"*

Lara didn't understand her question. She was about to ask Elena to explain when she spoke again.

"Go away," Elena said, her voice returning to normal.

Lara was confused, trying to make sense of Elena's statements. Elena continued, the tone of her voice alternating back and forth as she seemingly spoke to herself. Lara suddenly realized that Elena had a split personality. The second personality, the one Lara hadn't yet met, spoke next.

"Lara is the only thing standing between us and Jon. Kill her!"

"No!" Elena replied. "Jon will never forgive me."

"We have his line blocked. He won't be able to see what happened."

"She'll have a pulse blast through her head."

"You can say you accidentally shot her."

"That's too obvious. You're reaching."

"*You put on a good show back in the intersection, saving Lara's life. They will not suspect you.*"

"Jon may find out. I can't keep my line blocked forever, and if he follows it into my past, he'll discover what I've done."

"*You had the perfect opportunity a minute ago. You should have let the Korilian kill her. But I'm not surprised you couldn't follow through with our plan. You've never had the guts to do what it took.*"

"I tried to kill myself on Hellios—chewed the flesh from both wrists."

"*That was cowardly, not courageous. Thankfully, I discovered the ability to heal ourselves or we'd be dead. You owe your life to me.*"

"You owe your life to me! Without me, you would not exist."

"*Fine! The score is even. Now back to Lara. Kill her!*"

"I can't."

"*I should have known you wouldn't follow through on our plan. Let me do it. Give me control.*"

"No! I promised Jon. Plus, the Codex guidance on the One with no line is unclear. Lara might be critical to the House's survival."

"*McCarthy and the House. That's all you care about.*"

"It's all I have!"

"*What have they done for you, except ship you off to Darian and almost certain death, then let you rot for two decades on Hellios while the Korilians tortured you until you were too insane to resist?*"

"I am not insane!"

Elena's body began trembling, her eyes flitting about until they focused on Lara.

"*What's your opinion, Lara? Are we insane, or not?*"

The answer was clear in Lara's mind, but she hesitated, stalling while she chose her words carefully. "I was a counselor, not a psychiatrist."

"*Would you care to render a guess?*"

"I would not."

Elena stared at Lara for a few seconds, then spoke. "*Okay, Elena. Do whatever you want. But don't come crying to me when Jon takes Lara into his arms every night.*"

Elena stood rigidly for a moment, then lowered her pistol. She placed it

The End of Time 171

into its holster, then smashed an armored fist against the corridor wall, narrowly missing Lara's head.

"I can't kill you," Elena said, "but let me explain a few things. I don't like you—whatever you are—and I'll take every opportunity to make your existence as miserable as possible. Are we clear on that?"

"Like crystal."

The heat inside Lara extinguished as two drones flew down the passageway toward them, followed shortly by McCarthy on the run, leading the rest of the platoon.

When he reached her, he said, "I couldn't get the corridor portal open, so I found an alternate route." His eyes went to the dead Korilian, then to Lara's damaged chest armor and shattered helmet nearby.

"Are you okay?"

Elena replied instead. "I checked her out. She's fine."

McCarthy looked to Lara for confirmation, and she nodded, although McCarthy gave her an odd look. He must have realized something happened between her and Elena. Lara would fill him in later. Then her thoughts turned to Liza, and a lump formed in her throat.

"Sergeant Kalinin," she said. "We left her in the intersection."

A Marine at the back of the platoon stepped out, wearing scarred body armor splattered with blue Korilian blood.

"Major Harkins was kind enough to send a few Marines down after me," Liza announced.

Relief washed over Lara.

"Check her suit out," Harkins ordered.

Liza moved toward Lara, passing Elena.

Elena nodded her head slightly. "Sergeant," she said, which seemed to be a compliment, thanking Liza for her effort in the intersection.

"Major," Liza replied, her voice flat, which Lara figured could mean any number of things.

Liza examined Lara's suit controls on her forearm. "Her environmentals are good," she announced.

"Let's get going," Elena said. "Back to the seventh level. We're almost there."

33

The platoon retraced its path back to the intersection Lara had fallen into, then climbed back to the seventh level and over a pile of dead Korilians partially blocking one of the corridor openings. Elena returned to the front of the formation beside Harkins while Lara and McCarthy took their usual positions at the back of each squad, near Anjul. The man from the Special Intelligence Division hadn't said a word since entering the facility, although Lara noticed his eyes were wide with fright.

After traveling down the corridor, they reached another closed portal.

"This is it," Elena announced.

Two Marines took station on either side of the portal, then Elena pressed the colored controls.

The fibers wriggled back, revealing a large chamber. The two squads of Marines surged in, spreading out around its circumference. Upon entering the chamber, Lara's eyes went to the single object in the room: a six-foot-diameter multicolored pulsating blob floating in the air, the colors slowly swirling in random directions. Attached to the sphere and radiating out toward the chamber walls, floor, and ceiling were dozens of one-inch-thick strands of gray fibers.

"The central computer core," Anjul announced.

The End of Time 173

It was a good thing Elena and Anjul knew what they were looking for, because it wasn't what Lara had envisioned.

Anjul removed his backpack and retrieved what looked like a laptop computer, except it didn't open; a small display was built into its top instead. Attached to the side of the computer was an inch-thick strand of gray fibers resembling those that originated from the multicolored sphere. The strand was curled into a coil, but what caught Lara's attention was that the strand seemed alive. It moved on its own as Anjul unfastened the coil, the loose end floating through the air, moving toward the Korilian computer core. Anjul continued feeding the strand until its end embedded itself into the sphere.

Anjul watched various parameters update on the laptop computer's display. Five minutes later, he announced the data download was complete.

"We have everything."

He pressed one of the controls atop the laptop, and the strand detached from the floating Korilian blob. Anjul coiled it back up and returned the strand and computer to his backpack.

Elena led the platoon from the chamber, where they ran into Marines from 2nd Brigade, who had continued to spread through the seventh level, eliminating any Korilians they encountered.

The platoon's exit from the facility was uneventful, and they were soon back aboard their SAV, lifting off from the planet's surface.

34

After downloading the Korilian database onto Anjul's computer and retrieving all personnel from the planet, 3rd Fleet retreated from the Vormak star system to a nearby asteroid field, its four hundred starships dispersed within the drifting rocks. Inside *Surveillant*'s intelligence center, Devin Anjul worked diligently on the database extracted from the Korilian core, using algorithms to recode the data into a format usable by human computer networks.

With her services as a fleet guide not needed during the jump hold, Lara spent time with McCarthy, with periodic stops by the intelligence center to check on Anjul's progress. It was during one of those visits that Anjul announced the data conversion was complete.

Admiral Goergen and her intelligence officer, along with McCarthy and Elena, joined Anjul and Lara in the intelligence center. Upon Elena's arrival, Lara's thoughts went to their altercation in the Korilian complex, where Elena had almost killed her. After returning to *Surveillant*, Lara had revealed to McCarthy what had occurred, and he finally seemed to take her concerns regarding Elena seriously. Elena's dual personality wasn't something McCarthy was trained to deal with, and they agreed that until further notice, Lara would avoid interactions with Elena and under no circumstance be alone with her.

The End of Time   175

For her part, Elena behaved as if nothing untoward had happened on Vormak 4. Lara wondered if she even remembered the conflict between her two personalities. One consolation from the event was the revelation that Elena had taken to heart her discussion with McCarthy, when he'd made it clear that she could not harm Lara. Elena's other personality, however, appeared unrestrained. As long as Elena's primary personality remained dominant, Lara believed she was safe. But she had no idea if, or when, Elena's other personality could take control.

After Goergen arrived, Anjul explained that the tablet taken into the Korilian facility was essentially a data storage device, which he had then connected to a larger computer he'd brought aboard *Surveillant* for the mission. After receiving permission from Goergen's intelligence officer, he linked *Surveillant*'s central computer to the reformatted Korilian data.

"I've located the information we're interested in," Anjul said as he shifted to one of *Surveillant*'s computer terminals. After a few commands, a hologram appeared above the main data fusion table, filling almost the entire room with a map of a significant portion of the galaxy. After another command, yellow lines appeared, weaving throughout the star systems.

Anjul turned to Elena. "Is this what you saw in your view?"

Elena nodded.

"Fortunately," Anjul said, "I've done what Elena couldn't do. I've compared the Korilian data to our maps of the galaxy, finding an overlapping, identical segment, allowing us to orient the Korilian star systems and navigation routes. As you can see, the Korilian navigation routes go through hundreds of star systems. Whether all of this territory is part of the Korilian Empire or some of it is controlled by other species is unknown. What I can comment on is what the navigation routes say."

He activated a laser pointer on his wristlet, aiming it toward one of the yellow lines.

"The navigation routes go primarily through twenty-one star systems" —Anjul illuminated several stars—"with one system serving as a central hub, which is likely the seat of the Korilian government or their primary industrial center. Our astronomers assigned an alphabet-soup-and-number name to this star system a few hundred years ago, but the Korilian name of the system is *Korilia*. I don't think there's any doubt that this is the home planet of the Korilian Empire. I think the next step is to send a reconnaissance probe to take a look."

Goergen turned to her intelligence officer. "Send a recon probe at once, and inform Fleet Command of what we've learned thus far."

Korilia was another thirty jumps from Vormak, but the reconnaissance probe didn't have to conduct jump holds, waiting only for its jump drive to recharge, which took only a few seconds for an object its size, and the probe soon returned. After redocking with *Surveillant*, its data was fed into the starship's computer, and Anjul pulled up a hologram of the star system.

Five planets appeared, rotating around an orange-reddish star. Anjul zoomed in on each planet, but surprisingly, there was no indication of life or industrial activity on any of them.

"This can't be right," Anjul announced as he integrated the data into the Korilian map, using coordinates from the probe. "According to the navigation routes, this is the correct star system, and you can see that it is undoubtedly the focal point of Korilian transit."

As Lara stared at the holographic map, thin layers of fog began to slide across the floor, inward from the intelligence center's bulkheads. When they met in the center of the room, a column of mist rose toward the map, coagulating into a sphere in the middle of the Korilia star system, between two of the planets orbiting the star.

"It's between the third and fourth planets," Lara announced.

"What is?" Anjul asked.

"I'm having a vision," Lara said. "There's something hidden between those two planets."

The fog dissipated as Anjul zoomed in, but there was nothing there.

Anjul said, "Let's suppose that Lara is correct, and there's a planet we can't see for some reason. It would interact with cosmic radiation, either absorbing the energy or altering its path."

He entered additional commands to the computer, and a red circle appeared between the two planets, offset by thirty degrees counterclockwise and twenty degrees down.

The End of Time 177

"The computer agrees with you," Anjul announced. "Based on the recon data, there should be a planet in this location."

He zoomed in to the area, and this time, Lara noticed a spherical, hazy distortion.

"Bingo," Anjul said. He studied the distortion for a moment, then added, "This is amazing. It looks like the Korilians have the technology to cloak an entire planet, making it invisible." He turned to Admiral Goergen. "There's one way to find out. Send another probe to this location, just inside the distortion sphere."

Goergen agreed, and a reconnaissance probe made the trip, then returned to *Surveillant*.

Anjul accessed the data again, and this time, a mottled black-and-orange-colored planet appeared above the fusion table. But instead of a few minutes of video, only a single picture was recorded. After studying the photograph, Anjul concluded that whatever was cloaking the Korilian planet had likely interfered with the probe's equipment. To be sure it wasn't a probe malfunction, however, Goergen sent another probe, which returned with the same result—only a single photograph. However, they had sent the second probe to the other side of the Korilian planet, so they at least had full reconnaissance.

There were hundreds of starships traveling to and from the planet, plus four starship construction yards in orbit. Additionally, there was a large oval-shaped star base in a wider orbit, which Anjul surmised was the cloaking device. What was unexpected, however, was that there were no Korilian warships in the vicinity. The Korilians, it appeared, were overconfident in their cloaking device.

Upon further examination, however, they spotted a single Korilian cruiser in an even wider orbit, just outside the distortion field, apparently serving as a sentinel, watching over the planet. That raised the question— What nearby forces could the sentinel call upon? Goergen dispatched probes to the twenty other Korilian navigation hubs.

The reconnaissance probes returned, each relaying the same basic data: heavily populated Korilian industrialized planets, none cloaked like Korilia, and each with a single starship construction yard and a squadron of dreadnoughts and cruisers in orbit. The starship construction yard data was stunning. The Korilians had at least twenty-four yards compared to Earth's eight. Intelligence indicated the Korilian starship construction capacity was twice that of the Colonial Navy's, not triple. Perhaps the output of the yards was lower.

As Goergen absorbed the data, Lara sensed the admiral was running through the calculations. At a minimum, the equivalent of two and a half Korilian battle groups could arrive at Korilia within a few hours. But 3rd Fleet had four battle groups and could easily destroy the four starship construction yards before enough Korilian warships arrived to threaten it.

To verify her assessment, Goergen asked McCarthy, "What would be the outcome if Third Fleet attacked Korilia?"

Lara felt the chill from McCarthy's view as he attempted to assess the result.

"I cannot tell," McCarthy replied. "My view terminates once we enter the cloaking distortion field." He turned to Elena, and Lara felt the chill from her view.

"Same here," Elena said.

Goergen's eyes then canvassed her intelligence officer and the three Nexi. "I intend to request permission to destroy the starship construction yards at Korilia. Pending the outcome of that conflict, I plan to destroy as many of the other twenty construction yards as possible while we have sufficient starships to do so. Do you have any objections?"

There were none.

35

In a conference room atop the Council headquarters building, Fleet Admiral Nanci Fitzgerald's hologram flickered as it stood at the open end of a white V-shaped table populated with twelve other holograms in their seats. At the apex of the table sat Council President Portner, flanked by Morel Alperi to his right and Lijuan Xiang to his left, followed by the other nine regents.

"We need to strike now," Fitzgerald reiterated, "while the Korilian home planet is undefended. We don't know if this oversight is a temporary or permanent situation, but we need to take advantage of it, destroying the starship construction yards in orbit. Assuming the attack on Korilia is successful, I intend to target the other twenty construction yards using Third Fleet as a raiding force for as long as it has sufficient resources."

Regent Alperi was the first to respond. "What you're saying, Fleet Admiral, is that you intend to employ Third Fleet until it is reduced to an ineffective fighting force. In other words, until Third Fleet is destroyed."

"Destroyed is too strong a word," Fitzgerald replied, "but your assessment is essentially correct. Third Fleet will remain on the offensive as long as possible, then its remaining starships will retreat toward Colonial territory."

"You realize that both Nexus Tens are aboard the Third Fleet command ship, and your plan places them at significant risk."

Lijuan interjected before Fitzgerald could reply. "I believe Fleet Admiral Fitzgerald is well aware of that fact. But this isn't the first time McCarthy and Elena have been placed at risk. McCarthy led the Fleet in battle during the Final Stand, and the Council sent Elena to Darian 3 and then abandoned her. We could keep them safe in a padded room on Earth, but the more engaged our Nexus Tens are in battle, the greater their impact. Having McCarthy and Elena assist Third Fleet will give it a tremendous advantage. If we destroy enough of the Korilian construction yards, we can bring the Korilian War to a swift end."

"What if there are additional Korilian forces in the region that we haven't identified," Alperi asked, "and Third Fleet is destroyed while attacking Korilia?"

"The risk is worth the potential gain," Lijuan replied.

Council President Portner addressed Fitzgerald. "What is your assessment of success?"

"Regent Alperi's concern is valid," Fitzgerald replied. "There's the potential that there are additional Korilian forces nearby and the attack on Korilia could result in disaster. However, I agree with Regent Xiang. The risk is worth the gain. Additionally, even if the attack on Korilia fails to destroy the construction yards, the surprise assault will force the Korilians to more adequately defend their territory, diverting warships from their Liberation Campaign resistance. Win or lose at Korilia, we benefit."

Portner nodded, then addressed the Council. "Unless there are other questions, I suggest we put Fleet Admiral Fitzgerald's proposal to a vote."

There was a motion to do so, which was seconded, and the twelve-member Council cast their votes. The tally was unanimous.

Portner announced the result. "The Korilians have underestimated our ability to locate their home planet, and we will hopefully make them pay for that error. Fleet Admiral Fitzgerald, you are free to employ Third Fleet in whatever manner you see fit, for as long as desired."

36

Lara's vision cleared as the jump darkness was replaced with *Surveillant's* brightly lit command bridge, and she quickly assessed the sensor data as the expected reports were received.

"Shields are up!"

"No Korilian warships in this sector!"

Looking out the bridge windows, Lara spotted a barren planet framed by an orange star behind it. The starship's crew attended to their duties at their consoles, while Admiral Goergen, seated in her command chair, calmly examined the sensor displays. Admiral McCarthy stood near Goergen with—as usual—Elena beside him.

Whenever they were in the same compartment aboard the starship, whether it be the bridge, combat information center, or wardroom, Elena stood or sat beside McCarthy. He seemed not to notice or care, but Elena's habit grated on Lara, and she searched for a way to convince McCarthy to tell Elena to stay away. Considering his affinity for the unstable Nexus, she hadn't yet devised a persuasive reason.

During 3rd Fleet's transit toward Korilia, McCarthy had selected the planetary systems and asteroid fields to traverse though, ensuring their approach remained undetected. However, his view and Elena's continued to dissolve shortly after they arrived in Korilia's orbit.

They were now two jumps from the Korilian planet, and after another twelve-hour hold, 3rd Fleet would conduct a double jump to commence its assault. Goergen had periodically sent reconnaissance probes to Korilia, and thus far its status hadn't changed: a single Korilian cruiser in orbit, which wouldn't last long following 3rd Fleet's arrival. Whether the cruiser would be destroyed before it reported 3rd Fleet's arrival, or how long before sufficient Korilian forces arrived to force 3rd Fleet to disengage from Korilia were the primary questions at the moment.

The sensor supervisor announced, "No Korilian recon probes in this sector."

Goergen launched three more communication pods, relaying 3rd Fleet's status to Fleet command headquarters on Earth. Altogether, the communication chain extended for over fifty jumps, with three pods assigned to each location.

The reconnaissance supervisor announced, "Communication link with Fleet Command has been established."

Goergen and McCarthy reviewed the data relayed from Fleet command headquarters. To minimize the possibility the Korilians would detect 3rd Fleet's approach to Korilia, Fleet Admiral Fitzgerald had decided to keep the Korilians focused on the Liberation Campaign assaults. Over the last few days, Fitzgerald had kept the Korilians guessing as the Colonial Navy battle groups repositioned. Now that 3rd Fleet was twelve hours from its jump to Korilia, Fitzgerald gave the order: an all-out assault with sixteen battle groups against the Liberation Campaign planets.

Lara watched the displays as the Colonial starships engaged the Korilian armada.

Admiral Goergen rose from her chair. "Get some sleep," she said to Lara. "You're going to need it."

37

Inside the Korilian Fleet command compound on the planet Keorsn, Pracep Mrayev reviewed the latest sensor and reconnaissance probe details as the sixteen-battle-group armada prepared for the final leg of their journey to Earth.

Following the Rhysh's approval, twelve battle groups had been transferred from Pracep Meorbi's campaign as requested. Additionally, Mrayev had added four of his own to the pending assault against Earth, pulling them back from the front line ostensibly for refit and resupply, sending them instead toward Earth. All sixteen battle groups had just begun a jump hold at the planetary system the humans called Proxima, which was a treacherous location due to its fluctuating gravitational fields. Jump drives required moderate gravity vectors to function, but if they were too high, the drives wouldn't work.

Approaching Earth via Proxima could result in his entire armada becoming trapped for an unpredictable period of time, but Mrayev had little choice. The other approach routes to Earth were thoroughly monitored, and although Mrayev's forces had the ability to neutralize human reconnaissance probes, freezing the last image relayed by each probe, there was no guarantee the humans wouldn't be alerted.

Routing his forces via Proxima was dangerous, but it noticeably improved the odds of achieving a surprise attack, which was essential. His sixteen battle groups could defeat Earth's orbiting defense stations and a single fleet, but not five. He needed to keep the four human fleets engaged at the front line.

To minimize the potential their approach would be detected, Mrayev had also ordered a rare quadruple jump to Proxima. Mrayev's crews were still recovering from the physiological effects, but there was little to worry about. Only a single human fleet was within striking distance—the one in Earth's orbit. The sixth human fleet was still unaccounted for, but even if it was nearby and the humans attacked at Proxima with two fleets, Mrayev's armada would outnumber the humans two to one. Even at a reduced combat effectiveness while his crews recovered, they would prevail.

Proxima was another three jumps from Earth, and Mrayev planned to initiate the assault with a triple jump into Earth's orbit, once this jump hold was complete.

Standing beside Mrayev was Krajik, his executive assistant, who was also reviewing the sensor and reconnaissance data. When Krajik completed his assessment, he conveyed a thought to Pracep Mrayev.

There is no indication the humans have detected our approach. Everything is proceeding as planned.

38

In the north wing of Domus Praesidium, Rhea Sidener, the Nexus One, sat at the head of a rectangular conference table, flanked on one side by her eight Nexus primuses—heads of levels two through nine—and on the other side by the heads of the various Nexus departments: Defense, Intelligence, Operations, Engineering Design, Manufacturing, Finance, Human Resources, and Supply. Although each primus oversaw the personnel within their level, the departments were matrix organizations, tapping into the talents of those from various levels. Noah Ronan, seated on Rhea's right, was the only Nexus who was both a primus and department head; in his case—Defense.

Rhea was in the middle of her weekly meeting when her wristlet and that of Shika Parella's, head of the Intelligence department, vibrated, overriding Rhea's *Do Not Disturb* notice she had set for today's review. After reading the message, Rhea's and Shika's eyes met, then Rhea activated the holographic projector mounted in the conference room ceiling. A quarter-sized hologram of Jonuthin Berber, senior supervisor in the intelligence center's afternoon shift, appeared above the table's surface.

"We have a critical naviganti alert," Berber reported, referring to the level-nine Nexi on watch in the intelligence center, who viewed various prime timelines into the future.

"What is the issue?" Rhea asked.

"We've detected a pending Korilian assault."

"What system?"

"Earth."

Rhea pulled back slightly, stunned by the report.

"When and with how many starships?"

"Within the next twelve hours," Berber replied. "Starship quantity is difficult to assess, but it's between one thousand and two thousand."

There were shocked expressions around the table as they digested the information. The Korilians were about to attack Earth with between ten and twenty battle groups. There was only one Colonial fleet in orbit—four battle groups—with the Liberation Campaign's sixteen battle groups several days' transit away.

"Where is the Korilian armada now?"

"Unknown. We detect them after they jump into Earth's solar system."

Rhea's eyes went to Shika. "How is it possible that we are just now learning of this attack?"

"We've been focused on the Liberation Campaign and Third Fleet's transit to Korilia," Shika replied.

Rhea followed relevant timelines into the future to discern the most likely outcome of the Korilian assault. After a short moment, her face paled.

She turned to her operations department head. "Establish a link to Fleet Admiral Fitzgerald at once!"

39

"Order Sixth Fleet and all orbiting defense stations to Defense Alert One."

Fleet Admiral Fitzgerald spoke into her wristlet as she moved briskly through the corridors from her office toward the elevator, descending the one hundred floors to the ground level, plus the half-mile subterranean trip to the Fleet command center. After the elevator halted its descent and the doors opened, she stepped into the Fleet command center, registering the tension immediately; supervisors were hovering over data fusion tables or scrutinizing sensor screens, searching for the Korilian armada.

How many ships, and how far away are they?

The deputy fleet commander, Admiral Liam Carroll, met Fitzgerald as she approached her command console. "Nothing," he said. "All recon probes report negative. The nearest Korilian ships are those engaged in the Liberation Campaign."

Fitzgerald digested the news as she settled into her command console.

Could the Nexus One be wrong?

Although the future discerned by the Nexi was never set in stone, that the Nexus One could be wrong about something of such magnitude was unlikely.

"Run diagnostics on all recon probes," Fitzgerald ordered. "Ensure they're functioning properly."

Carroll relayed the order, and the command center personnel began analyzing their reconnaissance probe network.

A few minutes later, the sensor supervisor's hologram appeared before Fitzgerald. "We've completed diagnostic checks of all recon probes, and there seems to be an anomaly on several. The video and data appear to be looping."

Fitzgerald tapped commands into a semitransparent command panel floating by her right side, and a hologram of all recon probe locations—a partial map of the galaxy out to ten jumps—appeared before her.

"Which probes?" Fitzgerald asked.

The sensor supervisor annotated the probes from his console, changing the color of the affected probes to red. A path appeared from the probe perimeter to Proxima.

"I should have known," Fitzgerald muttered.

The Colonial Fleet avoided transit via Proxima due to its volatile gravity vectors, which could trap starships for an indefinite period of time. Only once in the last thirty years had Colonial warships journeyed via Proxima —a task force led by McCarthy just before the Final Stand. McCarthy had been able to time the passage during a safe period of low gravity oscillations.

It appeared the Korilians had risked trapping their entire armada, or perhaps their jump drives were more robust and could handle the higher gravity.

"Send replacement probes to Proxima and a new set of probes to all other locations within three jumps from Earth."

Fresh probes were launched from the orbiting defense stations, beginning their journeys to their programmed positions. A moment later, the sensor supervisor reported, "New probes have reached Proxima, but they either malfunctioned or were destroyed after completing the jump."

The Korilians are at Proxima.

Of that, Fitzgerald was sure. But she needed to know how many ships were approaching.

"Send replacement probes to Proxima, this time inside the nearby asteroid field, shielding them from destruction. Then maneuver them for a complete recon of the system."

The End of Time 189

Another pair of probes began their journey and successfully completed the trip, then began the round-robin data relay, jumping back and forth between Proxima and Ritalis, where another set of probes continued the data relay to Cygni, then Earth. A few minutes later, the probes at Proxima had gathered the necessary information.

Fitzgerald sat at her command console in stunned silence.

Sixteen hundred warships, in addition to over a thousand engaged by the Liberation Campaign fleets. How was that possible?

Before she had time to analyze the situation further, the sensor supervisor's urgent report focused her attention.

"All Korilian warships are spinning up their jump drives."

The Korilians had realized they had been discovered and were continuing their transit toward Earth. The critical question was whether they would hold one or two jumps from Earth or complete a triple jump, commencing their assault immediately. Fitzgerald had no idea how long the Korilian crews had been recovering at Proxima, but knew they were capable of being combat-ready even after three consecutive jumps.

Fitzgerald ordered all Fleet forces in Earth's solar system to Defense Alert One.

40

"Sixth Fleet and all orbiting defense stations are at Battle Stations."

Fitzgerald acknowledged the command center supervisor's report, followed by the announcement that the Korilian armada had completed its first jump, commencing a hold at Ritalis. They were now two jumps—four minutes—from Earth.

The command center computer completed its calculations, displaying the results on Fitzgerald's console screen. The computer had run a simulation using the worst-case parameters: sixteen Korilian battle groups opposed by only 6th Fleet and the planet's orbiting defense stations. Against sixteen battle groups, 6th Fleet would not last long.

Once 6th Fleet was eliminated, the Korilians would focus on punching a hole through Earth's formidable defense shield. The shield was robust, able to withstand the loss of numerous defense stations, collapsing in a sector only when a station, along with the two rings of bases around it—a ring of six plus the next ring of twelve—were destroyed. Altogether, the Korilians would have to destroy nineteen adjacent defense stations to puncture Earth's defensive shield. Korilian warships would then pour through the gap and begin destroying the construction yards.

If humankind had any hope of defeating the Korilians, they could not let their construction yards be destroyed. The loss of even four of their

The End of Time 191

eight yards would likely be too crippling a blow. Fitzgerald needed rein-forcements. By all measures, however, the Liberation Campaign fleets were too far away to reach Earth in time to assist. Still, she had to try.

She turned to Admiral Carroll. "I intend to order all Liberation Campaign fleets to disengage immediately and return to Earth." That part of her order wasn't unexpected. The next part, however, was. "I intend to give them six hours."

"That's impossible," Carroll replied. "A thirteen-jump trip would normally take six days. With a half hour between jumps, the crews will be incapacitated before they're halfway back."

"We don't have a choice," Fitzgerald said.

Carroll approached Fitzgerald. "We cannot lose those four fleets. If you push them too hard, what's left of the Korilian armada, once they're finished with Sixth Fleet and our construction yards, could destroy them as well. Our fleets could also be pursued by the Korilian battle groups along the Liberation Campaign front, catching our four fleets in a vise. You're setting the table for the complete destruction of the Colonial Navy aside from Third Fleet."

"Unless you have a viable alternative," Fitzgerald replied, "this is the only choice we have."

Carroll stared at Fitzgerald for a moment, then relented, his eyes going to the floor. "There is no alternative."

Fitzgerald turned to the command center supervisor. "Recall all Libera-tion Campaign fleets. Order them to return to Earth using thirty-minute jump holds."

The supervisor reacted with a shocked expression, replaced with concern once he realized Fitzgerald was serious.

The order went out, and shortly thereafter, a hologram of Admiral Kevin Shallcross, in command of 4th Fleet, appeared before Fitzgerald.

"Fleet Admiral Fitzgerald," Shallcross began, "I have received new orders, but there appears to have been an error in transmission. We've been ordered to return to Earth using thirty-minute holds."

"That is not an error, Admiral. The Korilians will commence a sixteen-battle-group assault in a few minutes. We need the Liberation Campaign fleets within six hours if we are to save half of our construction yards."

"I am aware of the situation," Shallcross replied. "You must also be aware that this order isn't executable. We won't make it halfway back. And Fifth Fleet, which isn't used to multiple jumps due to its previous assignment as an Earth defense fleet, won't make it a third of the way."

The gravity of their predicament and lack of solutions momentarily overwhelmed Fitzgerald, and her frustration bled through.

"I didn't ask if the order was executable! You will transit using thirty-minute holds until you either reach Earth or you and your crews are unconscious. Is that understood?"

Shallcross stared back at Fitzgerald, then replied tersely, "Your order is *well* understood." His hologram disappeared.

After Admiral Shallcross's image faded, the video displays mounted across the front of the command center lit up, peppered with over a thousand bright white flashes as the Korilian armada completed its journey to Earth. The sensor displays quickly updated, reporting what they were expecting: sixteen hundred Korilian warships, evenly split between dreadnoughts and cruisers, accompanied by sixty-four carriers that could launch a total of thirty-two thousand marauders. 6th Fleet, with its sixteen carriers, could field only eight thousand vipers in response.

The Korilian armada had completed its jump closest to Construction Yard Seven, and as Fitzgerald expected, moved to engage, the warships' main engines igniting. To counter, Fitzgerald ordered 6th Fleet to reposition to assist the planetary defense stations in that sector.

As the Korilians moved to within weapon range, Fitzgerald searched desperately for a solution. As she focused on the displays and prepared for battle, one thought occurred. It was a long shot that it would make a difference, but at this point, anything was worth a try.

Fitzgerald tapped her console, and an image of the command center supervisor appeared on her display.

"Order Third Fleet to commence its assault on Korilia immediately."

As the order went out, Fitzgerald evaluated its impact. 3rd Fleet was three jumps away, and there would be consequences from a triple jump without recovery holds. But if any fleet could manage, it was 3rd Fleet, with Goergen in command and McCarthy assisting.

There was no telling how the Korilians would react, but hopefully they

The End of Time

would recall the twelve battle groups along the Liberation Campaign front, addressing at least one of Admiral Carroll's concerns—preventing the four Liberation Campaign fleets from being caught between two Korilian armadas. Hopefully, at a minimum, 3rd Fleet's assault would be successful, destroying the four construction yards in Korilia's orbit. The Korilians would still have at least twenty yards, however, while there would likely be nothing left of Earth's yards by the end of the day.

A hush fell on the command center as the Korilian armada and 6th Fleet approached Construction Yard Seven.

41

"Man Battle Stations."

Lara was roused from her slumber by the announcement from the speaker in her stateroom ceiling, followed by the deep tones of the general alarm reverberating throughout the command ship.

She had taken Admiral Goergen's advice, getting as much sleep as possible during the jump hold. However, as she threw on her Nexus jump-suit while McCarthy donned his Fleet uniform, she glanced at the clock, realizing she had been asleep for only two hours.

They emerged from their stateroom into the corridor, hurrying toward *Surveillant*'s command bridge. As Lara wondered why *Surveillant*'s crew was being ordered to Battle Stations earlier than planned, she felt the chill from McCarthy's view.

"What's going on?" she asked.

"We've been ordered to proceed to Korilia immediately."

"Why?"

"The Korilians are assaulting Earth with sixteen battle groups."

"Sixteen hundred warships? How did they get so many?"

"That's a good question, but not one that affects us at the moment."

As they moved swiftly down the corridor, she sensed McCarthy was worried. His views had consistently dissolved after the jump to Korilia, but

The End of Time 195

he hadn't predicted this early order to commence the assault. Elena emerged from her stateroom shortly after they passed by, and she caught up, placing herself on McCarthy's other side.

They soon reached *Surveillant's* command bridge, which was fully manned. Goergen was already seated in her command console, and McCarthy stopped beside her, as did Elena, while Lara settled into her fleet guide chair beside Goergen.

The operations officer turned to Goergen. "All battle groups report ready for the jump."

Goergen ordered, "Jump at the mark."

The operations officer entered the command into his console, and a few seconds later, five deep tones reverberated throughout the command ship, followed by the computer's voice over the ship's intercom.

"One minute to the jump."

As the seconds counted down, a thin layer of fog began sliding across the deck, rising steadily until it filled the entire command bridge. The center of the mist began to spiral, opening a small hole within which appeared an image of *Surveillant*. As Lara wondered what the vision meant, thin tentacles of fog reached out from the sides of the spinning tunnel, wrapping themselves around the starship.

Although Lara didn't understand what the vision meant, she at least knew that tentacles portended danger. She glanced at the clock.

"Thirty seconds to the jump."

"Admiral Goergen, I'm having a vision. *Surveillant* is in danger."

"That's not particularly prescient," Goergen replied in a flat tone. "I think that's obvious. Do you have anything more specific?"

Unfortunately, Goergen was right. During battle, the Korilians typically focused on destroying the fleet command ship. At least her vision addressed one of the unanswered questions—Would the Korilians engage 3rd Fleet at Korilia?

Lara focused on her vision, trying to discern additional details, but the fog dissolved instead.

"Fifteen seconds to the jump."

There wasn't enough time to invoke another vision, if she could even do so.

Ten seconds before the jump, five deep tones reverberated throughout the ship again. When the time reached zero, Lara's vision went black.

"Shields are up!"

Lara was suddenly back on the brightly lit starship bridge again. After the long transit to Vormak and now Korilia, totaling fifty-five jumps, she barely felt the nauseating sensation when the jump wave passed through her.

She felt a tingle as the starship's shields formed, and a glance at the nearest console showed *Surveillant* at the center of a sphere of twelve battleships, their shields melded together to form a protective outer bubble. Additionally, *Surveillant* was embedded within 3rd Fleet's Kusanagi battle group of one hundred warships.

The other three battle groups materialized in the distance, shimmering shields forming around each warship. Korilia loomed directly ahead, while in the planet's orbit were four starship construction yards, hundreds of transports and cargo ships, and the space station hiding the planet. Everything appeared exactly as reported by the reconnaissance probes.

"All ahead full," Goergen ordered.

The main engines of four hundred warships ignited, and 3rd Fleet moved toward the nearest construction yard. Lara searched the sensor display and spotted the single Korilian cruiser in a wide orbit, positioned differently than in the recon photos, but essentially as expected.

A shrieking howl tore through Lara's mind. The same howl she had heard emitted by the slayer when it was wounded on Hellios, only a hundred times more intense. Lara placed her hands over her ears, hoping to block out the sound as she endured the pain. As she wondered if what she was experiencing was real or a prescient sign, Elena also clamped her hands over her ears and closed her eyes tightly, then fell to her knees, her body trembling. McCarthy stared at both of them with a quizzical look; he apparently heard nothing.

Elena scrambled toward one of the command bridge consoles and drew her knees up tight to her chest, her eyes glazing over.

Lara looked through the bridge windows, trying to discern what she and Elena were experiencing. The planet, space station, construction yards, and transports were exactly as depicted in the recon photos. There was nothing else noteworthy.

She looked closer, then realized the transports and cargo ships weren't moving.

McCarthy must have realized the same thing. He turned to Admiral Goergen.

"Reverse course!"

Goergen focused on McCarthy, then Lara and Elena. Turning back to her operations officer, she spoke, but her words came out slowly, like a recording on low battery power. Everywhere Lara looked, the crew was moving in slow motion.

And getting slower.

Finally, everyone on the command bridge stopped moving; they were frozen in place.

42

Vice Admiral Nesrine Rajhi, seated at her command console aboard the battleship *Intrepid*, examined the status of her Excalibur battle group after completing the jump to the Korilia star system. Of 3rd Fleet's four battle groups, arranged in a diamond formation, Excalibur was the farthest from the planet and would be the first to engage arriving Korilian warships. She scanned the sensor displays, and after noticing a single white flash—the Korilian cruiser departing the system, which was a wise decision in light of the arrival of four hundred Colonial warships—Rajhi turned her attention to the planet Korilia.

But what caught Rajhi's eyes instead was that the other three battle groups had halted, for reasons unknown. Rajhi had received no orders, nor had there been any communication from Admiral Goergen explaining or even indicating this change in plan. Was Excalibur expected to continue, or halt with the other three battle groups?

"Hail Third Fleet," Rajhi ordered her communications supervisor. "Request orders to Excalibur."

The message went out, and a moment later, the supervisor reported, "There is no response from Third Fleet."

Rajhi studied the other three battle groups as she tried to decipher

The End of Time   199

what was going on, then noticed the main engines of every starship in the other three battle groups were still firing, yet the ships weren't moving.

"What the hell?" Rajhi muttered under her breath as she tried to make sense of what she was seeing.

To her operations officer, Rajhi ordered, "To all Excalibur ships, all stop."

Excalibur's one hundred warships' reverse thrusters fired, slowing the starships until they stopped, while the other three battle groups remained motionless.

That was when she realized the Korilian merchant ships weren't moving either.

"Do we have communications with Fleet Command?" she asked.

"Yes, ma'am. The communication pods are active."

"Establish a video link, priority one transmission."

A moment later, Fleet Admiral Fitzgerald appeared on one of Rajhi's console displays.

"What is Third Fleet's status?" Fitzgerald asked.

"We've fallen into a trap. Some sort of force field has immobilized three of Third Fleet's battle groups. Excalibur's ships are unaffected at the moment, and I intend to determine the source of the immobilization and free the other three battle groups."

Fitzgerald was about to respond when she suddenly looked away from the camera, her face lighting up from white flashes emanating from the Fleet command center displays.

The command center supervisor appeared on screen, stopping beside Fitzgerald. "The Korilians are disengaging from the Liberation Campaign assaults."

"Which systems?" Fitzgerald asked.

"All systems, Fleet Admiral. The Korilians are taking significant losses during their jumps. They've not even waiting for optimal jump times."

Starships could not jump with shields up, and during the brief period the shields went down before the jump drive engaged, they were vulnerable. As a result, Korilian and Colonial disengagements were almost always sudden and simultaneous, occurring at the time, calculated by the command ship's computer, when there would be the fewest number of charged enemy pulse generators.

That the Korilians were disengaging from the Liberation Campaign assaults immediately, without waiting for the most opportune moment, spoke volumes. The Colonial Navy's assault on Korilia had struck a nerve, and Rajhi knew exactly where the Korilian battle groups were headed.

They're jumping to Korilia.

Twelve Korilian battle groups were on their way. However, they were a long distance away, and there were more immediate concerns.

Turning back to the camera, Fitzgerald asked, "What is the current Korilian order of battle at Korilia?"

"No forces at the moment," Rajhi replied. "The single cruiser in the system left as soon as Third Fleet arrived. However, there are twenty squadrons of Korilian warships within a few jumps, so it won't be long before we have company. If all twenty squadrons jump to Korilia, Excalibur will be overwhelmed."

"Then you'll need to figure out how to unfreeze the other three battle groups," Fitzgerald replied.

"I understand," Rajhi said as a dozen white flashes illuminated the darkness.

A squadron of Korilian warships had arrived, just outside weapon range. A few seconds later, another dozen flashes announced the arrival of a second squadron.

As Fitzgerald's image faded from Rajhi's display, she ordered her operations officer, "Redeploy Excalibur into a defensive screen between the Korilian warships and the rest of Third Fleet."

43

Seated in her fleet guide chair aboard *Surveillant*, Lara gazed around the command bridge; everyone was frozen in place. She stood and examined McCarthy, whose eyes were focused on Goergen, who had her mouth open, attempting to issue her next order. Throughout the command bridge, people were frozen in the middle of reports and gestures. She examined Elena, who was huddled with her back against a console with her knees drawn tight against her chest, her eyes squeezed shut and her hands clamped over her ears.

At least that dreadful howl was gone.

Lara then focused on the most pertinent detail of all—she didn't appear to be affected.

Why can I move, but no one else can?

Or was this all in her mind, and she was frozen in real life as well, each person locked into their own fantasy, like the Lost Ones at Domus Praesidium?

Returning her attention to what had happened to *Surveillant*'s crew, she realized that all of the electronic indications were also frozen. None of the sensor displays updated, and the time displays on the bridge consoles no longer changed.

The ship's crew—and *Surveillant* itself—was stuck in some sort of time stasis.

Bright white flashes pulled Lara's eyes toward the bridge windows. Three of 3rd Fleet's battle groups were frozen. Only Excalibur seemed unaffected for some reason, and she watched as the battle group redeployed into a planar screen between the other 3rd Fleet battle groups and dozens of white flashes in the distance. As more flashes appeared, announcing the arrival of additional Korilian warships, she realized the Excalibur battle group would soon be overwhelmed and the rest of 3rd Fleet destroyed.

Lara stepped forward and leaned against the data fusion table while she thought. As she studied the symbols on the display, representing 3rd Fleet, Korilia, and its orbiting star base, something tugged on Lara's mind, a nagging feeling that she was overlooking something important.

Then she noticed movement. The Excalibur warship symbols on the data fusion table were moving, and in the corner of the display, the clock was updating, the seconds ticking off again. Lara scanned the other equipment and personnel on the bridge, but everyone and everything else was still frozen.

She stepped back and took another look around for a clue that would help them out of their dilemma.

Nothing registered.

But when she looked back at the data fusion table, its clock was frozen again and the Excalibur symbols were no longer moving.

What the hell is going on?

She approached the data fusion table again, trying to figure out why it worked a few seconds ago but not now. When she touched the display, the clock began ticking again and the Excalibur symbols updated.

Lara looked around the bridge again. Still no change.

She stepped away from the console. The clock stopped, and the Excalibur symbols froze again.

It was her.

Whenever she touched the data fusion table, it was released from its time stasis.

Then she wondered—if she had the ability to free equipment from whatever was freezing them in time, what about people?

The End of Time 203

Lara stepped in front of McCarthy and studied his face, saw the danger reflected in his eyes when he had realized what was happening to 3rd Fleet. Then she embraced him.

McCarthy startled as she touched him, no doubt surprised by her sudden appearance before him. She felt him wrap his strong arms around her, and she pressed her cheek against his chest as he looked around the bridge.

"What happened?" he asked. "I can't view for some reason."

Lara explained what she had gleaned: that three of 3rd Fleet's battle groups were frozen in time, but there was something about her that released things and people from whatever was binding them. Additionally, and perhaps the more pressing matter, was that Korilian warships were jumping to Korilia and would soon overwhelm the Excalibur battle group.

"Do you know how you're doing this?" McCarthy asked.

Lara shook her head.

"We need to figure this out," he said. "We need to somehow leverage your ability and free the rest of Third Fleet."

"I don't *know* how I'm doing this," Lara said. "I don't even know *what* I'm doing."

McCarthy considered the issue for a moment, then asked, "Do you know why Elena reacted the way she did?"

"A dreadful howl," Lara replied, "like the one emitted by the slayer on Hellios when it was injured."

"That's odd," McCarthy said. "I heard nothing. It seems you and Elena are connected to the Korilians in some way. Elena spent nearly twenty years with them. Perhaps she can decipher what's going on. Let's see if you can unfreeze her."

Lara released one arm from around McCarthy, watching to make sure he didn't freeze again. Then she slid her other hand down his arm until his hand in hers was their only contact.

"Good so far," he said.

They knelt beside Elena, then Lara gently touched her shoulder.

Elena opened her eyes and screamed. Her eyes were still glazed over, though, seemingly unaware that McCarthy and Lara were beside her. But then her scream ended, and she focused on them. She released her hands from her ears and wrapped her arms around McCarthy and Lara, pulling them close. Her breathing was shallow and rapid, her face damp with perspiration.

"Elena," McCarthy said, "we need your help. The command ship and most of Third Fleet are frozen in time. Lara can free things or people if she touches them, but she doesn't know why."

Elena looked at Lara. "Don't you feel it? Don't you see it!" She shuddered in revulsion and squirmed as if she were trying to evade something.

Slowly, she pushed herself to her feet, joined by Lara and McCarthy. Elena peered through the bridge windows at the black-and-orange-mottled planet and the star base in orbit. She pointed to the Korilian star base.

"It comes from there."

"What does?" Lara asked.

"I can't explain. You have to see it."

Lara stared at the star base but saw nothing aside from the nearby Korilian space vessels, frozen in transit.

"I don't see anything," Lara said.

"Look harder."

Lara concentrated, squinting her eyes, then closing them, hoping to invoke a vision, but nothing materialized. "I still don't see anything."

Elena grabbed Lara's hair, pulling hard as she twisted Lara's head toward her.

"Harder! You need to see the lines."

"The lines?"

"Every living thing has a line. The same timelines we follow when viewing the future or past. You have to stop looking at us as people, but instead as lines. Then you'll understand what you're dealing with and perhaps be able to fight it."

"Like a view?"

"Yes. But instead of one line, all lines. You must simultaneously view the timeline of every human and Korilian in the system."

"I don't know how," Lara replied. "I don't know how to view even one line."

Elena grabbed Lara by her neck. "I didn't ask if you knew how. I told you to do it! You *must* do it!"

The End of Time 205

McCarthy gently pried Elena's hands from Lara's neck and hair. "Lara has a point. Viewing lines is easy for you and me. But Lara isn't even a Nine. She doesn't understand the technique."

"You're not helping, Jon." Elena glanced at the frozen men and women aboard *Surveillant*, then out the bridge windows at the Korilian warships advancing toward the Excalibur battle group, almost within weapon range.

McCarthy turned to Lara. "Treat it like a vision. Open your mind and see what happens."

Lara took a deep breath, then closed her eyes and attempted to invoke a vision.

Nothing materialized.

She tried again using a different technique Dewan Channing had taught her.

Still nothing.

Her pulse began racing as she realized she was ill-suited to do what Elena asked. She couldn't follow a line; she had no idea what one even looked like.

She was about to try again when a cloud of mist began to coagulate beside them, taking the shape of a human. After it formed, Lara's mother, Cheryl, stood before her.

"I cannot do this for you," Cheryl said quickly, "but I can show you what it looks like."

Cheryl turned translucent, then what was left of her body condensed into a glowing sphere that began to elongate on both ends, stretching into a pulsating strand that extended into the distance in two directions.

"To follow a line," the glowing strand said, "you must be able to follow a person's essence through space and time. That's what a Nine or Ten does. But you don't need to do that; your job is simpler. We're currently frozen in time, and thus all you must do is *see* the line."

Lara followed what Cheryl was saying, but didn't understand how it helped. Explaining that she only needed to see the timelines was akin to explaining to a caveman that he didn't need to do calculus to solve the problem, that algebra would do.

She closed her eyes and tried again, letting the image of *Surveillant's* command bridge in her mind fill with fog. As the fog began to dissipate, she imagined McCarthy, Elena, and the rest of the bridge crew exactly where they were standing or sitting.

This time, as the fog cleared, glowing orbs appeared where McCarthy, Elena, and *Surveillant*'s crew members were. The orbs began spinning and stretching out as Cheryl's had done, until only thin pulsating strands remained.

Lara opened her eyes, and the thin glowing strands remained. Lara was surrounded in space by the thousand timelines of the command ship's occupants. But the glowing strands weren't the only unusual objects present.

Thin white tentacles were hovering near her, Elena, and McCarthy, while tentacles were wrapped tightly around everyone else's timeline and the command ship itself. The timeline strands extending into the distance were dark, no longer pulsing with energy. The lines were being strangled by the white tentacles.

That she now saw the lines and tentacles must have been apparent on her face, because Elena whispered in her ear, "Follow the tentacles."

Lara followed the white tentacles from the command ship toward their origin: the Korilian star base.

It hung in orbit, the tentacles emerging from the center of the large oval. They weaved through space, and every line they came in contact with turned dark.

Time wasn't frozen. It was being strangled.

"I see it," Lara said, both excitement and dread permeating her voice. "I see what's happened. The tentacles are coming from the Korilian space station."

"The rest is up to you," Elena said, as she and McCarthy, along with the rest of *Surveillant*'s crew, materialized again.

The white tentacles remained, but Lara noticed how they hovered around the three of them, whereas they wrapped themselves tightly around everyone else on the bridge.

Lara let go of Elena's arm, and the tentacles immediately wrapped themselves tightly around the Nexus Ten's body. As Lara reached toward Elena, the tentacles retreated. She moved her hand in various directions,

The End of Time 207

the tentacles retreating in response to each of Lara's movements. Then she touched Elena's arm again, unfreezing her.

"Don't do that again," Elena said. "Others may not realize they're frozen in time, but I do."

"Sorry."

"What have you figured out?" McCarthy asked.

"I understand the problem and see what I'm doing, but I don't know where to go from here. I can't possibly touch everyone and everything at the same time."

"Perhaps you're thinking too literally," McCarthy said. "Nothing we do as Nexi is physical, aside from praetorian combat skills. It's all mental. Maybe you *do* need to touch everything, but not with your body. With your mind."

"You're right, Jon," Lara replied as an idea took hold. "This time, *you're* going to be the guinea pig."

Lara released his hand, and McCarthy froze. She closed her eyes and concentrated, imagining she was reaching toward McCarthy, touching his cheek.

"Well done," McCarthy said.

She opened her eyes. A bubble had formed around herself and McCarthy, and the tentacles had retreated. They probed the bubble, unable to reach McCarthy.

Lara then pushed the bubble toward Elena with her mind while trying to keep it from collapsing around McCarthy. The bubble slowly expanded and soon enveloped Elena as well. She let go of Elena's arm.

"That's a good start," Elena said. "Now you need to create a bubble large enough to free Third Fleet."

Lara's elation at her accomplishment turned to panic. It took a significant effort to create a bubble large enough to encompass McCarthy and Elena, and the larger the bubble, the more effort was required.

She took a deep breath, then mustered up the strength to proceed. Pushing the bubble outward, she created a slowly expanding sphere. It enveloped the equipment consoles around them, expanding to ten feet wide, then fifteen. But then the expansion slowed down. The larger the bubble, the more tentacles she came in contact with, and the bubble's expansion halted at a diameter of twenty feet. Lara struggled to maintain the bubble as the tentacles probed vigorously against it.

"That's the best I can do," Lara said, her words escaping briskly as she fought to keep the bubble stable, her mind and body straining with the effort.

Lara let the bubble collapse to just around the three of them as she gasped for breath.

"Twenty feet is as good as I can do, and only for a short period of time."

"That'll be good enough," McCarthy said.

Lara and Elena looked at him.

"Good enough for what?" Lara asked.

He pointed to the source of the white tentacles.

"We're going to the Korilian space station."

44

"One minute to ten-pulse engagement range."

Aboard the battleship *Intrepid*, Vice Admiral Rajhi's crew waited silently at their consoles as the Korilian warships closed on the Excalibur battle group. Rajhi monitored the sensor data on the displays, with the most important factor—time to engagement range—counting down on the bottom right corner of each screen. Starship tyranium pulses lost strength as they traveled, interacting with interstellar matter. The closer the starship was to the target when it fired, the stronger the pulse.

"Ten-pulse engagement range," *Intrepid*'s weapons officer announced.

The Korilians didn't attack; their warships continued closing.

Excalibur's fire control systems were in automatic for the time being. The systems of all ninety-six battleships and cruisers were tied together, with the computers calculating how many pulses were required to collapse a Korilian starship shield. At this range, it would take ten battleship or twenty cruiser pulses—or various combinations of cruisers and battleships—to collapse a Korilian shield, and the combat systems colluded to assign the requisite number of Colonial ships to a single target.

When the Korilians closed to within nine-pulse range, the combat systems would automatically retarget, assigning only nine Colonial battleships per target, and so on, increasing the shield-collapse rate for the first barrage as the Korilians closed. The Korilians, however, were doing the same, combining their firepower against a few unfortunate Colonial ships.

Now that the Korilians had reached the ten-pulse engagement range, Rajhi had to make her first significant decision—whether to deploy her vipers. Excalibur's one-hundred-strong warship complement included four carriers, each loaded with a wing of five hundred vipers. However, if Rajhi's Excalibur battle group jumped away from Korilia, the carriers would have to retrieve their surviving vipers first, which took time. Time they might not have.

Excalibur's flight officer was looking at Rajhi, awaiting orders for their viper wings. Finally, Rajhi made her decision. She would push her battle group to the limit, defending the rest of 3rd Fleet as long as possible, and couldn't afford to deal with the time-consuming viper retrieval.

Rajhi announced her decision. "We will not deploy vipers."

"Nine-pulse engagement range."

There was still no attack.

The Korilians would normally have engaged by now but were delaying their initial barrage while additional warships jumped to Korilia and joined the advancing armada. Finally, Rajhi decided to attack first; the longer she waited, the more the advantage swung to the Korilians.

"To all Excalibur ships—engage."

Immediately after her weapons officer entered the command, Intrepid's sensor displays lit up as tyranium coils energized. Explosions filled the bridge windows as ninety-six warships fired, the blue pulses speeding outward while the Korilian fire control systems reacted instantly, sending incoming red pulses toward the Colonial ships, their shields illuminating as they absorbed the pulse energy.

Korilian pulses collapsed the shields of ten battleships, with Colonial pulses penetrating an equal number of dreadnought shields. Shortly after the opposing forces engaged, sensors detected incoming Korilian marauder wings headed toward two of the Colonial battleships with down shields; the Korilian combined pulse had also penetrated their armor. There were no vipers to intercept the marauders; the damaged starships would have to rely on their suppression-fire batteries to take out the nimble fighters.

At the one-minute point—fifty-seven seconds to be exact—the Excal-

The End of Time

ibur ships fired again, with the Korilian ships counterfiring so quickly that their pulses appeared simultaneous. On Rajhi's display, the sectors in Excalibur's planar defense grid became colored, with green indicating the sector had a fully operational battleship and cruiser, yellow indicating only a battleship, orange—just a cruiser, and red—no operational Colonial ships.

By examining other colored grids on the bridge displays, Rajhi gleaned additional information: how many of her ships had a shield down, main engines inoperative, one or two reactors down, and how many had inoperable jump drives.

Rajhi touched various sectors on her display, with a two-finger tap selecting a supplying sector and a one-finger tap identifying the receiving one. Battleships and cruisers flowed toward the yellow and orange sectors, returning their status to green, but Rajhi could do so for only so long. She had only one battleship and one cruiser squadron in reserve.

45

McCarthy led Lara and Elena toward *Surveillant*'s spaceport, all three staying close together as they proceeded, while white tentacles retreated as Lara's bubble advanced. Along the way, they stopped in *Surveillant*'s armory, where McCarthy selected three pulse-pistols and waist holsters in case there were Korilians aboard the space station.

As they resumed their way to the spaceport, Lara wondered how they would exit the command ship. Although the corridor doors opened once within Lara's bubble, the spaceport doors were immense, large enough for supply ships to pass through the opening. There was no way Lara could create a bubble large enough to unfreeze the spaceport doors, allowing them to be retracted. When she queried McCarthy about the issue, he explained.

"We'll take one of the welding repair-bots. It has a cutting torch we can use to cut through one of the spaceport doors. It's designed for two operators, but we can fit three." He glanced at Lara, who was five foot six, then Elena, barely five feet tall and still quite thin, having not fully recovered from her incarceration on Hellios.

Upon reaching the spaceport, they entered the maintenance bay and boarded a repair-bot, which had several robotic arms with various attachments. McCarthy took one seat and Lara the other, while Elena jammed herself between them. McCarthy energized the repair-bot, and it lifted off, then he guided it toward the spaceport doors.

"You need to tell me how fast to go, Lara. I can't see the bubble you've formed or how fast you're pushing it forward."

Lara monitored the bubble in her mind, providing feedback as McCarthy adjusted the repair-bot's speed until the bot and bubble moved forward at the same rate.

After a short journey, they reached the spaceport doors and stopped five feet away.

"Okay, Lara, create a bubble as large as possible, and push as much of it as you can through the spaceport doors."

Lara increased the bubble's size back to twenty feet in diameter, pushing a large portion of it through the spaceport doors.

"That's the best I can do."

McCarthy manipulated one of the repair-bot's arms, and a cutting torch activated at the end. As the torch cut through the spaceport door, McCarthy moved the repair-bot in a circular pattern until a hole large enough for the repair-bot had been cut. Lara let the bubble collapse back down to fifteen feet, easing the strain on her mind.

The repair-bot moved forward again, and after passing through the hole in the spaceport door, McCarthy turned it toward the Korilian space station.

In the distance, Lara watched the multicolor battle between the Excalibur battle group and advancing Korilian armada. Starship shields lit up in yellow flares as they were bombarded by red and blue pulses, accompanied by purple flashes as shield generators disintegrated. Among the many colors was an occasional intense orange flash as a jump drive imploded, tearing a starship to shreds.

As a dozen white flashes lit up the darkness, announcing the arrival of additional Korilian warships, Lara knew the outcome was inevitable. The Excalibur battle group would be defeated.

It was only a matter of time.

46

Vice Admiral Rajhi continued filling the gaps in Excalibur's defense screen, allocating her dwindling reserve of battleships and cruisers. The Korilian and Colonial ships continued firing at one-minute intervals until they finally closed the distance, with the white and gray starships exchanging pulses at almost point-blank range as they passed each other. The opposing starships began maneuvering, turning and rotating as they attempted to hit their adversary on the same shield while presenting a different shield to their opponent.

The Excalibur battle group retreated as the Korilians advanced, ensuring that each Korilian ship remained engaged and that none slipped cleanly through to within firing range of the frozen 3rd Fleet battle groups. As they retreated, Rajhi kept a keen eye on how much territory she had to work with. She had launched reconnaissance probes toward the rest of 3rd Fleet, and the probes had frozen in space partway in their journey. Their locations marked the boundary the Excalibur battle group could not penetrate. Rajhi also calculated how long her dwindling forces could remain in the Korilia star system; how long before they reached the Departure Point —the time beyond which disengaging from battle would result in unacceptable losses.

In order to jump, each starship had to drop shields, and during that

The End of Time

brief period, the starships were vulnerable. During battle at relatively even odds, there was little concern, because opposing warships would fire as soon as their pulse generators recharged, leaving few ships on either side with charged pulse generators and a clear shot during those few seconds before the sudden and unexpected departure of their enemy. However, as one side gained a significant advantage, it could afford to hold warships with charged pulse generators in reserve, anticipating the inevitable departure of their defeated foe.

As the ratio of surviving warships tilted in one side's favor, the losses sustained during the departure jump would mount. To minimize those losses, Rajhi and other Fleet commanders monitored the DP—the Departure Point—calculated by the ship's computer and defined as the point at which ten percent of the departing warships would be heavily damaged or destroyed. If a defeated force remained beyond the Departure Point, losses would mount exponentially until no starship would survive after dropping its shields for the jump.

"*Five minutes to the Departure Point.*"

Intrepid's computer made the announcement, ensuring Rajhi and her staff remained apprised of the critical time. If desired, Rajhi could stay longer, sustaining additional casualties during the battle and when shields were dropped for the departure jump. They would be buying time by sacrificing ships, but for what reason?

Rajhi tapped her console display, establishing a connection to Fleet command headquarters. Fleet Admiral Fitzgerald's image appeared, the transmission flickering as *Intrepid*'s shields were hit with Korilian pulses. There were also intermittent delays as the communication pods relayed the data to and from Earth.

"Admiral Fitzgerald. The situation is critical. I've lost twenty percent of my battle group, and more Korilian ships are arriving. We'll reach the Departure Point soon, and there is no change in status of the other battle groups. All three remain frozen in place. Request orders."

"How long until the DP?" Fitzgerald asked.

"Four minutes."

Rajhi waited while Fitzgerald processed her request, realizing the Fleet Admiral had no good options: abandon the rest of 3rd Fleet, leaving it to certain destruction, or order Rajhi's battle group to stay longer, to achieve what?

Fitzgerald's eyes shifted to the right, no doubt monitoring the more important battle in Earth's orbit, then returned to the camera.

"Admiral Rajhi, jump at the DP. Return to Earth via the most expeditious route, minimizing losses along the way."

The screen went black, and Rajhi focused on her orders.

"Three minutes to the Departure Point."

Rajhi ordered her operations officer, "To all Excalibur ships, prepare for double jump at the Departure Point. Recommend jump coordinates."

The operations officer sent the order, then recommended dual locations for the double jump, which Rajhi approved.

"Two minutes to the jump."

"Jump coordinates verified. Drive spinning up. Initiating jump sequence in two minutes."

As *Intrepid's* crew made final preparations for their jump from the Korilia system, the sensor supervisor made an unexpected report.

"I have a new contact, leaving the Third Fleet command ship."

The report made no sense. *Why would a shuttle depart the command ship during battle, and how was that even possible? Had other ships freed themselves?*

"Is there any other movement within the rest of Third Fleet?" Rajhi asked.

"No, ma'am. Just this contact."

"On screen," Rajhi ordered.

The display zoomed in to the contact, which Rajhi didn't recognize at first; she had never seen a shuttle of that design before. Then she realized it wasn't a shuttle at all. It was a hull repair module. But it wasn't moving toward the Excalibur battle group, as Rajhi expected.

"Where is the contact headed?"

The sensor supervisor calculated the object's trajectory, and a yellow line appeared on the display, leading to the Korilian star base.

Rajhi had no idea why it was headed there, but she had a decent idea of who was aboard. If anyone could have freed themselves from whatever had frozen the rest of 3rd Fleet, it was one of the three Nexi aboard *Surveillant.*

The End of Time 217

Five deep tones reverberated throughout *Intrepid*, followed by the announcement:

"One minute to the jump."

Rajhi had a decision to make. If there was any hope for the rest of 3rd Fleet, it rested in the hands of whoever was aboard that module. If Excalibur jumped away now, the Korilians would no doubt spot and destroy the object moving toward their star base. That was something Rajhi could not allow. She had to keep the Korilians focused on Colonial warships.

"Thirty seconds to the jump."

Fitzgerald had ordered Rajhi to depart the Korilia system at the Departure Point, saving as many of her ships as possible. But Rajhi had new information that might change Fitzgerald's mind. Unfortunately, there wasn't enough time to contact Fleet Command.

"Ten seconds to the jump."

Five deep tones sounded throughout the ship again, announcing their pending departure.

Rajhi was out of time and made her decision. This wouldn't be the first time she had disobeyed a direct order.

"To all Excalibur ships," Rajhi announced, "abort the jump!"

47

Seated at her console at the back of the Fleet command center, Fleet Admiral Fitzgerald monitored the battle status on her displays. The Korilian assault in Earth's orbit had been intense, and despite the valiant efforts of 6th Fleet, the expected result was about to play out. The Korilian armada had focused first on 6th Fleet, since it was the only mobile component of Earth's defense system at the moment, with the four Liberation Campaign fleets still en route from the front line and 3rd Fleet stuck at Korilia. Outnumbered four to one, 6th Fleet had not lasted long. Not a single battleship or cruiser remained.

The only good news was that the powerful defense stations surrounding Earth and the construction yards had inflicted significant damage while the Korilian armada engaged 6th Fleet.

Over two hundred Korilian warships had been destroyed, and another hundred more as the Korilian armada turned its attention to the defense stations. But in the critical sector protecting Construction Yard Seven, only one defense station remained in operation. Once it was destroyed, the shield in that sector could not be maintained.

The defense station's shield was weakening as it was pounded by Korilian warships. Finally, the shield collapsed in a bright yellow flash,

The End of Time 219

leaving the defense station exposed. Fitzgerald watched as it was hit with a barrage of red pulses that tore the station apart.

The Korilians wasted no time targeting the construction yard. It wasn't long before red pulses sliced through all ten assembly lines, cutting them into pieces. The segments, which began spiraling apart, were then hit by successive pulses, obliterating them.

Fitzgerald now had a decision to make. Earth's orbital defense shield had been penetrated, and unless the hole was sealed, the entire Korilian armada could pour through the gap and attack the other construction yards and even the cities on Earth. She could close the hole by contracting the defense station bubble. However, the new, smaller sphere would be inside the construction and repair yard orbits, leaving all sixteen yards exposed.

A quick survey of the Korilian order of battle revealed that there were no troop transports in Earth's orbit or waiting in solar systems nearby, as far as Fleet Intelligence had discerned, which meant the Korilians weren't planning on landing combat troops on Earth any time soon. It was obvious —the goal of the Korilian assault was the destruction of the starship construction yards, which would be a fatal blow to the Colonial Navy. Without the Fleet keeping the Korilians at bay, a planetary invasion was inevitable.

It was a gamble, but Fitzgerald gave the order, widening the hole in Earth's defense shield instead of closing it. The defense stations near the hole began to descend, creating an open funnel toward Earth. In the process, however, they sealed off access to the rest of the construction and repair yards. The Korilian warships couldn't travel low enough to slip under the descending funnel.

Fitzgerald had left a portion of Earth, inside the funnel, unprotected. Nothing could stop Korilian warship pulses from raining down upon the exposed cities. As she and the other personnel in the Fleet command center awaited the Korilian response, the armada began moving away from the funnel toward Construction Yard Six. Fitzgerald's gamble had paid off.

There was a momentary reprieve from battle as the Korilian armada repositioned, but the battle's outcome hadn't changed. The Korilians would repeat the process, blasting another hole in Earth's defense shield, then destroying the construction yard behind it. The defense stations would take a toll on the enemy warships, but the Korilians would achieve their goal. Unless the Liberation Campaign fleets arrived in time, every construction and repair yard would be destroyed.

As the Korilian armada prepared to assault the next construction yard, a communications supervisor approached.

"Fleet Admiral," he said, "the Excalibur battle group hasn't jumped. Their transponders indicate they're still at Korilia, but they're not acknowledging any of our communications."

The supervisor's wristlet vibrated at the same time a message alert appeared on Fitzgerald's display. She opened the alert—a message from *Intrepid*.

ADMIRAL RAJHI ACKNOWLEDGES HAIL. SITUATION TOO CRITICAL TO REPLY.

Fitzgerald stood and approached the fusion plot of the Korilia system. Only sixty-two ships remained in the Excalibur battle group, opposed by just over one hundred Korilian warships, with eight more squadrons—almost another one hundred starships—en route from nearby planetary systems.

Rajhi had done a commendable job, destroying over forty Korilian dreadnoughts and cruisers, but the Korilian numerical superiority was too significant to overcome. Plus, the Excalibur battle group was already at DP-50, at which half of the remaining starships would be destroyed when they dropped shields for the jump.

What is Rajhi thinking?

Had her battle group been pinned down somehow, unable to disengage? Or was there some other reason Rajhi had decided to stay?

Fitzgerald examined the fusion plot and spotted a solitary blue symbol moving in the midst of the 3rd Fleet quagmire. When she examined the ID at the bottom of the blue symbol, she had no idea what it was. She had never seen this type of ship in combat.

She called to the nearest sensor supervisor. "What type of ship is this?"

The supervisor studied the display for a moment. "It's a repair-bot." He scratched his head, then added, "I have no idea why Third Fleet would be operating a repair-bot during battle."

Fitzgerald did. She followed the repair-bot's trajectory on the fusion plot.

Someone was headed to the Korilian star base.

48

The repair-bot moved slowly toward the Korilian space station, propelled by small thrusters instead of a main engine like Fleet transports. Despite the urgency of their situation, Lara was thankful for the slow pace; it took a tremendous effort to keep the bubble large enough to encapsulate the repair-bot and also move forward, pushing the tentacles out of the way.

Lara matched the repair-bot's speed but found it increasingly difficult to maintain the bubble as they moved toward the space station. The tentacles became denser the closer they got. She strained with the effort, beads of sweat forming on her face. Despite her determination, the bubble gradually decreased in size until it barely enclosed the repair-bot.

They were only halfway there.

"We have to slow down," Lara said. "I can't move the bubble this fast."

McCarthy slowed the module to minimum speed, but the effort required to maintain the bubble continued to escalate. A few minutes later, the repair-bot lurched to a halt.

Lara turned to McCarthy. "I can't keep the bubble large enough and moving at the same time. The tentacles are too dense. We have to turn back."

"That's not an option," McCarthy said. "We have to make it to the space station."

The End of Time   223

"I can't do it!" Lara shouted. "It gets harder the closer we get. I don't even know if we can make it back to *Surveillant!*"

"You have to figure out how to get us to the space station," McCarthy said firmly. "The rest of Third Fleet depends on us."

Lara's strength was ebbing, and her protective sphere had shrunk inside the repair-bot. The tentacles were now reaching through the module's hull.

"The bubble is collapsing. We have to head back now!" Tears formed as she strained to protect McCarthy and Elena from the probing tentacles.

"Both of you, shut up," Elena said.

She was scrunched between them, her eyes darting around as the tentacles closed in on them. She twisted toward Lara. "We're going to the space station."

Elena placed a hand on Lara's chest, and Lara felt a surge of energy flow into her body, restoring the strength that had almost completely left her. Elena was using her healing talent the normal way. Instead of draining someone's life force, she was flowing hers into Lara.

Lara expanded the bubble outside the repair-bot, then informed McCarthy.

The repair-bot resumed its trek toward the space station.

As Elena's life force flowed into Lara, Elena's face paled and the amount of energy flowing into Lara waned. The bubble began shrinking again. They were almost there, but at the rate Elena was fading, they weren't going to make it.

"I need more," Lara said. The bubble had shrunk to just outside the repair-bot again.

Elena planted her other hand on McCarthy's chest. The energy flowing into Lara surged as Elena drew on McCarthy's life force as well. His eyes widened when he realized what Elena was doing, but he said nothing as he guided the repair module toward the space station.

They were only a hundred yards away now, and McCarthy searched for a docking location. He spotted a force field guarding what looked like a small spaceport in the side of the space station and angled the repair-bot toward it.

The module passed through the spaceport's life-support field, and the tentacles disappeared. The bubble around the repair-bot expanded rapidly as Lara no longer met resistance. It was as if they had entered the calm eye of a hurricane.

McCarthy maneuvered toward a docking station and lowered the repair-bot onto the spaceport deck. Elena dropped her hands from McCarthy's and Lara's chests, then collapsed between them. McCarthy pulled Elena into his lap, cradling her head in his arm. Her eyes were cloudy, unresponsive. But they slowly cleared, and she touched the side of McCarthy's face.

"I'm sorry," she said, "for draining your life force without asking."

"It's quite all right," McCarthy said. "You did what had to be done. Are you strong enough to accompany us, or do you need to stay here and recover?"

"I'll be ready to go in another minute or two."

While they waited for Elena to recover, with Lara keenly aware of how McCarthy cradled Elena in his arms, they examined the spaceport through the repair-bot windows. It was empty; no Korilians or ships of any kind were in the spaceport. Unfortunately, they had no idea of how many Korilians were aboard the space station. The repair-bot had no sensors, no way to scan for Korilians. They couldn't even determine if the space station air was breathable. Korilians could breathe air suitable for humans—that was clear. But whether humans could breathe the range of air composition that could sustain Korilian life was unknown. Perhaps, now that they were inside the space station and the tentacles had disappeared, McCarthy and Elena could figure that out.

"Can either of you view now?" Lara asked.

McCarthy shook his head.

"Completely blocked," Elena replied.

Once Elena was ready to proceed, McCarthy cracked open the repair-bot hatch and sniffed the air. After experiencing no ill effects, he opened the door fully.

McCarthy was the first to exit, followed by Elena, then Lara.

As Lara stepped onto the space station's metal deck and looked around, her intuition tugged at her. There was something odd about this space station. Something...out of place. She tried to identify the important detail she was overlooking, but it eluded her.

McCarthy pulled his pulse-pistol from its holster, as did Elena and Lara, then approached the spaceport exit. The door slid open, revealing an empty passageway.

They moved quietly down the corridor until they reached an intersection. After peering around the corner, McCarthy whispered, "All clear."

They stepped into what appeared to be a main passageway running through the oval-shaped Korilian space station, with a corridor branching out on both sides at intersections as the passageway made its way around the space station.

After looking both ways, McCarthy hesitated.

Without being able to view, he couldn't answer the critical question— Where did they need to go? Was there some sort of control room aboard the space station where they could deactivate whatever was freezing the lines of time? And if so, where was it? He turned to Elena.

"Can you view?"

Elena shook her head.

The two Tens looked to Lara, wondering if she had received or could invoke a vision.

"I'll see what I can do."

She closed her eyes and imagined the intersection filling with fog, then waited for a path to form, showing her the way. Nothing materialized.

"No visions at the moment," Lara replied.

Fortunately, the Korilian space station was an oval design. Keep heading in one direction, and they would eventually explore the entire station.

McCarthy led the way, investigating both sides of each intersection they encountered. Finding the control room, if there even was one, was taking far too long, as the men and women in the Excalibur battle group fought for their lives, protecting the rest of 3rd Fleet. The only consolation was that thus far, they had not encountered any Korilians aboard the space station.

They reached a door much larger than the rest, which didn't open automatically when they approached. It had a control panel built into the bulkhead on one side. McCarthy took station on one side of the door, pulse-pistol held ready, while Elena positioned herself on the other side. McCarthy motioned Lara to move behind him, and once she was in place, he touched the control panel. As the door slid upward, McCarthy and Elena pivoted into the doorway, pistols aimed into the compartment.

"All clear," McCarthy announced.

Lara joined the two Nexus Tens, entering what looked like a control room with consoles lining the far wall. One large display showed the Korilian planet, its four assembly yards, and hundreds of Korilian ships frozen in time. Not far away, what remained of the Excalibur battle group was wilting under the Korilian onslaught, outnumbered two to one now. It wouldn't be long before the Korilians turned their attention to the trapped 3rd Fleet battle groups, destroying them as well.

Lara stopped a few feet into the control room, suddenly realizing what was out of place. It was the space station's construction: composite metal instead of the springy Korilian fibers, a spaceport not much different from starship spaceports, plus the control room consoles were similar to those aboard Fleet starships. Lara felt the hair on the back of her neck stand up, and something told her the key to everything was behind her.

She turned around, her eyes going to large metal letters above the doorway they had just passed through.

Her knees went weak as she read the words, written in the Colonial language.

PROMETHEUS ONE

Lara recalled the dissertation by Morel Alperi at Central and the comment by Devin Anjul from the Special Intelligence Division during dinner aboard *Surveillant*, when both had lamented the failure of the Prometheus Project, humankind's attempt several centuries ago to travel enormous distances across the galaxy through wormholes created by Prometheus portals—one at Central and another by a space station transported to a distant solar system, one that held the potential to support life.

The project had failed, and Lara now realized that what had occurred was far worse than failure. Prometheus One had somehow frozen the Korilian home world in time.

Five centuries later, after humans and Korilians met, the Korilians had figured out that humankind was responsible for this cruel attack on their home world, a blatant act of aggression. Lara recalled the Korilian obelisk that had been transported to Earth, and the meaning of the inscription at its base became clear. The Korilian symbols had been translated correctly after all.

Time will stop for you, also.

They just hadn't understood the context. And Lara finally identified the additional emotion embedded into the Korilian symbols on the obelisk. It wasn't just hatred and rage.

It was revenge.

49

Inside the Colonial Fleet command center, Fleet Admiral Fitzgerald monitored the deteriorating situation. Not that there was much she could do. The Korilian armada had destroyed half of the nineteen defense stations it needed to destroy in order to puncture Earth's protective shield again, exposing Construction Yard Six. With only nine stations firing back, Korilian losses were dwindling.

The Army artillery batteries on Earth's surface were doing what they could. Now that 6th Fleet had been destroyed and was out of the way, the artillery batteries had begun firing, sending blue pulses toward the Korilian warships. But the artillery batteries were built to destroy descending surface assault vehicles carrying Korilian combat troops and were ill-suited for attacking warships in orbit. The planet's atmosphere interfered with tyranium pulses even more than interstellar matter; the best the artillery batteries could do was temporarily neutralize a starship, encapsulating it in an electromagnetic storm that sizzled across the ship's shields.

Still, anything that slowed the Korilian carnage as they swept through the construction yards was welcome. Only the arrival of the four Liberation Campaign fleets could change the outcome. Unfortunately, no starship crew had accomplished what Fitzgerald had ordered: thirteen jumps in six hours. Thus far, the most completed by a starship crew in a single day had

The End of Time   229

been six, accomplished by the crew of the *Argonaut* eighteen years ago. The
Fleet supply corridor to Darian 3 had begun collapsing, and the Army had
rushed troops to the planet. The physical toll of the jumps had been enormous, killing ten percent of *Argonaut*'s crew and twenty percent of the Army
personnel aboard the troop transport.

However, warship crews were accustomed to jumping more than those
aboard troop transports, plus Fleet personnel were far more battle-hard-
ened today than they were eighteen years ago. But thirteen jumps in six
hours? In the back of Fitzgerald's mind, she knew that what she had
ordered wasn't achievable, yet she hoped that somehow, against all odds,
her starship crews would accomplish the impossible.

One of Fitzgerald's displays shifted to a new incoming message. An
image of Admiral Shallcross, in command of 4th Fleet, appeared. He was
slumped in his console chair aboard his command ship, staring at
Fitzgerald with dark pupils surrounded by red. His eyes had begun hemor-
rhaging, filling the whites of his eyes with blood. In another jump or two
without sufficient recovery time, his eyes would burst from the steadily
increasing pressure inside.

Shallcross spoke slowly, his words slurred.

"Fourth Fleet cannot continue," he said. "We just completed the fifth
jump, and ten percent of my crews are incapacitated. Our medical bays are
overflowing, and the conscious crew members are barely functioning."

"What is the status of the other three fleets?"

"Similar to mine," Shallcross replied. "We cannot complete another
eight jumps. If you do not cancel your order, we will be forced to disobey
it."

Fitzgerald considered Shallcross's statement. If she relented and
cancelled her order, it would seal humanity's fate. Their construction yards
would be destroyed, and without replacement starships, what remained of
the Colonial Navy would be overwhelmed by the Korilian armada. After
that, it was only a matter of time before Korilian combat troops assaulted
the remaining colonies and Earth itself.

Humankind would be exterminated.

The construction yards *had* to be saved, and the only way was with the
Liberation Campaign fleets. Yet she knew Shallcross's assessment was

correct. The four fleets could not reach Earth in time. If she continued pushing them, she risked their destruction as well, easy targets for what remained of the Korilian armada assaulting Earth.

Fitzgerald's thoughts began to cloud with despair; there was nothing more she could do. She had led the Fleet for eight years, guiding it through its most trying times as it abandoned planet after planet under the withering Korilian assault on their colonized worlds. During the Fleet's retreat, she had carefully crafted a plan that had saved humanity from annihilation during the Final Stand three years ago, destroying the entire two-thousand-strong Korilian armada that had assaulted Earth. But it had all been for naught. Tonight, the Korilians would inflict a wound from which the Fleet, and humanity itself, could not recover.

Then her resolve steeled. As long as the Fleet had ships, they would fight and somehow defeat the Korilians. As she searched for a solution, she latched onto a glimmer of hope. If the Liberation Campaign fleets couldn't reach Earth in time, then the only chance of salvation was with McCarthy in command of the four remaining fleets. If he survived 3rd Fleet's ensnarement at Korilia, perhaps he could pull off a miracle.

Fitzgerald pressed two buttons on her chair armrest, and her fleet deputy commander, Admiral Carroll, and the senior command center supervisor approached.

When they stopped before her, she finally relented. "Order all Liberation Campaign fleets to stand down until further orders are received. Get the medical ships to them as soon as possible."

50

Lara stood beneath the words forged above the control room doorway, realizing that the Korilian War wasn't the result of the Korilian Empire's ambition, resentful of humankind's expansion across the galaxy. The Korilians hadn't been the aggressors; they were simply responding to an attack occurring five centuries ago, when Prometheus One had frozen their home world in time.

Her thoughts shifted from the past to the present; the Excalibur battle group was now less than half strength and fully committed. They were well past the Departure Point, and their remaining ships would be targeted and destroyed if they dropped shields to jump away. While Lara wondered why Admiral Rajhi had stayed, she wasn't surprised.

The woman truly has a death wish.

But Rajhi needed help. Was there some way to reverse what Prometheus One had done and unfreeze the rest of 3rd Fleet?

Those thoughts and more raced through Lara's mind in only a few seconds, then she turned to McCarthy and Elena, who were studying the consoles and displays.

"I know what this space station is."

As the two Nexus Tens turned toward her, Lara pointed over her shoulder at the words above the door. She saw the realization on their faces as they grasped where they were, and what had happened.

McCarthy turned back toward the consoles, studying them for a moment, then smashed his fist into one of the glass control surfaces. She sensed his frustration from across the room. If he or Elena could have viewed, they could have easily determined whether they could deactivate Prometheus One and what that process was. They could have simulated thousands of permutations of commands entered into the various consoles, studying their effect until the proper sequence of commands into the appropriate consoles was discovered.

He looked to Lara—their one hope. Her premonitions didn't rely on timelines. Perhaps a vision could show her the way.

"It's up to you, Lara. You need to find a way."

Lara took a deep breath and focused, imagining she was on the 1st Fleet command ship during the Final Stand. During the crucial moments of the battle, she'd had a vision that had changed the outcome, leading the Colonial Navy to victory. She recalled with irony that Admiral Rajhi—then Captain Rajhi—had been part of that vision, noting that their fates seemed somehow intertwined.

Prometheus One's control room filled with fog, which began coalescing toward the center, taking human form. When the rest of the fog faded, a translucent form of her mother, Cheryl, stood before her.

"Can you help?" Lara asked.

Cheryl smiled. "I can't do it myself, but I can show you how. Come with me."

Lara followed Cheryl to the center console, larger than the rest, and stopped beside her.

"Step into me," Cheryl said.

Her words took Lara by surprise, but perhaps this was why Cheryl had appeared in translucent form as opposed to normal flesh.

She followed her mother's direction, stepping into the translucent shape. An odd sensation rippled through her body, foreign and yet familiar at the same time, as if whatever had manifested as Cheryl was already part of her.

"Follow my hands," Cheryl directed.

The End of Time 233

She moved her right hand toward one of the controls, and Lara followed, mimicking her mother's movements. Lara pressed a control, which shifted the glass surface to a different configuration of symbols, then touched one control after another.

After a dozen commands, a portal in the center of the console appeared and a red circle rose a few inches.

The OFF button, Lara guessed, hoping her assessment was correct.

Cheryl reached toward the button, holding her hand above it until Lara joined her.

"This is it?" Lara asked. "This will unfreeze Third Fleet?"

"This will stop whatever Prometheus One is doing," Cheryl replied. "What happens next, I cannot say."

"How do you know how to do this?"

"That also, I cannot tell you."

A purple flash lit up the main display, and Lara observed the aftermath of a pulse-generator implosion, shredding one of Excalibur's starships into pieces. The Korilians were closing in on what remained of the battle group, having surrounded the last four battleship and cruiser squadrons. Lara knew Rajhi was on one of those battleships; she didn't know how, but she could sense it.

Lara refocused on the control panel, then pressed the red button.

51

"*Siganella* has lost number three shield! Her armor has been penetrated!"

Admiral Rajhi acknowledged the shield supervisor's report, her eyes going to the wounded battleship, watching as *Siganella* began a port roll, turning its vulnerable starboard side away from the Korilians warships, toward *Intrepid* instead.

The Excalibur battle group was penned in and the battle had degenerated into a dogfight, with small groups of Colonial warships trapped in pockets. *Intrepid* was fighting in tandem with the battleship *Siganella* against four Korilian dreadnoughts, with *Intrepid*'s and *Siganella*'s shields gradually weakening under the onslaught.

Moments earlier, Rajhi had taken direct command of *Intrepid*. Although she was the battle group commander, there wasn't much strategic or tactical guidance she could provide to her remaining ships. However, she was a former battleship captain and the most experienced one in the Fleet. Her tactical prowess couldn't save *Intrepid*, but it might buy them time. At this point, it was a fight to the death, with Rajhi's ships taking out as many Korilian warships as possible before there was nothing left of the Excalibur battle group.

Intrepid's pulse generator completed its recharge, as did *Siganella*'s. Their fire control systems were linked, and the two battleships fired simul-

The End of Time   235

taneously, targeting the bow shield of the Korilian dreadnought they had been pounding. Finally, the shield collapsed, and what remained of their combined pulse punctured the Korilian warship's armor, traveling deep inside. Explosions rippled within the dreadnought, then its remaining shields flickered and disappeared, followed seconds later by an explosion that sheared the warship in half.

A bright yellow flash illuminated the bridge windows as *Intrepid* was hit with a dual-pulse from two Korilian dreadnoughts on its port side.

"Loss of number two shield! Armor penetration in several compartments!" *Intrepid*'s shield supervisor called out.

"Port roll!" Rajhi ordered. "Full power!"

Rajhi held onto the forward bridge railing as *Intrepid*'s topside port thrusters ignited, accompanied by the keel thrusters on the starboard side, shifting *Intrepid*'s vulnerable port side toward *Siganella*.

Both Colonial battleships were now wounded, each using the other as a shield from the powerful Korilian pulses. However, they could not protect each other from the small fighters, and several squadrons of marauders streaked toward them.

As the fighters sped between the two Colonial warships, firing into the gaps where their armor had been penetrated, *Intrepid*'s and *Siganella*'s self-defense batteries engaged, targeting the nimble marauders. Rajhi subconsciously listened to the damage reports as compartment after compartment was compromised by the fighter attacks, focusing her attention on the time remaining before *Intrepid*'s number two shield was regenerated.

Four more minutes.

A bright yellow flare on *Intrepid*'s starboard side caught Rajhi's attention, followed by the sensor supervisor's report.

"Shield-generator explosion aboard *Siganella*. Her forward reactor is down."

Siganella was now at half power, and the battleship could not recharge its pulse generator while recharging its shields.

Not that it mattered.

The three remaining Korilian dreadnoughts completed their pulse-generator recharges and fired again, this time sending a triple-pulse toward *Siganella*'s number four shield.

The shield collapsed, followed by a bright orange flash as *Siganella's* armor was penetrated and its jump drive imploded, vaporizing the battleship.

Rajhi checked the clock, counting down the time until *Intrepid's* number two shield regenerated.

Three more minutes.

Unfortunately, while facing three Korilian dreadnoughts, no matter which way she turned *Intrepid*, one of the dreadnoughts would have a clear shot through the missing shield before it regenerated.

Rajhi realized her time was up. She had escaped death many times throughout her career, but in less than a minute, the Korilian dreadnoughts would complete their pulse-generator recharges, and one of the pulses would melt its way through *Intrepid*.

There was nothing more she could do.

Except...

She might be able to take out one of the dreadnoughts.

"Helm, ahead flank! Fifteen degrees down, twenty to port!"

If she could intercept the nearest Korilian warship and ram it, she would destroy both starships in the process. Hopefully, the Korilians would be slow to decipher her intent and wait too long before beginning avoidance maneuvers.

The Korilian ship began maneuvering too soon, however, and Rajhi realized she would not be able to ram it. But as it turned away, that left only two dreadnoughts to worry about for the moment. If she could survive the next attack, *Intrepid's* shield would be back in only two more minutes. The Korilians would still be able to attack twice more, but Rajhi decided to focus on one challenge at a time.

After analyzing the trajectories of the remaining two dreadnoughts, Rajhi adjusted course, threading the needle between the Korilian warships while rolling to starboard, placing one dreadnought directly above *Intrepid* and one below. From those angles, their pulses would still slip inside *Intrepid's* missing shield, but they would be grazing blows instead of direct hits.

Rajhi's tactic proved successful, as both Korilian dreadnoughts fired, inflicting minor damage on *Intrepid's* port side.

The End of Time   237

But the third dreadnought had begun turning around, and Rajhi would soon have three dreadnoughts to contend with again. This time, the Korilian crews would take Rajhi's suicidal tactics into account, ensuring they could pass by without being rammed, with one of the three ships gaining a clear shot through *Intrepid*'s missing shield.

Two more minutes until the shield regenerated.

They didn't have two more minutes.

There was nowhere to turn.

Rajhi watched as all three dreadnoughts closed on *Intrepid*.

Still, *Intrepid* would get off one more shot.

"Target the weaker contact," Rajhi ordered, hoping she could collapse the dreadnought's shield, causing significant damage.

Intrepid's weapons officer called out, "Fire," and the pulse hit the nearest Korilian dreadnought squarely on the bow.

The shield held.

It was now the Korilians' turn to fire, with the three dreadnoughts spreading out so that no matter which way *Intrepid* turned, one would have a clear shot through *Intrepid*'s compromised armor.

Rajhi didn't bother to maneuver. It was pointless.

As the nearest dreadnought approached *Intrepid*, its pulse-generator doors opened. Rajhi realized that she and *Intrepid*'s crew had only seconds to live, and her grip tightened on the forward bridge railing.

Unexpectedly, the dreadnought's pulse-generator doors closed, and Rajhi watched as the Korilian warship sped past *Intrepid*, then turned away.

The other two Korilian dreadnoughts likewise passed by without firing, and Rajhi watched in amazement, perplexed by the Korilians' odd behavior.

"Ma'am!" *Intrepid*'s sensor supervisor called out. "The Korilians have ceased fire. They're retreating."

52

From her console at the Fleet command center, Fitzgerald watched as Construction Yard Six approached the end of its existence. Of the nineteen defense stations protecting its sector, only one remained. After it was destroyed, another gap would be created in Earth's defense shield. Korilian warships would then target Construction Yard Six, blasting its assembly lines into pieces, then the Korilians would move on to Construction Yard Five.

With 6th Fleet destroyed, 3rd Fleet frozen and also likely destroyed at Korilia, and the Liberation Campaign fleets unable to proceed toward Earth, Fitzgerald could only watch as humankind's only chance to win the war was demolished by the Korilian armada.

Suddenly, the Korilian attack halted.

A quiet fell over the command center as operators and supervisors studied the video displays and sensor screens, then cast curious glances between them. Over one thousand Korilian warships rested motionless in space as the remaining defense stations in the area continued firing, their blue pulses impacting Korilian shields.

The senior command center supervisor's image appeared on one of Fitzgerald's displays.

"Your orders, ma'am?"

The End of Time

Fitzgerald had no idea why the Korilians had halted their assault, but the longer the pause, the better. It was best not to provoke them into resuming their attack.

"Terminate defense station response."

The order went out, and a few seconds later, the defense stations stopped firing.

The tension inside the command center rose steadily as Fitzgerald and others awaited the next Korilian move. Were they about to pivot their attack and destroy industrial centers on Earth or critical infrastructure, such as power and water? Or would they attack the major cities, red pulses raining down through the atmosphere, eventually overwhelming the defense domes protecting the major population centers?

As Fitzgerald evaluated the possibilities, the command center lit up when the video displays monitoring the Korilian armada flashed bright white.

When the light subsided, the Korilian warships were gone.

Fitzgerald scanned through her sensor displays; the Korilian ships were no longer in Earth's orbit.

"Sensors!" she called out, contacting the senior sensor supervisor. "Where did the Korilian armada jump to?"

While she waited for a response, her thoughts went to the Liberation Campaign fleets. Had the Korilians detected their approach, and even more important, how incapacitated were the crews after six jumps in three hours? Was the Korilian armada on its way to engage while it still had sufficient strength to wipe out the four Liberation Campaign fleets, then return to Earth to finish destroying the construction yards?

Only now did Fitzgerald realize she had set the Fleet up for total defeat, not anticipating the possibility the Korilians would temporarily halt their attack on the construction yards to deal with the Liberation Campaign fleets.

As her heart sank from the realization, the sensor supervisor made his report. "The Korilian armada has completed a double jump to the Ritalis star system."

After the Final Stand, Ritalis had been repopulated, as had the other colonies that had been reclaimed. But without Fleet support, Ritalis was completely undefended and easy prey for the Korilians, especially if ground troops were on their way.

But why Ritalis?

"Have the Korilians commenced an attack?" Fitzgerald asked.

"No, ma'am. It looks like they're just in a jump hold."

Stunned by the sudden change in Korilian tactics, Fitzgerald wondered if the Korilians were retreating. But why would they do so when they were on the brink of victory?

Her thoughts were interrupted by the communications supervisor. "Admiral, incoming communication from Third Fleet."

Admiral Rajhi's image appeared on the display. "Fleet Admiral Fitzgerald, the Korilians have halted their attack in the Korilia system."

"Same here in Earth's orbit. They've retreated to Ritalis. Do you have any idea why?"

"I think so," Rajhi replied. "Whatever time stasis Third Fleet was trapped in has been terminated. The other three battle groups have been unfrozen, although Admiral Goergen and the rest of Third Fleet personnel are somewhat disoriented. Even more significant is that Korilia has also been unfrozen, including the ships arriving and departing the planet."

As Fitzgerald wondered what happened—how everything was unfrozen—she had an inkling.

"Where are the three Nexi?"

"They're no longer aboard *Surveillant*," Rajhi replied, "but I think I know where they are. Shortly after Third Fleet was frozen, we detected a repair-bot heading from *Surveillant* toward the Korilian space station. It's now heading back toward *Surveillant*. I don't know who's aboard, but I suspect it's McCarthy, Elena, and Lara."

After shifting her sensor display to the Korilia system, Fitzgerald spotted the repair module moving toward the 3rd Fleet command ship. She concluded that Rajhi had stayed past the Departure Point to distract the Korilians, preventing them from spotting and destroying the repair-bot. If her assessment was correct—that McCarthy, Elena, and Lara had freed 3rd Fleet and Korilia from the time stasis—then Rajhi's decision to sacrifice her battle group had been a critical move indeed.

Fitzgerald examined the status of the Excalibur battle group on her

The End of Time

sensor display: barely one third of the ships had survived. Rajhi seemed calm, but her face was covered in a sheen of perspiration. The final moments of the battle must have been harrowing.

"Well done, Admiral Rajhi. Have Admiral Goergen and McCarthy contact me as soon as they're able."

53

It was a long, slow journey from Prometheus One to *Surveillant*, but this time it was far less stressful and taxing without the tentacles trying to strangle them. McCarthy and Lara had taken their seats in the repair-bot, with Elena jammed between them again. Lara noticed how Elena avoided touching her while squishing her body against McCarthy. For his part, McCarthy seemed not to notice or mind Elena's proximity.

The repair-bot didn't have standard Fleet radio equipment; it was able to communicate only with the host ship's maintenance department when within range of *Surveillant*. Until then, it was quiet inside the repair-bot, the three Nexi lost in their own thoughts: about what Prometheus One had accidentally done to the Korilian home world and the ramifications of that mistake—billions of lives lost in the three-decade-long Korilian War. Lara had undone that error, but the correction had come thirty-three years too late.

Unfreezing the Korilian home world had produced an unexpected benefit. The Korilian warships decimating the Excalibur battle group had ceased firing and retreated. Just over two hundred Korilian warships were now faced by the entire 3rd Fleet—three full-strength battle groups arranged in a defensive sphere surrounding the remaining and heavily damaged Excalibur ships.

The silence inside the repair-bot was interrupted by a crackly radio transmission. "Repair unit four-zero-four, this is *Surveillant*. Do you copy? Over."

McCarthy activated the radio. "This is repair unit four-zero-four. Received your last. Request you inform Admiral Goergen that Admiral McCarthy, Elena, and Lara are aboard, returning to *Surveillant*."

54

After the repair-bot landed in *Surveillant*'s spaceport, McCarthy, Elena, and Lara headed to the command bridge. Activity aboard the starship seemed normal, aside from encountering a few crew members who seemed somewhat disoriented as they walked through the starship corridors. If that was the result of being frozen in time for a few hours, Lara wondered how difficult things would be for the inhabitants of Korilia, working through the fog —and surprise—after having been frozen in time for five centuries.

Upon reaching the command bridge, there was no indication the starship had been stuck in a time stasis; any disoriented personnel had been replaced with new watchstanders. Admiral Goergen sat in her command chair assessing the situation: 3rd Fleet, facing just over two hundred Korilian warships, currently had the advantage with 330 operational starships, but twelve Korilian battle groups had departed the Liberation Campaign star systems, jumping toward Korilia at a rate never seen before.

When Goergen turned her attention to McCarthy, he explained what they had learned and done—that Prometheus One had been transported to the Korilia star system five centuries ago and accidentally frozen the Korilian home world; that with Lara's help, they had deactivated the wormhole star base, freeing Korilia and nearby starships from the time stasis.

Goergen established a communication link with the Fleet command center on Earth. After Fitzgerald's image appeared on the display, Goergen informed the Fleet Admiral that the three Nexi had returned to *Surveillant*, then McCarthy provided the details on Prometheus One.

"That explains why the Korilians halted their assaults on our construction yards and Third Fleet," Fitzgerald replied. "It also answers the primary question that has lingered since this war began—*Why did the Korilians attack us?* We now know why. They believed that we attacked them first."

After a short pause, Fitzgerald continued. "The immediate course of action is clear. Return Third Fleet to Earth as quickly as possible, in case the Korilian pause in this war is temporary. The longer-term issue is more complicated—how to explain to the Korilians what happened and why it took us so long to fix it. I'll inform the Council, and I'm sure we'll be reaching out to the Korilians soon. Hopefully, they'll respond this time. Any questions?"

There were none, and Fitzgerald's image disappeared.

Goergen wasted no time, turning to her operations officer. "What is the status of Excalibur ship jump drives?"

"All jump drives are operational."

"Order all Third Fleet ships to prepare for jump at time four-two-one." To her navigator, Goergen directed, "Plot the most direct course to Earth."

A moment later, the operations officer announced, "All ships report ready for the jump."

"Jump at the mark," Goergen ordered.

The operations officer relayed the order, and five deep tones reverberated throughout the command ship, followed by the computer's voice over the ship's intercom.

"One minute to the jump."

As the seconds counted down, Lara prepared herself for the long return trip to Earth, which would hopefully be far less stressful than their journey to Vormak and Korilia.

55

On the planet Krykag, Pracep Mrayev and his executive assistant, Krajik, stepped from the military transport and lumbered into the Leruk, temporary home of the Rhysh, the ruling body of the Korilian Empire. For over five centuries—while the original location of the Rhysh on Korilia was inaccessible—the Rhysh had met on Krykag instead.

After a short traverse through the mountainside complex, Mrayev and Krajik entered a dimly lit chamber, illuminated by twenty-one globes hovering above and evenly spaced behind a semicircular table behind which the twenty-one members of the Rhysh sat. Within the globes, each representing one of the Korilian worlds that had formed the Empire eons ago, burned a replica of the planet's sun. The center globe, larger than the rest and representing Korilia, had been dark for over five centuries, its sun extinguished when the planet had been frozen in time by the humans. Tonight, its sun burned brightly, now that the original Korilian home world had been freed from the time stasis.

At the center of the curved table beneath Korilia's glowing orb sat Khvik, the oldest member of the Rhysh and the only Korilian still alive from the Time of Freezing—the day Prometheus One had frozen Korilia in time.

The End of Time 247

Mrayev and Krajik stepped onto a stone dais, their figures illuminated by a dim blue light from above, facing the rulers of the Korilian Empire.

Members of the Rhysh, Mrayev said telepathically, *I humbly stand before you, at your service.*

While awaiting a response from the Rhysh, Mrayev sensed the relief felt by its members, as well as their apprehension. Freeing their original home planet and its inhabitants from the time stasis was a joyous event, but one that created many complex issues. One of which was that members of the Rhysh from five centuries ago were still alive. Technically, the Rhysh that Mrayev stood before today was null and void; the members of the Rhysh who were unfrozen on Korilia were the legal rulers of the Empire. However, despite the potential loss of power and prestige, Mrayev sensed a unanimous commitment from the Rhysh members seated before him; each would step aside if requested by the more senior representative from its planet.

Mrayev sensed the same from Krajik, who was slated as the next Rhysh member from the planet Kdosir. Krajik, a rare royalty-combat crossbreed who had learned much serving under him during the war against the humans, would step aside if another was deemed the next representative from Kdosir. That was yet to be determined, however, as the Rhysh they stood before tonight had just started sorting through the significant effort required to reintegrate Korilia's inhabitants—including its previous Rhysh members—back into the Empire.

That would not be the topic of tonight's meeting, however. The discussion would focus on what had occurred in the Korilia star system after the arrival of the human fleet, along with the implications. Khvik was the first to speak.

Pracep Mrayev, we have evaluated your preliminary assessment and have no issue with the details provided; what the humans did in the Korilia star system is clear. Your report, however, does not explain why.

Mrayev replied, *I provided the facts I am aware of. Answering your question —Why did the humans deactivate the machine?—requires speculation.*

This is true, Khvik conceded. *We request your assessment, speculation or not.*

I do not have sufficient insight to answer that question. However, I believe we can conclude that one of our assessments three decades ago was correct; the machine was manufactured by the humans—because they knew how to deactivate it.

I cannot speculate with confidence on the more important question, Mrayev continued. *Why did they attack Korilia five centuries before we made contact with them? This is an issue that has troubled me during my time as pracep. The humans gained no advantage from freezing Korilia. Nor did they attack once we made contact. We attacked them; we started this war. Perhaps not all assessments concerning this machine were correct. Perhaps it was not an attack.*

A Rhysh member to Khvik's left replied, *What happened at Korilia is a ploy to deceive us. You must remember that deceit is integral to human nature. The humans are losing this war and have unfrozen Korilia to end the conflict and prevent their annihilation.*

Another Rhysh member asked, *If humans could have freed Korilia from its time stasis whenever desired, why did they wait until now? When we assaulted their home planet three years ago, they were one battle away from extermination. If the intent of the human intervention at Korilia was to convince us to end the war, they would have done so prior to their final stand.*

More comments were shared between Rhysh members over the next several minutes, concerning what the humans had done and the way forward, until a consensus was reached. Khvik then addressed Krajik, standing beside Mrayev.

The humans have requested a negotiation to end this war. There are several questions which must be answered before we can respond appropriately. You will lead a delegation and engage the humans in discourse to clarify our understanding of events in the Korilia star system and propose a response. After your report, the Rhysh will provide further direction.

Krajik bowed his head. *I will do as you command.*

56

3rd Fleet was halfway to Earth, having just begun a jump hold in the Altaria star system in the outer realm of human colonized planets. After completing the jump, Admiral Goergen had requested Lara's presence, along with McCarthy's and Elena's, on the command bridge. Lara stepped from the elevator and took in the view through the bridge windows: a blue-and-green planet with white swirling clouds. A lump formed in her throat as she stared at her home planet of Altaria, which she had been forced to abandon at the age of seventeen when the Korilians advanced into the Pleaides star cluster. By then, her parents were dead, casualties in what had already become a horrific war against the Korilian Empire.

McCarthy and Elena arrived a moment later, stopping beside Lara and Admiral Goergen. The 3rd Fleet commander looked up, shifting her attention from her displays to the three Nexi standing before her.

"We received an update from Fleet Command," she began. "The Korilians have responded to the Council's request to begin peace negotiations. Discussions have commenced between Korilian emissaries and Council staff, our first discourse since the war began."

"This is good news," McCarthy replied.

"Can you offer any insight on the outcome?" Lara asked.

"Not at the moment. The relevant timelines are too distant for me to latch onto."

Lara turned to Elena. "What do you see?"

A look of pain flashed across Elena's face for a second, then her features hardened. "I prefer not to view any Korilian lines unless required. If one crosses my path, I'll deal with it." Then her voice dropped a notch, her eyes locking onto Lara's. "Don't ask me again."

There was an uneasy silence until Elena's demeanor suddenly changed. She offered Lara a smug smile, then leaned toward McCarthy, whispering into his ear. His gaze shifted to Lara. When Elena finished, he slowly nodded.

Elena pulled away, then headed toward the bridge exit. As she passed by Lara, she said, "Enjoy the conversation."

Lara turned to McCarthy. "What conversation?"

McCarthy replied, "There's something I should have told you a long time ago."

It was a short distance from the command bridge to their stateroom, but it was an excruciatingly long journey as Lara imagined several devastating conversations they might have. The leading contender was that McCarthy was going to tell her that their relationship was over, that he was in love with Elena and not her. Why else would Elena have whispered in his ear, prodding him to have this talk? Why else would she say, "Enjoy the conversation," unless that twisted, sadistic mind of hers knew she wouldn't?

The door whisked closed after they entered their stateroom, and McCarthy gestured to the side of the bed. Lara stopped before him instead.

"Whatever you have to say, you can say it directly to my face."

McCarthy tried to pull Lara into an embrace, but she knocked his hands away. "Don't touch me!"

"This isn't what you think," he said.

"Then what is it? And before you start, do you mind telling me why Elena already knows what we're going to talk about?"

The End of Time 251

McCarthy answered, "During one of my visits to Sint-Pieters, I let her follow my timeline into the past."

"Why would you do that?"

"Elena has trust issues. For years, she convinced herself that I knew she was on Hellios and did nothing. I needed to convince her that I didn't know."

"I don't understand. What does that have to do with today?"

"When you let someone view your past, they can see—everything."

"Everything? Even our most intimate moments?"

McCarthy nodded.

"How could you?"

Lara's anger and resentment flared. She was going to ask—*Why do you care so much about Elena?*—but already knew the answer. He had been in love with her since they were teenagers, and now that Elena had returned from the dead, he had finally decided between them.

McCarthy sank onto the side of the bed and patted the bedspread beside him. Lara refused again, folding her arms across her chest instead. "I'm waiting."

His eyes held hers for a moment, and Lara sensed pain and regret escaping the normally ironclad control of his emotions. Whatever he was about to tell her was difficult for him. Lara's façade softened somewhat, and she sat beside him, waiting for him to begin.

"When we first met," he said, "you still wore your wedding ring. I know how much you loved Gary and how difficult it was for you to deal with his death. I regret how I treated you aboard *Mercy*, attacking you where you were most vulnerable."

Lara recalled the tense first week interacting with McCarthy aboard the Fleet hospital ship *Mercy*, after he'd been injured and his fleet guide killed during the battle at Ritalis, just before the Final Stand. Lara had used her Touch without asking, looking into McCarthy's mind to determine the root cause of the issue. That McCarthy—a Nexus Ten—had failed to predict the attack on his command ship. That his fleet guide, Regina, was dead because of this failure. Lara had also failed. Three years after Gary had been killed in a Fleet battle in the Tindal star system, she had still not come to terms with his death.

"It's not like I didn't ask for it," Lara replied. "I was a grief counselor unable to deal with my own loss, while I lectured you on your inability to deal with Regina's death."

"You have no line," McCarthy said. "Without the ability to predict your reaction, I didn't want to tell you, afraid of what might happen. But I promised myself that I would tell you before the war ended. I suppose I could wait a few more days..."

"Tell me what?"

"I once told you about Teresa, my fiancée, who was killed in battle."

In McCarthy's stateroom aboard the 1st Fleet command ship before the Final Stand, Lara had seen a video clip on his desk of an attractive brunette. She wore a sparkling diamond engagement ring, and her face beamed with excitement.

"She served on a starship in my battle group, and during one of the battles, her ship's jump drive was damaged. We reached the Departure Point, and I should have ordered the jump, leaving Teresa behind, but I couldn't. I stayed until her ship's jump drive was repaired, and that decision cost me five battleships. Thousands of men and women dead, sacrificed for one woman.

"Afterward, when I realized what I had done, I swore that I would never let that happen again. That the life of one woman, no matter how important she was to me, was not worth the lives of thousands. Unfortunately, that decision was too late for you."

Lara had trouble following him, wondering where he was headed. "I don't understand."

"Take my hand," he said, holding it out to her, "and look into my mind."

Slowly, she reached toward him and placed her palm atop his, then used her Touch.

Her vision clouded in a white mist, and when it cleared, she was on the bridge of an Atlantis-class battleship, in McCarthy's body as he sat in the battle group commander's console. She realized she was reliving one of McCarthy's memories from the time he was the commander of the Normandy battle group, before he became the 1st Fleet commander. She felt the tension in his body and the concern in his mind as his hands moved rapidly, sending orders to his ships via the three-dimensional hologram before him.

The End of Time

253

McCarthy's eyes scanned the displays. His battle group was engaged in a furious battle against two Korilian battle groups, and the clock was at negative eight minutes and counting—they were past the Departure Point and would take additional casualties during the jump away.

On the main display was a battleship with a missing shield, surrounded by four other battleships protecting it while they traded pulses with a squadron of Korilian dreadnoughts. The battleship shields were weakening, all less than twenty percent and draining.

"Time to Versailles's jump-drive repair?" McCarthy asked.

"Repairs are almost complete," the operations officer replied. "It should be ready to jump in three minutes."

Lara sensed that McCarthy's concern was focused on Versailles. That Teresa was aboard the wounded battleship. That this was the battle where he had stayed past the Departure Point to save her life.

The squadron of Korilian dreadnoughts fired in tandem, targeting one of the battleships protecting Versailles. The combined pulse collapsed one of its shields, and the pulse continued on, vaporizing a path through the battleship. Seconds later, a brilliant blue explosion consumed the ship, shredding it into fragments hurtling into space.

McCarthy's operations officer reported, "We've lost Vancouver."

Lara pulled her hand away as she sucked in a sharp breath.

Gary had been aboard *Vancouver*.

The realization swept through Lara's mind: *McCarthy* was responsible for Gary's death, plus the years of grief that followed. Tears formed in her eyes as she realized McCarthy's selfish act had killed her husband.

He tried to pull her close.

"Stop," she said, dropping her gaze to the floor as she struggled to sort through what she had just learned.

McCarthy sat beside her, waiting quietly.

After a long moment, Lara said, "I need to be alone for a while."

"I understand." He went to kiss her on the cheek, but she pulled away.

He pushed himself to his feet, then left the stateroom without another word.

57

Seated in her fleet guide chair on *Surveillant*'s command bridge, Lara barely felt the jump wave as 3rd Fleet completed the last leg of the long journey from Korilia to Earth. Beside her sat Admiral Goergen, while McCarthy and Elena stood nearby, gazing out the bridge windows, taking in the scene. The other four fleets—all except 6th Fleet, which had been destroyed by the Korilian armada—were assembled in Earth's orbit, while the remnants of Construction Yard Seven were still being cleared by scavenger ships.

During the return trip to Earth, Fleet Command had kept 3rd Fleet updated. Discussions between Korilian emissaries and Council representatives had rectified a crucial Korilian misunderstanding: Prometheus One had not been an attack on the original Korilian home world; it was humankind's first attempt at interstellar travel, to a planet that could likely support human life, which had failed with devastating effects. Follow-on negotiations had resulted in an agreement in principle: an armistice would be signed tonight at nine p.m. Brussels Time, with formal peace negotiations to follow.

Fleet Admiral Fitzgerald had invited her senior staff, including McCarthy and the five surviving fleet admirals, plus Elena and Lara, to her home in Brussels tonight to celebrate the formal cease-fire. It would be a black-tie affair, and neither Lara nor Elena had appropriate attire, so a

The End of Time

quick trip to Domus Praesidium was in order, where they would be joined by the Nexus One, who had also been invited to Fitzgerald's celebration.

Lara considered skipping the event; she wasn't in the mood for a festive occasion. She hadn't yet worked through McCarthy's revelation that he was responsible for Gary's death. However, to decline the event, she would need the Nexus One's approval, and she didn't want to discuss this issue with anyone, nor did she think The One would approve her request. She resigned herself to attending the event, smiling and conversing not far from McCarthy while mixed feelings for him churned inside.

58

Three Nexus shuttles descended through the clouds in the darkness, angling for the brightly illuminated but crowded Brussels streets. In each shuttle rode a Nexus Ten—Rhea in the lead transport, followed by McCarthy and Lara, then Elena. With the Nexus House's three Tens simultaneously in one location outside the safety of Domus Praesidium, Rhea had directed that each Ten travel in a separate shuttle and be accompanied by a full ten-member praetorian guard in case a minor house had nefarious plans or a Corvad cell had survived.

Prior to departing Domus Praesidium, all three Tens and the level-nine naviganti in the intelligence center had viewed all pertinent timelines into the future, verifying there was no indication of a threat. However, timelines could change quickly when manipulated by other Nines and Tens. Although the Nexus House was the last major house remaining—the only one with Tens—Rhea had proceeded with caution, especially in light of the attack upon McCarthy and Lara on Darian 3.

Sitting beside McCarthy, Lara took a deep breath and let it out slowly. The tension between them following his revelation had taken a toll on her, and she wasn't up for socializing tonight. McCarthy's words had replayed in her mind countless times since their discussion on *Surveillant*, and she had not yet come to terms with how that knowledge would affect their relation-

The End of Time 257

ship. Although she sat beside him as usual, she refused to hold his hand or offer any affection. McCarthy respected her wishes, waiting for her to work through the issue.

Rhea's shuttle touched down first, and she emerged with her guard, led by Ronan. McCarthy and Lara landed next and were escorted by one of Fleet Admiral Fitzgerald's aides to her twentieth-story penthouse. During their transit, Lara noticed how she turned men's heads. The side trip to Domus Praesidium for proper attire for tonight's event had been brief, but the results, spectacular.

The Nexus dresses they wore tonight were made of a lustrous, shiny blue fabric with full-length sleeves and a neck collar. They were tailored to accent their figures and had a diamond-shape cutout beneath the neck exposing the top of their breasts—just enough to be tantalizing without being scandalous. Ten large diamonds were embedded in the collars of Rhea's and Elena's dresses, while eight pure-white diamonds adorned Lara's. Each woman wore matching diamond earrings, plus a platinum medallion forged into the intricate Nexus House symbol, containing a large diamond in the center cut into the shape of an eye, which hung just above their cleavage.

Lara's hair was up tonight, pulled back to reveal the sleek lines of her neck, while Elena's blonde hair was still cropped short, having been sheared off after her rescue from Hellios, cutting away eighteen years of a tangled, matted mess. Lara had to admit that despite Elena's waifish appearance and lack of makeup—she had declined to wear any—she was quite attractive.

Upon reaching Fitzgerald's residence, the Fleet Admiral greeted her guests as they arrived, directing them to mingle on the open-air garden terrace as the Nexus praetorians placed themselves in strategic positions.

It was almost nine p.m., so instead of dinner, waiters in tuxedoes carried silver platters of drinks and hors d'oeuvres throughout the crowd. Lara selected a glass of champagne as a tray passed by. McCarthy chose a glass of red wine that almost matched his mess dress uniform, the Colonial Navy's version of a tuxedo, albeit in the Fleet's burgundy and crimson colors rather than black and white.

McCarthy stayed by Lara's side for a while, introducing her to the fleet admirals and a host of others she hadn't yet met, and they were soon approached by Regents Morel Alperi and Lijuan Xiang, who complimented both on their efforts aboard Prometheus One. Alperi soon drifted off to converse with other officers and dignitaries, and although Lijuan lingered longer, she eventually moved on, headed toward Elena. Lara noticed that Lijuan spent quite a while talking with the Nexus Ten and wondered what they were discussing; at one point, Elena turned and stared at Lara briefly before returning her attention to Lijuan.

The effort to smile and socialize tonight was quite draining, so Lara retreated to the far corner of the penthouse terrace, her thoughts returning to the issue she had been struggling with. As she stared at the city skyline, she processed what McCarthy had revealed to her on *Surveillant*. The issue wasn't just that he was responsible for Gary's death. He had also kept it a secret from her for three years. He had courted her and let her fall in love with him while withholding that crucial detail.

Her internal debate swirled around a central question—*Did it matter?* Did the fact that McCarthy sacrificed Gary for Teresa have a bearing on their relationship? Did it matter that he hadn't told her earlier? Did it affect whether she did—or *should*—love him?

It took a while, but she finally arrived at the conclusion she had hoped for. *It didn't matter.* People made mistakes, and McCarthy was no exception. Instead, she decided she was fortunate to be in a relationship with a man who was willing to do almost anything to save the woman he loved. She could not condemn him for that.

She spotted McCarthy talking with Fitzgerald and several others, and she moved beside him. When he spotted her, he offered an inquisitive look. She smiled and wrapped an arm around his waist. He pulled her close, and she felt the tension ease from his body. He'd been worried. She wondered what it must be like for a man who can see the future of all things except her.

Fitzgerald spotted their embrace and smiled. Lara doubted McCarthy had discussed the matter with Fitzgerald, but she was intuitive enough to notice that things hadn't been quite right between them when they arrived this evening, and that whatever the issue was, it had been resolved.

The End of Time 259

The Fleet Admiral gestured to a waiter and ordered a round of champagne for everyone. Once the drinks were dispersed, she stepped onto the ledge of a nearby firepit so that all in attendance could see her.

"In a few minutes," she said, her voice carrying across the open-air terrace, "we will enter a time that most of us remember as a distant memory, and many on Earth and its colonies have never experienced—a time of peace! In a few minutes, the thirty-three-year war against the Korilians will finally be over.

"Before we begin that new era, I want to offer a toast to several in attendance tonight. I must start with Regents Morel Alperi and Lijuan Xiang, without whose dedication we would not have had the personnel and material to defend Earth and our colonies."

She raised her glass of champagne into the air. "To Morel Alperi and Lijuan Xiang, we toast."

The crowd repeated the toast and took a sip of champagne.

"To Rhea Sidener, the Nexus One," Fitzgerald continued. "We asked for her assistance, and she provided it, regardless of the impact to her House or its members." Fitzgerald's eyes shifted momentarily to Elena, then returned to Rhea. "To Rhea Sidener, we toast."

Lara repeated the toast, then sipped her champagne.

"To Admiral Jon McCarthy, I speak not only as Fleet Admiral but as a citizen of Earth when I say we owe you an unrepayable debt of gratitude. Without your talent and leadership, we would not have defeated the Korilians during the Final Stand, nor would we have discovered what Prometheus One had done to the Korilian home world. On a personal note, you were only sixteen years old when we first met, and I did my best during those days as a starship captain, offering both professional and parental guidance. I have to admit, you turned out okay."

There was a ripple of laughter through the crowd.

"I also speak as a mother who has lost both children to the war, when I say—you are the closest thing to a son that I have."

Fitzgerald lifted her glass. "To Jon McCarthy."

Lara pulled McCarthy close as she repeated the toast, looking into his eyes. She could hardly believe that he loved *her*, of all women.

"To Major Elena Kapadia," Fitzgerald said, threatening to sour Lara's mood, "we are also indebted. You did what was asked of you on Darian 3, although leading Third Army Group to victory was an impossible task. For what happened over the next eighteen years, we both share a burden. I cannot imagine what you endured, but I know it was our fault." She gestured to those in attendance. "We failed you, not by conscious decision, but we failed you nonetheless, and that error can never be undone. Despite what you endured, however, when we called upon you to assist Third Fleet, you did, and your talent proved invaluable—we would not have been able to reach Prometheus One without you."

Fitzgerald lifted her glass. "To Elena Kapadia."

The Fleet Admiral then turned to Lara.

"To the enigma of Lara Anderson—the One with no line."

Lara was surprised by Fitzgerald's toast, referring to her in a way relevant only to a Nexus. She and the Nexus One were obviously close, discussing issues not germane to the Korilian War.

"Your assistance was instrumental during the Final Stand, and as I stand here today, I wonder if there is anyone we are more indebted to. Without your help, we would not have been able to deactivate Prometheus One and unfreeze the Korilian home world. Had that not been done, we would still be at war and humankind itself on the brink of extinction."

Fitzgerald raised her glass. "To Lara Anderson."

After the crowd repeated the toast, Fitzgerald announced, "Ten more minutes until the armistice!" then stepped down from the ledge.

Those around Lara showered her with more compliments, and the attention was too much. Eventually, she pulled McCarthy from the crowd, off to the side of the terrace. There were more important things to discuss at the moment. She had finally worked her way through what McCarthy had done.

She was about to speak when McCarthy pulled her close and kissed her, holding her in a long, passionate embrace. When she pulled back, she smiled and decided there was no need for words.

At least not between them.

Her thoughts shifted to Elena. That was another matter.

On *Surveillant*'s command bridge, before McCarthy had revealed the

The End of Time 261

devastating details of what he had done, Elena had waltzed past her, offering a gleeful *Enjoy the conversation* comment. Elena had known what they were going to discuss and had derived pleasure from Lara's pain. Ever since Elena boarded *Surveillant* for their journey to Vormak and then Korilia, Lara had avoided the unstable Nexus Ten, fearful of what Elena might do if provoked.

Not tonight.

Lara searched the crowd for Elena, spotting her standing by herself in a corner of the rooftop terrace.

Lara moved toward the Nexus Ten.

McCarthy grabbed Lara's arm. "Where are you going?"

"It's time Elena and I had a talk."

"I don't advise it."

"I've had enough of her. She needs to stop meddling in our relationship. She needs to accept that we're together and move on."

Lara saw the concern in McCarthy's eyes, but pulled from his grip anyway. He watched her closely as she approached Elena.

The Nexus Ten was leaning against the railing with her back to the crowd, so Lara stopped behind her.

"Over the last few weeks," Lara said over Elena's shoulder, "I tried to be nice to you. I tried to be thoughtful of what you went through on Hellios and gave you pass after pass. Not anymore. Tonight, I'm putting ground rules in place. If you violate them, your relationship with Jon will be over."

There was no response from Elena, which stoked Lara's anger.

"Did you hear me? Or did the Korilians destroy your hearing as well as your mind?"

"I have excellent hearing," Elena replied, still facing away. "It was dreadfully quiet on Hellios, and my hearing has become quite acute."

"Then here are the rules," Lara said, "which should be simple enough even for you to understand. If you interfere in my relationship with Jon or hurt me in any way—including verbal jabs like *Enjoy your conversation*—I'll force Jon to decide between us. Either a relationship with me or friends with you, but not both."

"That would be unwise."

"How's that?"

"If you destroy my relationship with Jon, I'll have no reason not to kill you. And at this moment, nothing would please me more than to put an end to that nonexistent line of yours."

"How can you talk so flippantly about murder? What's wrong with you?"

Elena ignored Lara's questions, which caused Lara's anger to build. She wanted to slap Elena in the face, knock some sense into her. But not while she was looking away.

"Turn around, you miserable excuse for a human being."

Elena slowly turned around. There were tears in her eyes, reflecting the terrace lights.

"All those years on Hellios," Elena said, her voice quavering, "the only thing that kept me going was my love for Jon, hoping we would someday be together. Even when I hated him for abandoning me, I still loved him. You've taken him away from me, and now all I have is the House. I don't know if that's enough...if I can keep going."

Her response took Lara by surprise. She had intentionally engaged Elena tonight knowing how dangerous she was, hoping the altercation would ignite the strange heat inside her, unleash whatever talent lurked within. She wanted to inflict physical pain to repay Elena for the emotional agony she had put her through. What she hadn't taken into account, however, was the pain Elena was enduring, her hopes destroyed by another woman.

Lara's anger dissipated, replaced with sympathy, wondering how she would feel if the situation were reversed. Before becoming a Nexus, she had spent her entire adult life as a grief counselor, plus she was an empath. How had she not recognized Elena's pain?

Mentally, she shifted gears, approaching the situation as a grief counselor. Lara stepped closer, moving to embrace her.

"Stop," Elena said as she burst into tears. "I'll take a hug from anyone but you."

Still, Elena needed consolation, and Lara reached tentatively toward her. Elena didn't react, so Lara gently pulled her into an embrace.

Elena wrapped her arms around Lara, pressing the side of her face against her shoulder. As she held Elena in her arms, Lara searched for ways

The End of Time 263

to console her. It was a complicated matter, since she was the source of Elena's grief. She decided to hold Elena instead, offering nonverbal support.

After a while, Elena finally spoke.

"Jon will love me one day. I have seen it."

Lara's body went rigid. Just when she started to feel empathy for Elena...

But Lara decided to remain in a grief counselor role, realizing Elena was stuck in the denial stage. Rather than antagonize Elena, it was better if she helped her through the stages. The sooner she reached the acceptance and hope phase, the better.

"Perhaps," Lara replied, then added the standard Nexus farewell, *"the future is not set*. Maybe after my relationship with Jon has run its course, you will be together."

Elena pulled back, her eyes widening. "Yes, of course. It's just a matter of time." She wiped the tears from her cheeks. "Until then, I'll just have to endure."

Their conversation was interrupted by loud explosions and cheers as fireworks filled the night sky.

It was nine p.m. The Korilian War was over. The only thing left was the paperwork.

Lara took in the amazing scene. Growing up on the fringe planet of Altaria, Lara had never seen fireworks, and the celebrations on Ritalis were paltry in comparison. As far as she could see in every direction, a brilliant array of colors exploded, then danced toward earth.

She watched the colorful display for a while, then bid Elena goodbye, offering her another hug, which Elena accepted. She searched for McCarthy and found him standing by the edge of the terrace where she left him; his eyes were still on her.

She pulled McCarthy into an embrace, holding him tightly. "I'm sorry," she said, regretting what she had put him through after his revelation about Gary.

Lara kissed him, and they let it linger. When she stepped back and looked up at him, his eyes were filled with relief. Thirty-three years of carnage were finally at an end, and their relationship was secure.

She signaled one of the waiters wandering through the crowd and selected another glass of champagne. With her arm around McCarthy's waist, she looked over the terrace ledge, mesmerized by the throng of people below flowing out from the bars and restaurants onto the sidewalks and streets. As she took a sip of her drink, she thought about the time she had stood on the balcony of her apartment on Ritalis as the planet was being evacuated. She could never have imagined what had occurred over the last three years.

The fireworks and cheers finally faded, replaced with a somber silence. Lara didn't know where everyone's thoughts were, but she felt the emotions. Elation and joy, mixed with grief and sadness. There was likely not a single person here tonight who hadn't lost a loved one in the war.

A bloodcurdling shriek pierced the night air.

Lara turned toward the source. Elena screamed again as she fell to her knees. Then she scrambled against the terrace wall and pulled her knees against her chest, wrapping her arms tightly around them. Her eyes glazed over as she rocked back and forth.

McCarthy pushed his way through the crowd, then knelt beside her.

"What's wrong?"

Elena didn't respond, so he caressed the side of her face. "It's me, Jon."

Her eyes slowly cleared, and after she focused on him, he asked again, "What's wrong?"

"Krajik is coming." Her lips trembled as she spoke.

"Who is Krajik?"

"The Korilian in charge of my interrogation."

"He's probably part of the peace negotiation envoy," McCarthy offered.

"You don't understand. Krajik is coming...for *me*!"

Elena covered her face with her hands and started crying, rocking back and forth again.

McCarthy turned to Rhea, and Lara felt a chill as The One viewed the future. When Rhea finished, a cold, hard look settled on her face.

"The war," she said, "is just beginning."

A moment earlier, Lijuan Xiang's attention had been drawn to Elena's scream. As Rhea's announcement was digested by those in attendance, she saw the concern and fear on their faces. Lijuan, however, repressed a smile. Rhea's assessment was more correct than she envisioned.

The war between the Nexus and Corvad Houses was just beginning.

The Synthec War: A Colonial Fleet Novel
Nexus House Book 4

From a distant region of the galaxy, a new threat forces old enemies to unite.

The war was finally over, or so Admiral Jon McCarthy thought. But the emergence of a new enemy—the mysterious Synthecs—leads to an uneasy alliance between humans and Korilians. McCarthy finds himself navigating a dangerous landscape both in space and in the halls of diplomacy to keep the coalition from falling apart before the real battle even begins.

As the Colonial and Korilian fleets prepare for an epic confrontation against a synthetic life form intent on exterminating all intelligent biological life, Lara Anderson and Elena Kapadia attempt to infiltrate a Synthec starbase on a covert mission that could turn the tide of the battle. But Elena's unstable dual personality and jealousy of Lara and McCarthy's relationship make her a dangerous wildcard in an already perilous operation.

Back on Earth, Fleet Admiral Fitzgerald faces a moral dilemma when ordered to betray her Korilian allies. Her decision could alter the course of the war and humanity's future. With time running out as the Synthec fleet prepares its assault, McCarthy and his allies must navigate a minefield of political deceit, shifting loyalties, and planned betrayals that will determine the fate of billions.

Get your copy today at
severnriverbooks.com

COMPLETE CAST OF CHARACTERS

<u>NEXUS HOUSE</u>
Rhea Sidener Ten (Placida) / Nexus One (The One)
Jon McCarthy Ten
Elena Kapadia Ten
Noah Ronan Nine (Primus) / Legion Commander / Department Head - Defense
Dewan Channing Eight (Deinde)
Lara Anderson Eight / Nine trainee
Angeline Del Rio Eight / 3rd Fleet guide
Jonuthin Berber Eight / Intelligence Center supervisor

<u>CORVAD HOUSE</u>
Lijuan Xiang Ten (Placida) / Princeps
Gavin Vaus Ten (Impetum)
Nero Conde Primus Nine / Legion Commander / Department Head - Defense

<u>COLONIAL COUNCIL</u>
David Portner Regent - Inner Realm / Council president
Morel Alperi Regent - Inner Realm / Director of Personnel

Complete Cast Of Characters

Lijuan Xiang Regent - Terran (Earth) / Director of Material
Salma Zaph Regent - Fringe Worlds

COLONIAL FLEET
Nanci Fitzgerald Fleet Admiral / Colonial Fleet Commander
Liam Carroll Admiral / Colonial Fleet Deputy Commander
Jon McCarthy Admiral / Colonial Fleet staff
Natalia Goergen Admiral / 3rd Fleet Commander
Kevin Shallcross Admiral / 4th Fleet Commander
Nesrine Rajhi Vice Admiral / Excalibur Battle Group Commander
Tom Wears Captain / Colonial Fleet Staff - Intelligence Liaison

COLONIAL MARINE CORPS
Drew Harkins Major / Nexus escort platoon leader
Ed Jankowski Sergeant Major / Nexus escort platoon
Narra Geisinger Sergeant Major / Nexus escort platoon
Liza Kalinin Sergeant / Nexus escort platoon
Troy Dansing Sergeant / Nexus escort platoon

KORILIANS
Mrayev Pracep (war campaign commander)
Meorbi Pracep (war campaign commander)
Krajik Pracep Mrayev's executive assistant (royalty-combat crossbreed)
Khvik Rhysh Representative (home world Korilia) / Senior Member
Korem Rhysh Representative (inner world Keorsn)
Kovar Rhysh Representative (inner world Kovirm)

OTHER CHARACTERS
Devin Anjul Special Intelligence Division agent
Elijah Guptah Director, Sint-Pieters Sanitorium
Cheryl Johnson Lara Anderson's mother

AUTHOR'S NOTE

I hope you enjoyed *The End of Time*!

The six-book Colonial Fleet series can be divided into two parts, and you've just finished the first half—the Korilian War. Regarding the second half, I've dropped a few hints in books 2 and 3, referencing a second Korilian pracep (war campaign commander). I've hopefully hinted clearly enough that the Korilians have been engaged in a two-front war, with Pracep Mrayev commanding the war against the humans while Pracep Meorbi oversees a vastly larger engagement.

Although *The End of Time* ended on an upbeat note regarding the Korilian War, it's probably apparent that the Korilians aren't going anywhere. Additionally, the next book in the Colonial Fleet series introduces an ancient enemy, a synthetic life form, about to overwhelm the Korilians in their centuries-long war. As the Synthecs prepare to turn their attention to the next civilization in their path—the human colonies— Admiral McCarthy leads the Colonial Fleet to the far reaches of the Korilian Empire, while Lara and Elena embark on a dangerous mission into Synthec territory that will determine the outcome of the pending battle.

I hope you enjoy the next novel in the series—*The Synthec War*!

ABOUT THE AUTHOR

RICK CAMPBELL, a retired Navy Commander, spent more than thirty years in the Navy, serving on four nuclear-powered submarines. On his last submarine, he was one of the two men whose permission is required to launch its nuclear warhead-tipped missiles.

Upon retirement from the Navy, Rick was contracted by Macmillan / St. Martin's Press for his novel The Trident Deception, which was hailed by Booklist as "The best submarine novel written in the last thirty years, since Tom Clancy's classic - The Hunt for Red October". His first six books became Barnes & Noble Top-10 and Amazon #1 bestsellers.

Rick lives in the Washington, D.C. area and continues to work on new books across the submarine and science-fiction genres.

Sign up for the reader list at
severnriverbooks.com